C000098757

TILL

THE

SUN

DIES

H.M. DARLING

Copyright © 2023 H.M. Darling

All rights reserved.

No part of this book may be reproduced or used in any manner without written permission of the copyright owner, except for the use of brief quotations in a book review.

This is a work of fiction. Names, characters, places, and incidents either are the product of the author's imagination or are used fictitiously. Any resemblance to actual persons, living or dead, events, or locales is entirely coincidental.

ALSO BY H.M. DARLING

CONTENT WARNING:

Till the Sun Dies is a new adult novel and contains materials that may be triggering to some readers, including depression, off-page domestic violence and emotional abuse, suicide, and explicit sex scenes (all consensual). Please do not read if any of this is triggering to you.

For the girls who dream with their eyes open

And for a boy made of sunshine

CHAPTER 1

There were two round-trip tickets, but only one seat was occupied.

I stared at the back of the seat in front of me and tried to pinpoint exactly where everything had gone wrong. My chest ached and dried tears stained my cheeks as I mentally combed through mornings that began with screaming and midnights that ended tangled in bed together. A lump formed in my throat as I remembered long locks of blonde hair tickling my face while she kissed me, soft pink lips delicate against mine one moment and spewing rage the next. If there was a time before the venom, I didn't remember it.

I knew she planned to leave. I prepared for it, even, because I was just as much to blame for this as she was. When she was angry, I was absent. She screamed, and I stayed silent. She begged... and I ran. She raged... and I built walls.

I proposed because she asked me to. I thought it would fix things.

Even on one knee, I felt nothing at all.

Our wedding came closer and closer, and I let myself hope. I convinced myself things would get better after we were married. There would be nowhere for me to run. Perhaps she would be kinder to her wife than she ever was to her girlfriend or fiancé. My gown was extravagant, flowing and full of lace, with pink butterflies sewn into the train. I stood in front of our families, and our friends, and I waited. I waited until the crowd stared at me with pity and my mother cried.

She never came down the aisle.

Five years of my life washed away in the rain.

Everything after that was a haze. I ran to the bridal suite, calling her name. Screaming it, even. No one stopped me. They all just *watched* as tsunami waves of grief dragged me down. My sister cut me out of my damned dress so I could breathe again.

I couldn't go home... home was her apartment, with her things and her friends and her dog. Instead, I wallowed on my sister's couch. When I was awake, I stared out the window at the desolate summer sun. At some point, I stopped feeling anything at all. I slept for long hours when I couldn't stand to exist anymore.

We were supposed to have a honeymoon. We saved for months to afford the hotel and plane tickets for five days in a city that was supposed to fix us. Somewhere in the fog of my broken mind, I remembered what day it was. I drank too much red wine, trying to forget about it. One moment, I scrolled through unread emails on my phone, pausing on the one that mentioned checking in for our flight. In a drunken stupor, I packed a single carry-on suitcase full of shit I hated, and took an Uber to Sky Harbor. I stepped onto a plane by myself.

I ran from every problem I ever had in life, and this was no different. Only this time, I was running further than ever before and I refused to look back.

Truthfully, I wasn't leaving much behind. The apartment had

been in her name and all my things were stuffed in boxes and abandoned in my parents' garage. My corporate job was nothing to brag about; my boss would log on Monday morning to find my resignation letter in his email. The summer heat in Phoenix was unbearable, I would not miss it.

I wondered how long it would take for my family to realize I was gone. When I left, my sister was in the middle of a twelve-hour nursing shift. She would come home and fall into bed without remembering to check on me. I hadn't spoken to my parents since the wedding; I only expected them to call after my sister realized I wasn't drowning on her couch anymore.

When I was young, before I had any concept of bills, rent, or expenses, I believed I would move across the world one day. I bragged about how I would be the first family member to escape the dreary, hot Phoenix summers and start a wonderful life some-where else.

Instead, I went to college. I fell in love. I got a job and an apartment. I proposed to the woman I loved. Everything I was supposed to do, I did. My dream of leaving Arizona faded like a candle in the wind.

Now, I had nothing.

That wasn't true. I had an overflowing savings account and a bleeding heart.

I opened the window cover, peering out over the ocean thou-sands of feet below us as it met land. I swallowed thickly, my heart ringing in my ears. The plane would land soon, and I would be... home. This foreign country, with a language I could barely speak, would become my home - at least for a while. I rested my head against the back of my seat, ignoring the aggressive flip of my stomach.

For the first time in my life, I was doing something for myself. I wasted so much time worrying about what others would think. My fiancé hated my tattoos, so I wore pants to hide them.

When my mom commented on my weight, I set down whatever I was eating. My sister told me she didn't think I was creative - I never picked up a paintbrush. It was time to stop worrying about what others would think. My family would be shocked and my boss would be furious. My friends... I didn't really have any of those. I had *her* friends. They were all gone, one after the other disappearing with her.

It was just me.

I hated airports. As I dragged my carry-on after me, I dug my nails into my palm, trying not to scream. I flinched away from people too close to me, and gritted my teeth at every harmless conversation I passed. Rolling my shoulders back, I focused on the pain in my palm as I wound through crowds of clueless people.

I stopped in a bathroom to brush my teeth and hair and reapply deodorant. On top of all the hustle and bustle of the airport, I couldn't stand the feeling of being unclean. I wiped makeup from under my eyes, blinking at myself in the mirror.

I didn't recognize the sad girl that stared back at me. I'd lost weight. My cheeks seemed more hollow than they ever had. My shirt and pants hung loosely over my shoulders and hips. I was still curvier than most, but something about me seemed - empty. My hair was supposed to be bright copper; it had faded to a dull brown, even flatter than the bark color of my eyes.

Deep in my backpack, I found my silicone earplugs. With them in, most of the noise faded to a background lull. I gathered my things and left the bathroom, feeling more prepared to make my way through the airport. I found the cab station and showed the driver the address to my hotel. He grunted in response and set the meter without so much as a greeting.

I stared out the window the entire drive. At first, it didn't seem like anything spectacular. Just a lot of traffic and dirty highways from the airport into the city. When the highway turned to city streets, I perked up. Bright trees lined boulevards and avenues, gray rooftops and wrought-iron balconies became the signature style of every building I passed. Streets overflowed with tourists, despite the overcast sky.

It started to rain just before the cab arrived at my hotel. It was a small Best Western, nothing impressive, but cheap enough for me to stay a while without worrying about money. I stared at it, something unfamiliar blossoming in my chest - excitement, maybe.

People scattered and stood under awnings, watching the rain come down. With an aching heart, I paid the driver and stepped out into the storm. Rain pattered against my face; I stared up at the sky and fought the urge to cry. I made it.

I was alone, but I was here.

Maybe tomorrow the thought of being alone wouldn't hurt so much.

When the throb in my chest subsided, I dragged my things into the hotel lobby. The receptionist greeted me with a smile on her face.

"*Bonjour*! Welcome to Paris."

CHAPTER 2

"Hi - uh, *bonjour*," I stuttered, moving closer to the receptionist's desk. A flash of annoyance crossed her face, but she maintained her smile. "Checking in for Adalyn Aldridge."

Once I checked in with an indefinite checkout date, I dragged my things into a minuscule elevator and up to a decent hotel room. I dropped both my carry-on and backpack on the ground, falling back onto the bed with a shaky breath.

I made it.

I was in Paris.

I was going to live in Paris.

I needed a job. I probably needed some sort of visa, an apartment, and about half a million other things I hadn't considered yet in my hasty escape. For the time being, though, I had a hotel room with a shower and a bed. That was enough.

I pulled out my phone, turning it on for the first time in nearly twenty-four hours. While I waited for my plane, I made sure my data service would work here. It would cost a fortune - I'd figure out a more permanent solution later. *One step at a time*, I reminded myself when my throat felt a little tighter.

As I expected, I found a dozen calls from my sister to accompany nearly fifty texts. There were a couple from my parents, inconsequential compared to Indy's frantic messages. I called my sister back first, setting the phone on speaker next to my head as I stared up at the ceiling.

"Where the hell are you?" Indy answered, her voice frantic. "I come home, and you're gone and you're not at Mom's. Fuck, Adalyn, I thought you hurt yourself."

I started in surprise. "Why would I hurt myself?"

Indy scoffed, indicating she wouldn't elaborate. Discomfort settled deep in my stomach. Through all the pain and numbness, I never once thought about hurting myself. Was I so far gone that Indy would believe something like that?

"Where are you, then?" Indy growled.

"I'm in Paris."

Indy was quiet. I pictured her wide eyes as she tried to piece together the steps that led me here. Abandoned in front of everyone who ever knew me... wallowing on her couch for a few days... Paris. She cleared her throat. "I can be there Friday. I can have some of my shifts covered and maybe stay for a week-"

"Indy," I interrupted. "I'm fine."

One of these times, I would mean those words. Today was not one of them.

"Why are you there?" She asked, her voice an octave too high.

"I think I'm going to stay here for a while." It wasn't really an answer, but it was all I had.

I didn't know why I was here, in the hotel room I was supposed to share with my wife, on a trip that should have been my honeymoon. All I knew was that I had the tickets, and the reservations… and it was far, far away from anything that ever hurt me.

"I don't know about this, Addie."

I pursed my lips. "I don't either, but I'd rather be here than drowning at home. Someday, I'm going to have to learn to stand on my own. Paris seems like a good place to start, I guess."

"You don't have to learn so soon," Indy said. "You were with her for five years."

I flinched, clearing my throat and sitting up. "This has nothing to do with her," I croaked.

Indy snorted, probably rolling her eyes. She didn't argue. "How long are you staying?"

"I don't know."

"You want me to come?"

"No."

She let out a long breath; her voice cracked when she spoke. "You'll come home eventually, though, right?"

My heart ached. I wished I could hug my little sister. Out of the two of us, she was the brighter and louder one. She smiled more. She was more ambitious. In a room with both of us, she outshined me every time. Yet, no matter how dark I became or how many rainstorms threatened to drown me, she always brought me back to the light. Always.

I couldn't give her the answer she wanted, because I didn't know. It was too early to know whether Paris would be enough for me, or if I would go running home at the first wave of darkness. So, instead, I said, "I promise, if I need you, I'll call you the minute I do. I'll check in every day."

"You better."

I promised her again, yawning. "You'll deal with Mom and Dad for me?"

"Of course."

I sat on the phone with Indy for a while longer, laying back on the mattress. She told me about her day at work, her annoyance with her almost-boyfriend, and updated me on the cat she was on the waitlist to adopt. My sister talked joyously and relentlessly. I was like that once too. My eyes drooped, and I wondered what happened to me.

"Addie!" Indy exclaimed.

Indy had been calling my name for a few moments. I'd dozed off. "Sorry," I mumbled. "I'm exhausted."

"What time is it there?"

I checked. "It's only six."

"Go find some food, then go to bed."

I agreed half-heartedly, resting back on the pillows. After I said goodbye to my sister, I didn't bother to call either of my parents. Indy would relay the message and deal with the backlash I was too cowardly to face. I didn't particularly have the energy to leave and find food like she suggested, but as soon as I thought about it, my stomach roared. Groaning, I pushed myself out of bed.

I brushed my teeth and hair again and didn't bother to change. I didn't know anyone here anyway, so there was no one to care about my wrinkled airplane leggings and sweater. I pulled my hair into a high ponytail as I opened the hotel room door, biting my room key as I fixed my hair. Turning to walk down the hall, I ran bodily into another person as she left the room across from me.

"Shit, sorry, uh-" she stuttered in a thick Southern accent, trying to apologize in French.

"It's okay," I laughed once.

Immediately, a warm smile spread across her face. She had a small, charming gap between her two front teeth, and the bluest eyes I'd ever seen. She brushed her large brown country curls out of her face and adjusted her white crop top. Everything about her screamed Southern charm.

"A fellow American!" She exclaimed. "Did you just get in?

9

There was this awful Italian couple in that room a few days ago, they argued so loud in the middle of the night and left their garbage bags in the hall."

"Yeah, I was going to find some food," I interrupted, overwhelmed by the onslaught of information. I felt myself tensing up, my heart beating faster. I took a slow step back.

"I'm Willa, and I know the best crepe place in the Latin Quarter. I'm headed there now. Would you like to join me?" She held out her hand in greeting.

I stared at her for a moment, my nerves curdling in my stomach. Every muscle in my body screamed for me to take two steps back into my room and lock the door. Any other day, any other time, that's what I would have done. I reminded myself I was here for a new start. A new life. A new me. I reached out and took her hand. "Addie. I'd love to."

Willa beamed and shook my hand before leading the way to the elevator. Instinctively, I patted my pocket where I kept two silicone earplugs in case the world grew too loud. I had never introduced myself to anyone so willingly, or agreed to go out with them. But, Willa had a wonderful smile, and I was alone here in this big city. Plus, I was starving, and I couldn't bring myself to turn down crepes in France.

Already, I was a different person in Paris than I'd ever been in Phoenix.

How strange.

"Where are you from?" Willa asked in the elevator. I told her I was from Arizona. She was born in Texas, but moved away to Michigan for college as soon as she could. She fixed her hair in the reflection of her phone. I noticed the large, glittering engagement ring on her finger, and resisted the urge to comment on it.

"I've been here a week," she said as we walked out of the hotel. "Still can't figure out the French thing, do you speak any?"

I shrugged. "I took it in high school, and for two semesters in college. So, basically, I can say hello and ask how you're doing."

Willa laughed, nodding. She led the way up the hill away from the hotel. Her Western boots clicked on the cobblestone street, and a couple of silver bracelets jingled around her wrists. I felt under-dressed next to her in my leggings and sweatshirt, but it was too late to change.

"How long are you here?" I asked before I could back out of the question. "Are you alone?"

Willa glanced at me with a glint in her eyes. She held up her enormous diamond ring. "I'm running from an engagement I'm not sure I want. So I'm here as long as I want to be. What about you?"

A lump grew in my throat. My eyes burned as I opened my mouth a few times before telling her the truth. "I was left at the altar. I'm here until... until I remember how it feels to be me."

Willa slowed her step, taking a deep breath. "Do you need a travel buddy?"

I paused, staring at her.

She shrugged and rubbed her hands together. "That was forward of me. It seems like maybe we could help each other. I talk a lot, and sometimes I walk really fast, but I won't ask about your pain if you don't ask about mine. I have a law degree, a candle business back home, and I'm allergic to kiwi and avocados."

I surveyed the busy Paris street, swallowing my heartbeat as I considered her offer. I was here to forget about the parts of me people ran away from - the dark parts, the sad parts, the drowning parts - to be happier, brighter, and free. As if she could sense my answer already, Willa smiled.

"What kind of candles?" I asked.

Willa beamed, looping her arm through mine as we continued to walk. I was grateful she talked so much. I'd forgotten how. She sold candles that smelled like dessert. She started in college to make a little extra money, but after she graduated with her Master's degree, she realized she hated law school and wanted to do something she loved instead.

The walk to the crepe place was a little over half a mile. Instead of waiting, Willa walked right in and sat us at a table on the patio beneath a bright yellow awning. When the server approached, he smiled and told Willa it was nice to see her again. A blush crept over his cheeks.

"You brought a friend this time," he said shyly.

"I made a new friend," Willa said, lounging back in her chair. "This is Addie. Addie, this is Thierry."

Thierry offered me a gentle smile. He was tall, with yellow hair and brown eyes. Everything about him seemed kind. His English was hesitant and broken through his thick French accent. I smiled back at him.

"Thierry, sweetheart, we're going to need some tap water, and two glasses of champagne," Willa said, placing her hand on his arm. He blushed and walked off with our order. She looked at me with a mischievous glint in her eyes. "I could just dunk him in my coffee."

I laughed.

"So, let's eat," Willa cheered, leaning over my menu and pointing. "Here's what's good."

CHAPTER
3

I met Willa in the lobby the next morning. She mentioned a great breakfast place she wanted to try, after admitting she hadn't visited too many of the tourist sites yet. We agreed to explore the city together. I dressed in a slightly wrinkly pair of flare jeans and a blue blouse.

When I met her downstairs, Willa wore her Western boots over tight black jeans, and a blue tank top. Her hair was voluminous and curly again, the exact opposite of my lifeless locks.

She handed me a wad of metro tickets. "I had an extra set. I thought we should try to get Navigo passes today."

I nodded in agreement. I read about those in bed last night. Instead of using a metro ticket every time I went in and out, I could scan the pass and go anywhere while it was valid. It would be helpful, especially since I'd be here for a while.

Willa led the way out of the hotel, humming and dancing while she walked. Apparently, it was only a quick metro ride, then a walk to the restaurant. I didn't mind. There was a slight chill in the late summer air, and it was overcast. I followed Willa into the metro, mimicking her movements to scan our tickets. The metro smelled like body odor and rot. I watched in fascination as the huge subway train screeched into the station. The noise ripped through me and I flinched, almost reaching up to cover my ears. Willa took my hand and dragged me onboard. I nearly fell when the train took off again.

"What do you want to do today?" She asked.

I blinked, reeling from the agonizing noise and rush of movement. "Oh, whatever you want is fine."

Willa tilted her head, her brow furrowing. "I'm asking you."

With a jolt, I realized I couldn't remember the last time someone asked what I wanted. Of course, I spent all my time with *her*, and she never cared. We did what she wanted, or what her friends wanted. When I was with Indy, she knew I wasn't always comfortable making decisions, so she did it without ever asking.

I pulled out my phone to show Willa the long list of things I wanted to do while I was here. It was alphabetized, with notes for locations and why I wanted to do them - if they weren't obvious. Willa took my phone and read through it, her eyes wide. I suddenly felt embarrassed by the list and wished I knew how to be spontaneous.

"You're very organized," she said. "How about we hit Notre Dame and the Sainte-Chapelle after breakfast, and take it from there?"

I agreed.

We ate breakfast at a cafe called *La Favorite*. It was decorated in pink cherry blossoms and was one of the prettiest restaurants I'd ever eaten at. I ordered salmon eggs benedict and a mimosa with a flower garnish. Willa flirted with the servers, and one of them knelt next to her to teach her words in French. I watched in amazement.

She could talk to anyone. I had no idea how to do that. I wondered if I could learn by spending more time with her.

I had friends at home, once. I had them in high school until I went to a different college than most of them. I had them in college until I graduated a year earlier than the rest. I worked too much with people twenty years older than me. And when I wasn't working, I had social obligations with *her* and her friends. It wasn't until it was too late that I realized I lost everything I built for myself.

Willa drank two large glasses of champagne at breakfast. I let myself absorb the sound of her laugh and the warmth of her smile, thinking it had been a long time since I laughed so easily. When we left the restaurant, she looped her arm through mine. I skipped through the street next to her, shaking my head in amusement. A slight buzz from the mimosas dulled my senses and made it easier to laugh with her when she pointed out a French bulldog in a bumble bee costume.

It rained on our walk to Notre Dame. Neither of us had thought to bring an umbrella. Willa didn't seem to care that the rain would ruin her curls, dancing through the streets as rain seeped into her clothes. It made my flat hair frizzy, and I brushed it away from my jaw, shivering at the unpleasant tickling sensation of hair on skin. Willa offered me a hair tie without questioning my disgusted sigh. Then, she took my hand and dragged me along after her with the brightest smile.

Notre Dame was surrounded by enormous security fences, and the back half was covered in scaffolding while it was repaired from the fire damage. Willa and I sat in the courtyard in front of it, staring up at the front of the cathedral. She pointed out the gargoyles, and I shared that they were added after Victor Hugo wrote the Hunchback of Notre Dame.

Almost immediately, I apologized, worried she wouldn't care about those kinds of facts like I did. Willa wrinkled her nose, taking my hand and asking me to tell her more. We sat in the rain and I told her everything I knew about how Victor Hugo brought the public's attention and devotion back to the grand cathedral.

When it rained harder, we took shelter in a little green bookstore across the street. I wandered away from Willa, lost in stacks of books. When I found her again, she sat in the children's section, talking quietly with Thierry the French server. I smiled, backing away from them and making my way upstairs. I hoped Willa found joy in this city. She ran from a life she was scared of. I ran from a life that broke me. Perhaps we were more similar than I imagined.

I sat in a window upstairs and watched the rain.

Willa found me a while later. Her lips were pink and swollen. She sat on the window seat next to me with a guilty look on her face, crossing her hands in her lap. "Will you hate me if I go with Thierry?"

I waved her off with an easy smile. "Go, have a nice afternoon with a cute French boy."

"Where will you go?" She asked, brows furrowed.

I shrugged, peering around the room, desperate for an answer. I didn't think she would accept that I wanted to stay here in my quiet corner forever. My eyes settled on a book by Gaston Leroux and an idea formed in my mind.

"I'm going to the Palais Garnier," I bluffed.

Willa grinned. "Fine, I'll text you tomorrow and we can do something, yeah?"

"Sure, Willa."

She skipped off. I heard her giggle downstairs and rolled my eyes. When she was gone, I almost stayed curled up on the window seat. I wanted to. It would be so easy to spend the rest of the day in a tiny bookstore, without talking to anyone or seeing anything new.

That wasn't why I was here. I was here for a new life.

So, I gathered my bag and left the bookstore.

CHAPTER 4

I traveled across the city by myself and was proud of it. I nearly cried in the metro. Even with my earplugs, too many people brushed against me and the screech of the trains sent splinters through my veins. I hoped it would at least get easier the more time I spent here. Right now, the different metro lines and the bulging crowds that pushed in and out of the trains was overwhelming and frustrating. I hardly understood the automated voice announcing which stop was next, and I almost missed the one for the opera house.

I stumbled out of the metro station, barely avoiding a couple of pickpockets lingering at the entrance. I clutched my purse to my chest, raising my eyes to look at the enormous building in front of me. Something like awe blossomed in my chest, only to be immediately shattered by a car alarm. I shook the sound out of my head. Determined, I crossed the street, following a group of tourists into the opera house. It was cooler inside, a welcome relief from the humidity and the on-again-off-again rainstorm.

Immediately after the ticket booth, an enormous marble staircase greeted me. My eyes widened, and I ran my hand along the banister as I climbed the steps. At the top of those, there was an even bigger staircase, and the words to a song about a masquerade echoed through my head. I watched a few others sing it out loud and pose on the grand steps with giant smiles. I raised my eyes to admire intricate chandeliers and sconces and paintings on the ceiling. A huge skylight let daylight into the room, illuminating even the darkest of corners.

With each step I took, I wondered how I'd gotten here.

Five years ago, I fell in love with a girl. Her hair was like gold and her smile made my heart ache. I loved her with everything I had - which wasn't much. I loved her until I couldn't stand the sight of her.

I didn't know when she stopped loving me. It could have been the day she left me at the altar, or it could have been long before. I was too shut down to notice.

I wondered if I was someone before her. Someone bright. Someone who smiled.

Or, maybe I wasn't. Maybe I was born someone who ran away when things got hard. I was doing it now.

Running.

I wasn't sure how long I wandered through the opera house. When I finally came to a room of gold, the sun was setting. The room seemed like it had caught fire, even the air particles around me glowed in the sunlight. I raised my hand to a cloud of sunshine, feeling the warmth on my pale skin.

"All these beautiful things, and somehow you still look sad."

I turned towards the deep English voice, raising my eyes to take in the man behind me. Immediately, I clamped my jaw shut to keep it from hitting the ground. Black boots and tight pants led up to a half-open, red silk shirt. His face was both boyish and chiseled like a statue of a Greek god. His eyes were the color of burnt honey, practically glowing in the sunset that poured through the windows and illuminated the golden room. He had light brown hair, like cocoa powder, and the messy waves shimmered in the sun.

I swallowed thickly. "I'm not sad."

The stranger dragged his tongue over his lips. "It's in your eyes. You want to love this so much more than you do."

I tried not to let my shoulders slump at his words, but he was right. Here I was, exploring a building I dreamed of since I was a child watching Gerard Butler and Emmy Rossum in the movie theater, and all I thought about was how desperately I wanted to go home. Exhaustion and loneliness seeped into every muscle in my body. My feet ached. My heart hurt. And I'd only been here for one day.

When I said nothing, the stranger straightened, his eyes brightening. He held out his hand. "I'm Holland."

I hesitated only a moment before taking his hand, which felt cool against mine. For the second time in as many days, I introduced myself to a stranger. This time, though, I used my full name without even meaning to. "Adalyn."

Holland whispered my name like he tasted it on his tongue. I wasn't prepared for the shiver it sent down my spine. I looked down at where we held hands, gulping.

"Would you like to dance?" Holland asked.

I raised an eyebrow, looking around the people milling around the large, golden room. "I don't-" I started.

Except Holland was already pulling me after him, into the middle of the room. A few people glared at us as we traipsed around them. I stumbled lightly, eyes wide when I ended up with my chest pressed to Holland's. He offered me a dazzling smile, wrapping one arm around my shoulders and holding my opposite hand. He started with a slow step into me, then sideways. I recognized the steps of a waltz and fell into step with him. My heart beat so loud I worried he could hear it pounding against my ribcage. A smile tugged at the corner of Holland's lips. My eyes lingered on his mouth for a moment too long before I forced them back to his endless eyes.

Everyone stared at us. My cheeks burned bright red and I couldn't catch my breath. Holland repeated the same steps, his eyes never wavering from mine. With each step I took with the stranger, I melted further into the honey gold of his eyes. After a couple more boxes, he raised one arm and spun me in a quick circle.

A smile tugged at my lips as I missed the last step and stumbled into him. He grinned.

"Again," he whispered.

This time, I was more ready for the turn, catching myself on the last step and moving up into him. Holland beamed, his steps quickening. I tilted my head curiously, watching the joy roll off him in waves. Step after step, his gaze never broke from mine. If we danced too close to annoyed tourists, he spun me away, guiding me with his steps. I barely knew how to waltz, but following him was as easy as breathing. Holland spun me around again, this time catching me and tilting me back slowly. I gasped, watching his eyes trail down my face, to my throat, and back to my eyes. I wasn't sure I'd ever been looked at like that.

He looked at me like he was a starving man, and I was everything he ever needed.

Time moved slower when he stood, pulling me with him. A foreign smile spread across my face, burning my cheeks with joy. Holland reached up to tilt my chin up so I'd stare directly at him.

"You have a lovely smile," he said.

Then, he turned on his heel and walked away.

I placed my hand on my chest to slow my racing heart, shaking my head. Holland disappeared around the corner, and I turned to look around the room. Half the crowd had moved on from the dancing disturbance, back to their own worlds. The other half stared at me with a mixture of emotions - including shock and annoyance, but there were also a couple of soft smiles.

I took one step to follow Holland, then paused and shook my head.

Instead, I turned and smiled up at the golden ceiling. It really was one of the most beautiful places I'd ever seen.

CHAPTER 5

I sat at a cafe across the street from the Palais Garnier, sipping a hot chocolate and resisting the urge to eat my whipped cream with a spoon instead of topping my drink like I was supposed to. My phone buzzed on the table next to me. I leaned back and answered my sister's video call.

Indy's hair was a mess, and she wore her scrubs. "Hey!" Her eyes widened in shock and she squinted at her phone. "I thought I'd find you in bed."

I flipped my camera to show her my view of the opera house. The shadows from the last of the day made it seem even more beautiful. Indy whistled in surprise. I turned her back to me, resting the phone on the table and sipping my drink again.

"What's up?" I asked her.

"I wanted to check on you to see if you were wallowing," Indy said. I watched her unlock the door to her apartment and promptly drop her bag on the ground. She kicked the door shut.

"Not wallowing," I responded. "I made a friend."

Indy's eyes popped out of her head. "You didn't!"

I nodded. "Her name is Willa. She's staying in the same hotel as me. We had breakfast together this morning, and she let me geek out over Notre Dame."

Indy plopped down on her couch and whooped in joy. I smiled softly in response, glancing back up at the Palais Garnier. A blush crept across my cheeks as I thought about dancing with a stranger inside. I opened my mouth to tell Indy about it, but she would never believe me. I kept the memory to myself, instead asking her how things were going at home. Indy embarked on a rant on how some old man groped her at work today. Mom and Dad were fighting again. Her application for the cat was denied, and her maybe-boyfriend was bringing lasagna for dinner tonight.

I alternated between actually listening to her and watching the busy Paris streets. Willa texted me asking if I wanted to grab dinner. I sent her back my location and told her to meet me; we could find somewhere new together.

I was still on video call with Indy when Willa arrived. Thierry was on her arm, smiling and watching her like she was his next meal. It might have been weird if she didn't beam up at him with utter joy. I waved at them.

"I want to see your friend!" Indy squeaked. "I need to know you're safe."

Willa ducked into the camera view, waving and introducing herself to my sister. Indy grilled her with questions about whether she was a serial killer or a Republican. Willa only laughed, sitting down next to me and answering my sister's obnoxious questions without hesitation. Thierry sat down on her other side, his brow furrowed while he watched Willa.

"Don't let my sister fall in love with anyone!" Indy blew a kiss when she finally hung up.

"I'm sorry about her," I said, shaking my head in amusement.

"She has spunk! I love her!" Willa clasped her hands together.

"Why can you not fall in love?" Thierry asked, tilting his head. "Paris is the City of Love."

"Love hurts, my dearest," Willa took his hand and kissed his knuckles. He watched her curiously. Willa wrinkled her nose at him before sitting back and giving me a knowing wink.

Thierry suggested a great cafe nearby for dinner. I paid my bill for the hot chocolate. Before we left, I scooped the last of the whipped cream on my spoon and plopped it in my mouth. Willa laughed hysterically as I covered my mouth to keep from spitting it out. I followed my new friends down the street.

Hours later, we sat on the grass at the Champ de Mars with champagne and chocolate-covered strawberries. Thierry left us since he had to work early the next morning, so it was just me and Willa sitting on the slightly damp grass. I reached for a piece of chocolate, staring up at the Eiffel Tower as it went dark, then burst into a million glittering lights.

All around us, collective gasps and cheers filled the air like the sweetest music.

My heart swelled at the sight. For half a second, I thought I would cry.

"I'm engaged to a man," Willa blurted. I turned toward her. She stared up at the Eiffel Tower wistfully. "A man who wants me to sit down, shut my mouth, and be his pretty little wife."

I blinked. Just yesterday, she said she wouldn't talk about her pain. Yesterday, though, she hadn't spent a whole day with a boy who looked at her like she was his universe.

"We're high school sweethearts. He's never physically hurt me," Willa paused, taking a shaky breath. She continued before I questioned her. "He wants to take away who I am. He doesn't know I'm here. I have ninety-three missed calls on my phone, and a couple hundred texts from him - not including my family."

"Why are you here?" I asked.

"The same reason you are, I think. To find myself," Willa said. "I thought, maybe, if I know myself a little better, I can make a better decision about being a man's wife."

I gulped down the rest of my champagne and poured myself another glass. Willa did the same. We both gazed up at the glittering Eiffel Tower, and my chest ached.

Donna would have loved this.

The thought of her name was a punch to the gut. I lost my breath. In one blink, I remembered every time she danced around the kitchen and talked about our honeymoon. She talked about how she wanted to kiss someone at the top of the Eiffel Tower, though she never said she wanted to kiss *me*. She saved every picture and video of Paris she came across on social media, and sent me all of them.

I thought of each time it was time to add money to our trip fund. My stomach twisted at the thought of her dropping to her knees and crying over not having her half - every month. She made more money than I did, and somehow never had her portion. Still, I smiled. I added extra from my paycheck. And, later, when she asked me to pay for dinner, I did, even though it over drafted my bank account.

I wasn't sorry for being here. It hurt to be here without her, but not in the way I expected. She wouldn't have gone to *La Favorite* for breakfast, she hated the color pink. And she wouldn't have listened to me ramble on about Victor Hugo and Notre Dame.

She definitely wouldn't have danced with me in the Palais Garnier.

A blush crept over my cheeks as I thought of Holland's smile as he spun me in a circle. I would likely never see the dashing stranger again, but I would always have the feeling of dancing in golden daylight. I could have drowned in that kind of freedom.

"I'm on my honeymoon alone," I told Willa. As soon as the words were out of my mouth, I brought my champagne glass to my lips and swallowed the rest of it with one breath.

She snorted. I turned to her in shock. We stared at each other - then both burst into laughter at the same moment. I fell back against the grass, laughing as I stared up at the sky. Willa patted her knees and kicked her feet, barely able to hold on to her full glass of champagne.

We laughed until we cried.

As soon as the tears started, they were hard to stop. My chest convulsed in sobs. Willa hiccuped, burying her face in her hands. I crossed my arms over my chest, holding myself tight and rocking back and forth as everything fell apart.

I loved her.

I did everything for her.

And she didn't show up.

She should have left me before the wedding. I wished she would have left a long time ago, because I was too much of a coward to ever do it myself. I wished she wouldn't have said 'yes' when I proposed. Instead, she waited until I genuinely believed everything would be okay, and left me standing up there alone.

It had been a week without one word from her.

I knew she was safe, her mother hugged me when I finally stepped off the altar. She told me Donna was... *sorry*. I didn't remember shoving her mother away, despite Indy telling me I did.

Willa reached over to grip my hand. I peered down at our hands, then up at my new friend. Her makeup was smeared down her face, her eyes as wet as mine. "We start tomorrow without regret," she said. "We're in Paris, let's make the most of it."

I squeezed her hand. "Deal."

CHAPTER
6

I wore a purple sundress the next day, the only semi-decent article of clothing I brought. It exposed the thick curves of my hips more than I typically would have liked, and the leaf and fern vine tattoos that laced up my left leg were completely on display. I clicked the heels of my tennis shoes together, hoping I didn't look ridiculous in a dress and travel pack. I made a mental note to ask Willa if she wanted to go shopping; I couldn't wear clothes that didn't fit properly forever.

"I didn't know you had tattoos!" Willa cried when I met her in the lobby downstairs. She knelt to inspect my leg. The leaves and ferns began at the top of my foot and laced all the way up my thigh. I got them after I graduated high school as a gift to myself. Only a few months later, I kept them hidden because Donna hated them.

Donna wasn't here anymore.

I accepted Willa's compliments, turning in a circle so she could see all the details.

"Hey," I asked when we left the hotel. "Can you ask Thierry if he knows any good hair stylists around here? Oh, and if he'd be willing to help translate?"

Willa beamed, pulling out her phone. "I'll ask. What do you want to do?"

I tugged at the tip of my hair. "I usually have it dyed a super bright copper color. It's been over a year. I'd like to get it back."

She gave me a thumbs up, leading the way to our metro station. This time, we stopped for our Navigo passes and pictures, activating them instantly and going on our way. Through the streets, we walked with linked arms, laughing and enjoying every moment.

We waited in line at the Louvre for a selfie with the Mona Lisa.

We wandered through Napoleon III's apartments.

Willa told me all about Greek mythology as we stared at sculptures that looked more human than I felt.

We got lost in the massive museum... twice.

The day went by in the blink of an eye, and we found ourselves in the Tuileries Gardens with cold sandwiches after several hours in the Louvre. My legs ached and my mind reeled from everything I'd seen and learned... and with the realization that this was my life: dancing around Parisian streets and snickering about nude statues with a girl I barely knew but might be my best friend.

Thierry joined us when he finished his shift at the creperie. Willa's eyes brightened when he kissed her knuckles. I wandered away from them, admiring the topiaries and hedges while Willa laughed and flirted with her French boy. It was the end of summer, and a lot of the green had begun to fade to orange or brown. Still, every step I took was breathtaking. I hummed as I walked, enjoying the warm breeze on my skin.

"You look happier."

I jumped, turning a corner and nearly walking directly into Holland.

A smile spread across his lips when I looked up at him, again dazzled by the gold in his eyes. He wore a black shirt and a blue sweater today and his expression was soft and warm. I glanced around the garden, wondering where he'd come from. I'd wandered away from Willa and Thierry; I couldn't hear her laugh anymore.

"Strange coincidence to run into you again," I said quietly.

He shrugged, offering me his arm. "Walk with me?"

If Indy were here, she would grill him about being a serial killer. There was, of course, that possibility. But, I couldn't stop thinking about the freedom I found dancing with him and wondered if he could offer me that feeling again. After a moment of hesitation, I laced my arm through his. His eyes widened in surprise. He recovered quickly, leading me through a set of hedges into a new section of the garden.

"Tell me one thing that makes you happy," he said.

I paused, glancing between the stranger and the garden in front of me. It seemed like such a simple question, but nothing came to mind. A lump formed in my throat, and I lowered my eyes.

Holland hummed, reaching up to place his hand over where mine held onto his arm. I stared at where our skin touched, surprised I felt no revulsion at the sensation. "I like a fresh *pain au chocolat*, the way it smells after it rains, the quiet awe of an art museum, the blush on a pretty girl's cheeks."

I jolted to meet his eyes, aware of how bright my cheeks burned. Holland smiled again, and I swore my heart skipped a beat. "That's a lot of things," I whispered.

"The world is full of beautiful things, might as well appreciate them." He squeezed my hand.

We walked quietly while I thought about his question. I

watched others live their lives around me - joggers, readers, dreamers. The park was full of people and none of them knew I was drowning. Finally, I slowed to a stop and turned to Holland. He blinked, his lips parting like he anticipated my answer more than anything.

"I like tulips, sour candy, and," I trailed off for a moment, reminding myself not to get lost in Holland's eyes. "Midnight," I said. "When the entire world is finally quiet, but the people who are still awake are the truest versions of themselves."

Holland held my gaze for a long moment, so long I thought time stopped. "Who are you at midnight, Adalyn?"

I sucked in a breath and shook my head. "I don't know anymore."

"Would you like to find out?"

I opened my mouth to answer him when Willa and Thierry came skipping around the corner. Willa's eyes widened in shock. The smile fell from Thierry's face. I watched him hold tighter to Willa's hand, pulling her close to him. She winced, wrinkling her nose to brush off whatever bothered her. She raised an eyebrow at me, her eyes dragging over Holland for an extended moment.

"Wow," she breathed before gathering herself. "We're heading back to the hotel. Are you coming?"

"You should come, it's getting late," Thierry said stiffly. His eyes remained fixed on Holland.

I paused. Willa gave me a wide-eyed, excited look. She gave me a small go-for-it motion with her hands. The dark look on Thierry's face made me hesitate. He seemed nervous, his hand nearly outstretched to reach for me and bring me back with them.

He was right; it was getting late. I was tired and my body ached from being on my feet all day. Going back to the hotel was the comfortable option, the one I would have chosen any other time. If I was at home, I would never consider it. But, I was tired of doing what others wanted me to and this new, broken version of me longed to feel something. And Holland made my heart race.

I raised my eyes to look at Holland again, this stranger I hardly knew. He stared back at Thierry. His smile faded and there was something challenging in his eyes, like he dared Thierry to say something else. When he felt me watching him, his eyes lowered to meet mine and melted. My breath caught.

"I would love to find out," I told him quietly.

He grinned.

"Location, please," Willa said cheerfully. I pulled out my phone and shared my location with her. She beamed in approval, tugging on Thierry's hand. "I want details later!"

I watched Thierry, confused. He stared at Holland as if he knew him... like he hated him. When I glanced at Holland, he nodded to Thierry with something like triumph. Finally, Thierry turned to follow Willa.

"Do you know Thierry?" I asked Holland, chewing on my lower lip.

He shook his head. "No, I don't." I paused, glancing after my friends. Holland stepped forward, tilting my chin up again and bringing my attention back fully to him. The gesture sent shivers through me. "I would like to know you, though."

"There's not much to know," I admitted.

"I doubt that."

"What makes you so sure?" I challenged, nearly clamping my jaw shut after the words escaped me. Too loud, too much, too brave, I reminded myself.

Holland only smiled. "I'm not, but won't it be fun?"

"Where are we going?"

Holland stepped impossibly closer. I thought, for a moment, he was going to kiss me. I might have let him. "Let's not spoil the fun," he whispered.

He stepped back swiftly. I nearly gasped at the lack of contact.

Holland held out his hand, offering me a mischievous smile. He bowed low, his eyes never leaving mine, drawing me into this world he offered. I didn't let myself hesitate. I took his hand.

As Holland led me away from the garden, I had a distinct feeling that nothing was ever going to be the same again.

CHAPTER
7

I gripped Holland's hand as he led the way onto the boat. Immediately, I resented the rock of the floor beneath my feet. My stomach flipped. For half a moment, I worried I would be sick and thought of how that would be a terrible way to start a date... if that's even what this was. Holland took a few steps forward, coaxing me after him. I hadn't told him I hated boats and water, but it was as if he heard my heart racing. His eyes were patient, never leaving mine, as he led me to sit on a bench near the railing.

A breeze whispered through the air; I shivered. The summer sunshine transformed into gold, taking the warmth with it and leaving the cool night behind. My sundress blew around my legs in the wind; I resisted the urge to grip the fabric to keep it still. Behind me, someone's child whooped in joy. I flinched away from the unexpected sound, shaking my head to rid myself of the sensation.

Holland traced his thumb over my knuckles, tilting his head in concern. I offered him a weak smile, squeezing his hand. Around us, Paris twinkled under the new night sky. The lights reflected on the river, and everything seemed to glow warm and golden. When I looked at Holland again, he admired the same thing I did - his eyes bright and fascinated.

"How long have you been in Paris?" I asked.

"A while," he responded. "I love this city." It wasn't an answer, but I watched his lips move while he talked. The boat lurched forward, and my stomach flipped again. I must have squeezed Holland's hand, because he moved closer, his thumb still rubbing circles over my fingers. "Why are you in Paris?" he asked, reaching over with his free hand to tilt my head up to focus on him.

It was like the whole world faded - all the noise and move- ment was gone. I didn't worry about the rock of the boat, or the fabric of my dress tickling my leg. The only thing I could focus on was the flecks of gold in Holland's eyes.

"Vacation," I lied. "I've always wanted to see Paris."

Holland hummed. "Okay, what's the actual answer?"

I stiffened, watching the lights twinkle in his eyes. "What makes you think that's not the answer?"

His fingers traced my hand, to my wrist where my pulse throbbed. "Your heart flutters when you lie."

Holland flicked his tongue over his lips while he waited. I stared down at his fingers on my wrist, suddenly aware he could feel my heartbeat. "To find myself," I answered finally. "Which is a lame answer, I know, but I tend to run away from things that scare me." I paused. "Sorry, that was a lot."

Holland chuckled, rolling his eyes. His fingers moved on my wrist and I jolted in surprise, shivers rippling through me. I rubbed my free hand on the fabric of my dress in an attempt to ignore the rocking of the boat and the slosh of the surrounding water. "Tell me something that scares you," he said.

I swallowed thickly.

I didn't know what it was about him that made me talk so openly. Perhaps it was because I did not know who this handsome stranger was, or how I'd run into him twice. All I knew was dancing with him made me feel more like myself than I could ever remember, and I would spend the rest of my life chasing that feeling.

Indy would scream at me about talking to strangers and getting kidnapped. She was right about being careful, of course. Except, I leaned closer to Holland each time I watched him talk. I longed for him to smile again, to laugh again, to touch me again.

I didn't even know him.

I answered him anyway. "I'm scared that I don't know how to be happy anymore."

"Why?"

"I told you. I'm a runner," I breathed.

Holland raised an eyebrow. "I think there's more to it. Do you have a family?"

I turned toward him with a flutter in my chest. "Yeah, my parents and younger sister. My parents are overbearing, and they don't understand a lot of things, but my sister is the light of my life. Do you?"

Holland took a deep breath. "I haven't seen them in a long time. My mother was a dancer and my father a pianist. My younger sister is my best friend." I smiled, and Holland's eyes strayed to my mouth before he asked another question. "Where are you from?"

"Arizona. Born and raised."

He wrinkled his nose.

A laugh escaped me at the sight of his distaste. "Have you been?"

He nodded once. "I went in the middle of summer. I thought the heat would be the death of me."

I laughed, leaning into him when the boat rocked more than I was comfortable with. "I don't think I ever want to go back," I murmured.

"So don't," Holland said.

He stood from our bench, holding his hand out in a grand gesture. I stood hesitantly, whimpering at the rock of the boat. Holland pulled me along behind him without another moment's hesitation. I followed him to the front of the boat. Holland stepped behind me, essentially trapping me between him and the very front of the boat.

"Close your eyes," he murmured.

I did, with a start. Holland placed his hands on my hips, turning me so my back pressed against his chest. His warm body shielded me from the breeze. I tried not to think too long about how his fingers felt on me. I realized, a moment later, that the wind on my face and through the skirt of my dress and holding onto the front of the boat felt a little like flying.

I smiled.

One of Holland's hands fell to rest on my waist. Sparks shot through me. I kept my eyes closed as he instructed, yelping when he coaxed me to step up onto the railing - like Jack and Rose in the Titanic. I opened my eyes when I stood on the railing, laughing once. Holland's hands gripped my hips, holding me up as I let go of the railing and laughed into the Paris night.

"Don't run, Adalyn," Holland said. "Fly."

I let my head fall back, hair whipping around my face.

Freedom. Flying.

Happiness.

Until a boat attendant yelled in French. I lost my balance in shock, falling back into a snickering Holland. He pulled me against his chest, muttering half-hearted apologies back to the boat attendant, who yelled over him. He was red in the face, yelling about how dangerous that was. I only caught every other word of his fast French; it was enough to send me scrambling. Holland shook his head, dragging me back to our seat on the bench. I laughed, blushing and resting my head on his shoulder while he tried to apologize to the French man.

When the boat ride was over, the French attendant cursed at us again. Holland laughed, waving goodbye to him as he led the way off the platform.

"Mean old man." He shook his head, winking at me. "Care for a treat?"

"Isn't it late for treats?" I raised an eyebrow.

"Not in Paris."

Holland moved a mile a minute, pointing out bouquets on balconies and couples kissing in corners. I was amazed; I would have walked with my head down, my silicone earplugs in - taking in the least amount of stimulation I could - and noticing none of it. Holland welcomed it all, and he made it look easy. We walked a couple of blocks to a bakery with lights still on. I missed what Holland ordered, unable to keep up with the fast French. My eyes widened in delight when he pulled a *pain au chocolat* out of a brown bag.

"Best pastries in Paris," he told me.

I bit down on the corner, unable to suppress a moan of delight at the taste. It was buttery, flaky, chocolatey, and it practically melted on my tongue. Holland grinned, biting into his as we kept walking. I enjoyed every bite of my pastry, frowning when it was gone. Holland offered me another.

The little voices in the back of my head told me I didn't need another treat. I wanted another one, though. I took the pastry. Holland smiled and pulled a second one out of the bag for himself.

We turned a corner, and Holland motioned for me to wait, raising the brown bag he carried. I paused, watching Holland step into the shadows. An elderly couple sat in a dark corner, curled around each other with raggedy blankets. Holland knelt in front of them, offering them the bag.

"Thank you, creature," the man said in a raspy voice.

Holland seemed unnerved when he returned to me. "That was nice," I told him.

He shrugged. "It's nothing."

When we walked away, Holland glanced back to make sure the couple was eating their croissants. They were.

"Penny for your thoughts?" I asked when I laced my arm back through his.

He smiled. "Wondering how you're holding up."

"It's after eleven," I said. "I'm an early sleeper. And every muscle in my body hurts."

"But we're on a mission to discover who you are at midnight," he countered.

"I know," I said with a smile. "One more hour. Give it your best shot."

Holland's grin was almost feral. "Is that a challenge, dear Adalyn?"

"If you want it to be."

"I do."

When I was nine, I told my parents I wanted to be a Lost Girl. I stood up from watching Peter Pan, stormed into their room, and declared I never wanted to grow up.

I wondered what happened to that girl.

When the clock struck midnight, I stood on a bench near the Seine, laughing and holding the hand of a boy I hardly knew. His sweater hung over my shoulders; it smelled like chocolate. He held a rain-soaked copy of Peter Pan in his free hand, reading it out loud as I walked back and forth on the bench. We found the copy on top of a trash can about half an hour ago. I mentioned it was my favorite story as a girl.

Holland started reading.

"Would you like to live forever?" I asked him when he finished a chapter.

He paused, closing the book and looking up at me. Something haunting flashed in his eyes. "I don't think it's all it's chalked up to be."

"Really?" I sat down on the bench. "Why?"

Holland cleared his throat. "I imagine it's lonely. Imagine all the time passing, never getting to fall in love with anyone because you're going to live forever and they aren't."

I pursed my lips, kicking my feet back and forth. "Is love your only argument? Because that's not a very good one. Love hurts whether you live forever or not."

"Most things that live forever are monsters," Holland countered.

"Like what? Vampires? Ghouls?" I teased.

He was quiet.

I paused, watching his face fall. My heart sank and my chest felt heavy. "I'm sorry, I don't know what I said. I didn't mean it."

"What do you mean?"

"You seem upset now. I didn't mean to make you upset." I gulped, fiddling with my thumbs in my lap.

Holland knelt in front of me, taking both of my hands in his. "I am not upset, only thinking." He stared up at me in concern. "Follow-up question," he said. "Would you live forever if you were a monster?"

"Only if I had someone to love," I teased, wrinkling my nose.

Holland shook his head in amusement. His eyes seemed to

glow in the dim streetlight. I wanted to lose myself in the molten gold over and over again.

"I should get you back to your hotel," he said.

I checked the time. It was twelve-thirty. As soon as I saw how late it was, my feet and back ached with renewed intensity and I winced. I was thirsty and had a slight headache. I'd forgotten about all of that with him. For a while, I'd been free.

We walked the rest of the way to my hotel.

Out front, I shrugged out of Holland's sweater and handed it back to him. "Thank you," I said. "For tonight, not just for the jacket."

He offered me a sweet, boyish smile. "It was my pleasure, Adalyn."

I watched, entranced, as he bowed low to kiss my knuckles. His mouth lingered a moment longer than it should have. He straightened and nodded politely. I took a step back into the hotel lobby, making sure my room key was in my pocket.

When I turned back, Holland was gone.

It was only then that I realized I never asked for his phone number.

CHAPTER
8

"So, you didn't kiss him and you didn't ask for his number? Girl, what were you thinking?" Willa whined.

I huffed out a long breath, watching the stylist paint my hair copper. I'd been kicking myself since last night for not remembering to get Holland's phone number. He appeared out of nowhere both times, whisking me into his arms and reminding me how it felt to smile. I couldn't count on it happening again, though. Paris was a big city. Holland could be anywhere. It seemed unlikely I would find him again. The thought hurt more than I expected it to.

I felt alive with him, walking through the Paris streets at midnight.

"Why didn't you kiss him? Hell, why didn't you jump his bones?"

"Willa!" I exclaimed, blushing bright red.

She leaned back in her chair, laughing and clasping her hands together. "My friend, he was *so* into you."

"I don't even know him."

"You spent all night with him, what did you learn?"

I thought about every time Holland laughed, and his eyes seemed to melt into mine. His hands were always cold, but it was warm in his arms. I groaned and almost buried my face in my hands. I definitely should have kissed him.

The stylist gripped my head and forced me to look straight forward. I flinched from her harsh touch, resisting the urge to join in on Willa's snickers. The stylist said something in French to the stylist at the station next to us, too quickly for me to understand. They both rolled their eyes and went back to work. I exchanged a look with Willa and smothered my laugh with a weak cough. She snickered, staring down at her phone in determination.

"We should go on a city-wide search," Willa said. "He has to be somewhere."

"There are millions of people in Paris," I countered.

She crossed her arms. "It can't end like this!" My heart twinged with regret. Willa leaped out of her chair. "I know! I'll ask Thierry!"

"Why would Thierry know?" I asked.

"He said he knows Holland," Willa said, skipping outside before I could respond. Thierry dropped us off at the hair salon earlier, mumbling something about coming back to help with payment when we were done. He was across the street at a cafe. I watched Willa skip to the crosswalk and frolic away before I lost sight of her in the waves of people.

I paused, remembering Holland said he didn't know Thierry. Why would Holland say he didn't know Thierry, but Thierry knew Holland? The thought soured in my stomach. I sat back in the chair, impatiently waiting for Willa and Thierry to return.

By the time they did, the stylist was drying my hair. Willa glowered in annoyance. Thierry clenched his jaw in frustration. Neither of them looked at the other, and Willa wore a scarf she

43

didn't have earlier. I watched them in confusion. Willa sat back down on the couch across from me. Thierry sat next to her. She rested her head on his shoulder, wincing at the movement. Willa's eyes met mine, and she shrugged. I said nothing, discomfort crawling across my skin.

Thierry translated when I paid the stylist, but said nothing when we left the salon. As soon as we were outside, he walked in the opposite direction we were supposed to go without looking back.

"What was that about?" I asked Willa.

Her shoulders slumped. "He says Holland is bad news."

I scoffed. "So, he's taking it out on you?"

Willa looped her arm through mine, beckoning me along. "I called him a misogynistic asshole for trying to make that assumption. He didn't like that."

I snorted. Willa bit down on her lower lip and shifted in her seat. "Wait," I said. "Do you believe him?"

She shrugged. "I don't know Holland. You don't either."

"It's unlikely he'll show up again, anyway," I said, nudging her with my shoulder.

"A one-night Parisian love affair," Willa teased, tossing her head back wistfully.

I grimaced. "I should have kissed him."

"Remember that for the next one. Let's go shopping."

I looked more like myself than I had in a long time, but I still barely recognized myself.

I caught sight of my reflection in the windows at Pink Mamma for dinner. My hair was brighter, in curls over my shoulders. It brought out the faded freckles on my cheeks. I stared at myself for a moment while Willa rambled about what wine to order. My cheeks were hollow, my shoulders slumped forward. The dead look in my eyes had begun to fade.

Three days in Paris and I already felt different.

Lighter. Free.

"So, what did you go to school for?" Willa asked, setting down her menu. She must have decided on a bottle of wine to order.

"Marketing," I said.

"Do you work in marketing?"

"No, I worked as an office manager for an insurance company," I said, wrinkling my nose.

"Got it. Not your calling," Willa laughed. She adjusted the scarf she wore, wincing as it moved. "What is your calling?"

I opened my mouth a few times before my shoulders felt heavier. I looked down at my menu, sucking in a deep breath. "I don't know."

"Hey, I paid for law school before I discovered I enjoy making candles and sitting on social media," Willa said. "I think it's perfectly okay to just exist without knowing what you love."

The server approached our table, greeting us in English. Willa ordered a bottle of wine and we both chose a pasta dish for dinner.

I tried to remember what I wanted to be when I was young. Besides believing I would live forever with Peter Pan, I went through a phase where I thought I would be a veterinarian. Before that, I wanted to be a ballerina, even though there wasn't an athletic bone in my body.

What did I even like?

I enjoyed marketing well enough, though it had been a few years since I kept up with the trends. I wasn't creative, and I didn't have the urge to help people like Indy did.

Or, maybe I was, and I'd always been a little too sad to find out.

I needed to find a job soon, something remote if I wanted to stay in Paris. I wondered if I could find a boring, data entry job as long as it paid well enough for me to stay in this city if I loved it enough.

If I could find a job…

If I loved Paris…

My whole life seemed like one big question mark.

The thought made my hands shake.

"Did I lose you?" Willa's questioning voice brought me back to reality.

"Sorry," I muttered. "It's loud in here, I'm struggling to focus." I fumbled for a topic to continue the conversation. "How are things with Thierry?"

Willa paused, straightening and offering me a smile. "He's a constant surprise."

"Do you like surprises?" I asked.

The server returned with our bottle of wine. Willa didn't answer until after he'd gone. "Sure," she said. "Especially blonde ones that make great lovers."

I smiled.

"Oh, hey, tomorrow, I want to find the French equivalent of Barnes and Noble. I need some books that aren't classics." Willa changed the subject.

"What do you like to read?" I asked, sipping my wine.

Willa smirked. "Spicy romance."

"Hey," I teased. "What you do in your own time is your business."

We both burst into laughter.

And just like that, I remembered what it was like to have a friend.

CHAPTER
9

I lay in bed, staring at the ceiling and waiting for something to happen. Willa went to bed hours ago. When I turned my head, I watched the clock tick past two in the morning. I was wide awake, unsure why the anxiety ripped through me so intensely. I felt fine during dinner with Willa, and even the metro ride back to the hotel seemed less jarring than usual.

As soon as Willa said goodnight and returned to her room, my heart beat faster… and faster. I paced for a while, braided my hair, and showered. Nothing helped keep the anxiety at bay. Now, I lay in bed and it felt like a boulder crushed my chest. Silent tears stained my face, relentless despite my internal reminders that everything was fine. I was safe.

My phone rang.

I sat up quickly, staring at it where it buzzed across the hotel room on the TV stand. My hands shook as I pushed myself out of bed and padded across the room to pick it up.

Once it was in my hand, I almost dropped it.

It was Donna's name on the screen.

I hadn't heard from her since the night before we were supposed to get married. Not a word when Indy packed up my things from the apartment. Not a word for the days I wallowed on the couch at Indy's house. Nothing in my days in Paris.

Until this.

I found myself unsure if I wanted to hear what she had to say. Perhaps it would be easier if I never heard her voice again. As soon as I considered that, a little voice in the back of my mind screamed that I was running again. The little voice was angry.

I slid the green button across the screen.

"Adalyn?"

At the sound of her voice, my flash of anger faded and my knees went out from under me. I sank to the ground, my breath catching.

"Why are you calling me?" I croaked, placing my hand over my galloping heart.

"Where are you?" She ignored my question.

I repeated myself.

Donna was quiet for a moment. I hated how steady her voice sounded when she spoke again. Forever strong while I was breaking down. "I miss you."

I shook my head, hiccuping. "I don't miss you."

"You do, though. Where are you? Come over."

The rest of my heart shattered. She didn't miss me. She wanted me for sex.

Did she even regret what she'd done to me?

"I'm in Paris, Donna," I said coldly. Tears burned down my cheeks.

"What?" Her voice turned to ice. "You would never go without me."

"I did," I breathed.

The room spun around me. I placed one hand on the floor to keep myself oriented.

"Wow," Donna said. "How brave of you."

I looked across the room at the clock, wishing I could turn it back a few moments and not answer the phone call.

"There were pink butterflies on my dress," I whispered.

Donna said nothing.

My lips quivered. I was collapsing in on myself, becoming smaller and smaller with each passing moment. I wanted to disappear. "There were pink butterflies on my dress," I repeated. "And the lilies you wanted in our bouquets gave me a headache. Your great-aunt wore white, like you said she would. I was angry for a moment. I waited for you to join me. And you never did."

Still, nothing.

"Why did you do it?" I cried. My anger rose like a tidal wave, giving my voice a sharp edge.

Donna hummed, like she could hardly be bothered to have this conversation. "I wanted you to know how it felt to be me."

"What?"

"You were never there. Always absent. Never listening. Just once, I wanted you to know how it felt to be invisible."

I clenched my fists. "Except I wasn't. I stood in front of our families, all of your friends, and watched them look at me in *pity*."

Donna laughed once. "I needed you to listen to me. It was the only way I knew how to make you listen."

I flinched. "I always listened."

"You *never* listened, Addie!" She yelled. "I tried to tell you I was hurting, and you brushed it off. I told you my mother was dying. Again, you brushed it off. I told you I wanted to go back to school, and you said some bullshit about affording rent."

I didn't remember any of that.

"You never-" I started.

"You're still not listening!" Donna screamed. "I loved you and you never listened!"

It took everything I had not to drop the phone. *Loved*. Past tense. She loved me. She didn't anymore. I dug my nails into my palm, trying to feel something other than the sting of her words.

"I love you now," I said. As soon as I said it, I wished I could take back my lie. I loved Donna once. I loved her in the beginning. I loved the way her hair glistened in the sun, and the way her lips felt on mine. I loved the sound of her laugh, and her hip dips. I loved her glasses and the scars on her knees.

I loved her when she hurt me. I loved her when she tore me to pieces.

I loved her until she drowned me.

But, I didn't love her now.

I wasn't sure when I started running from her. All I knew was I never stopped.

"No, you don't. You're in Paris without me," she sneered.

"You left me at the altar," I snapped, pausing. I'd never snapped at her before and instantly regretted it. "You could have left me before. You could have told me you wouldn't marry me when I proposed. Instead, you waited to humiliate me."

Donna was quiet.

"Why did you call me?" I asked harshly.

"I told you. I miss you," she growled.

"Do not lie to me, Donna."

She chuckled. "Look who finally grew a voice." It was my turn to growl through the tears. "I'm horny, I wanted you to come over."

"Don't call me again, Donna," I snarled.

"I hope you drown."

She hung up the phone.

There it was. The phrase I heard a hundred times before. She

TILL THE SUN DIES

used it at the end of every argument because those words cut the deepest. She was the only person I ever told about...

I wrapped both arms around my chest and let the phone fall to the ground. I couldn't catch my breath. Little black dots swam in my vision. I pushed myself to my feet, stumbling towards the bed.

I couldn't breathe.

The walls closed in around me. The room felt smaller than ever.

Broken pieces of my heart faded with each tear I shed. I gulped down air like it was water. It felt the same.

I let the grief drown me.

CHAPTER 10

I wasn't sure how long I drowned beneath waves of darkness. Incessant knocking on my door dragged me out of my stupor. My body ached as I pushed myself out of my fetal position. Makeup crusted onto my face and my eyes burned. I spluttered and brushed knotted hair off my neck and mouth. My heart raced, and every movement made me want to break down.

When I opened the door, Willa stood in the doorway with wide eyes. Over her shoulder, I saw it was still dark outside. Confused, I stepped back and let her into my room, barely able to focus on her sobs through the ringing in my ears. Mechanically, I locked the door. Willa sat down on the edge of my bed, clutching her chest and mumbling reminders to breathe.

"What happened?" I asked, my voice cracking after my hysterical sobs.

"My fiancé knows where I am," she hiccuped. "He threatened to drag me home."

I sat next to her. She gripped my hand so tight I thought she'd break it.

"When I was twelve," I whispered. "Indy and I almost drowned. We were tubing on the Salt River with our family and some family friends. The rapids were more than we could handle and we fell out of our tubes. I remember being terrified. I remember water in my lungs. Then, I woke up in the hospital. I hate water and boats because of it. It was the scariest experience of my life. Whenever I argued with my fiancé, she used the same line to win. She tells me she hopes I drown."

Willa sniffled. "Did you talk to her tonight?"

I sucked in a deep breath and shook out my hands. I didn't want to talk about me, or Donna. "Willa, did your fiancé ever hurt you?"

Willa shook her head. I waited. She trembled. "He only threatened to."

I wrapped my arm around her shoulders. Willa leaned into me, shaking uncontrollably. The longer I held her, the more she dissolved into hysterics. I felt nothing at all, staring at the designs on the carpet.

I never intended to hurt Donna, especially in the beginning. I wanted to be everything to her - the sun, the moon, and all her stars. Once she started with the cruel comments, the only way I found to defend myself and hurt her in response was to ignore her. When she was mean, I built walls. The few times she was kind, I turned a blind eye. It was easier. At some point, we stopped being a couple and started being two people who wanted to hurt each other.

I let her hurt me because I was incapable of feeling anything else.

"Can I ask you something?" Willa whispered. "And you promise not to tell anyone I asked you?"

"Who would I tell?" I sighed.

"Seriously, Addie," she begged.

The desperation in her voice sent chills over my skin. I straightened. "Okay, sure."

Willa cleared her throat. "Do you believe in anything supernatural?"

"Like ghosts?"

She sat back. Her eyes darted around nervously. "Anything, really. Ghosts, mermaids, vampires, fae?"

"When I was ten, I wanted to marry Peter Pan and live forever." I shrugged.

"I'm serious, Addie."

I narrowed my eyes, watching her fidget and rub her hands together. I opened my mouth to ask her what was happening, but stopped. She didn't want my questions. She wanted an answer.

"I like to think there are things out there we don't see or don't understand," I started. "I think it makes the world more interesting."

"Even if those things are monsters?"

"Willa, what's going on?"

She burst into tears again, shaking her head. I watched as she climbed further up my bed, burying her face in my pillows. Bewildered, I turned to check the time. It was four in the morning. We were supposed to meet Thierry for breakfast at nine.

While Willa cried into my pillow, I washed my face in the bathroom and brushed the knots out of my hair. I placed a glass of water on her nightstand, then one on mine. Willa's hysterical sobs faded into sniffles as I crawled into the bed next to her.

Eventually, everything fell quiet.

The next morning, Willa said nothing about her breakdown when we left to meet Thierry at a nearby cafe. Her eyes were bloodshot and swollen, but she plastered a smile on her face as she sank into the chair next to the blonde Frenchman.

I didn't have the same energy to pretend. I hardly did my makeup and opted for a pair of shorts and a t-shirt instead of the new clothes I bought the day before. The day seemed too loud and too bright; I resisted growls of frustration while Thierry ordered coffee for the table. I sank into my chair, flinching every time a car horn went off or someone rushed by on a motorcycle. I hunched over my coffee, burying my face in my hands and trying to maintain my composure.

"What is wrong with you both?" Thierry asked. He glanced between me and Willa, who sank into his shoulder like she didn't have the strength to stand up again. My eyes met Willa's. Her eyes widened, and she shook her head ever so slightly, silently begging me to lie.

I crossed my arms. "We're hungover, sorry."

Thierry narrowed his eyes. He took a deep breath and narrowed his eyes at Willa. If I didn't know any better, I would have thought she seemed defeated by my bluff. Thierry only hummed, taking a sip of his coffee.

I excused myself to go to the restroom, slipping inside the cafe. The downstairs restroom was quiet and dark. I sank to the ground in the corner, burying my face in my hands and trying to contain my discomfort.

I only had a moment of relief before someone banged on the door. I washed my hands and skirted past them to return to my friends. Willa and Thierry were talking; their voices quiet and sharp. I paused to listen.

"She doesn't know about Holland, please leave it alone," Willa whispered.

"All I'm saying is she looks like she lost blood," Thierry responded.

"Drop it, Thierry," Willa snapped.

Know what about Holland?

I looked like I'd lost blood?

I shook my head in confusion. I would have lingered longer, but a loud car rushed by, shattering my concentration. I wrung out my hands to shake off the noise. Both of them shut their mouths when I stepped around the corner. I sank into my chair and reached for my coffee like I had heard nothing suspicious.

"What do we want to do today?" I asked Willa quietly. I wanted her alone so I could ask her what they talked about. Some part of me also worried about the possibility of her abusive fiancé showing up to take her home.

Willa reached up to adjust the green scarf she wore. "Actually, I just want to rest today. Is that okay?"

"Sure," I said, deflated.

Willa glanced between me and Thierry. He narrowed his eyes and I swore she almost rolled hers, then corrected herself. "We can grab some books and go on a picnic in the park for the day. Maybe a nap in the sun will do us some good."

I agreed.

CHAPTER 11

Thierry didn't leave like I hoped he would.

I resisted the urge to glare at him as I lay on my blanket in the half-dead grass. He kept one arm around Willa while she lounged in the sunlight. She'd changed into a tank top and shorts, still wearing the green scarf. I lay on my stomach, alternating between dozing and reading the book I'd brought along. It was a cozy mystery, not interesting enough to keep my attention - and I was hyper-aware of everything around me. The crunch of footsteps. Strands of hair on my neck. Every time someone laughed too loud.

Too much. Too much. Too much.

I huffed, closing the book and resting my head on my forearm.

"We should get tattoos," Willa said suddenly.

I turned to her. "Do you have any?"

She shook her head.

"What would you get?"

"Daddy's Girl," she giggled, motioning across her chest. I snickered, shaking my head. "Is that the only one you have?"

I rolled onto my back and sat up to stretch my left leg out over our blanket. Willa peered at the leaves and ferns trailing up my leg. I motioned it went all the way up to the top of my thigh, beneath my shorts. "I got it after I graduated high school, it was everything I ever wanted. My ex hated it, so I never got any more."

"How did she let go of a sexy fox like you?" Willa said dramatically.

I burst into laughter, shaking my head. I expected the thought to sting. It didn't.

"We should go," Thierry said, sitting up. He looked around with wide eyes, like a startled deer.

"I don't want to go," Willa growled, gritting her teeth together. Her demeanor changed immediately, her eyes darkening as she turned back to Thierry.

The hostility between them was startling. Thierry shifted, seeming uncomfortable while he surveyed the surrounding park. I reached for my book, prepared to bury my nose in it and pretend to ignore whatever couple's catfight they were about to have. Before I could, though, I recognized the next person to walk around the corner.

Holland.

My stranger.

My heart fluttered as I sat up straight, my lips parting. Holland held a book in one hand and a pencil in the other; he paid no attention to where he walked. A rushed tourist skidded around him, and only then did he look up. Directly at me.

He stopped in the middle of the walkway, and there it was again - his dazzling smile that made the sun shine brighter.

"Willa," I breathed. "That's Holland."

Willa turned to follow my gaze. "Holy fuck," she blurted, then cleared her throat. "That's impossible."

Holland crossed the pathway, his eyes flicking from me to Thierry. Thierry wound an arm around Willa's waist tightly. Annoyance flashed on her face, but she nestled herself against his chest. I glanced at my friend, partially expecting to find concern or hesitation on her face. There was none. Willa shot me a wink.

"We meet again," Holland said, stopping at the edge of my blanket.

The world was quieter in his eyes.

"We were just leaving," Thierry interrupted, pushing himself to his feet.

Willa let her head fall back onto the blanket with a single sob. My attention snapped from Holland to her, and my heart lurched.

"Then, leave, Thierry!" Willa yelled, jolting up from where she lay. I flinched away from the loud noise. "Addie can handle herself."

Thierry opened and closed his mouth a few times. Then, reluctantly, he sat next to Willa. His eyes remained on Holland, who didn't seem the least bit bothered by their strange behavior.

When I turned back to Holland, he extended his hand. "Walk with me?" he hummed.

I took his hand.

"Don't go far without sharing your location, please," Willa said quickly.

"I won't," I told her.

Holland placed my hand on his arm. The movement brought me closer to him, and I blushed.

"Is everything alright with Willa?" Holland asked as we turned the corner.

I shook my head, dragging my fingers through my hair. "I don't know. It's been a long day." I paused. "Where did you come from?"

Holland reached into his pocket, pulling out two small pieces of chocolate. He offered one to me. I took it with a small smile, watching him unwrap it and place it on his tongue. My eyes dropped to his red-tinged lips for a moment longer than I would have admitted.

"I live up the street," he said. "I enjoy the parks."

"You live here?" I paused.

Holland raised his eyebrow. I remembered him telling me he'd been in Paris for a while, I just hadn't realized he lived here. I shook my head. I had no reason to be suspicious of Holland. Surely Thierry's hesitation had nothing to do with him and everything to do with his fight with Willa.

"Something's bothering you," Holland said.

I unwrapped my chocolate and swirled it on my tongue. It tasted like mint. "I don't want to talk about it."

Holland hummed, squeezing my hand. "What would you like to talk about instead?"

I paused, stopping mid-step and turning to face him. "Who are you?"

Holland tilted his head. "What do you mean?"

I shrugged. "I've coincidentally run into you in Paris three different times. My sister would be screeching that you could be a serial killer. I don't even know you and yet I enjoy being with you."

Holland licked his lips and held out his hand. "Give me your phone, please."

I fished it out of my pocket and handed it to him. Holland moved to take it, then paused and smiled at me. I stared at his mouth, unsure where the tingle in my stomach came from. After a moment's hesitation, I unlocked it. He opened the contacts.

"My name is Holland Hawthorne," he said, entering his phone number. "I was born in London, but I've lived in Paris for a few years. The parks are my favorite, I spend most of my free time in one or another with a sketchbook or my guitar. I won't keep you for too long today, it seems your friend needs you. But, I would like to run into you *coincidentally* again."

His smile was dazzling as he handed my phone back.

I raised an eyebrow. "You didn't say you weren't a serial killer."

Holland laughed. "Not your type?"

I shook my head, laughing softly. Holland moved my hand to rest on his forearm. I leaned into his touch. He still rolled the piece of chocolate on his tongue, his jaw clenching from the movement. I watched the daylight dance across his face, illuminating the honey gold of his eyes. Holland tilted his head to offer me a small smile.

"I should take you back to Willa and Thierry," he said quietly, his smile falling.

I opened my mouth to argue. The words never came. Instead, an earth-shattering scream broke the calm of the park. The noise pierced through me and I flinched, instinctively reaching up to cover my ears. Holland turned towards the noise, his eyes darkening.

It took me an extra moment to understand the French words over the hysteria.

Elle est morte.

She was dead.

Someone died.

Panic rose in my throat. People ran through the park, voices growing louder. Another scream... then two. I shook my head, struggling to process the extra stimulation. Holland pulled me against his chest, replacing my hands with his over my ears. I pressed my face into his shirt, whimpering.

"Addie!"

I turned away from Holland. Willa skidded around the corner, her eyes wide. Thierry was one step behind her. His eyes were wild and frantic, then furious when he saw Holland.

"Are you okay?" Willa reached for me. I let her take my hands. She looked over my face as tears escaped me. "Are you hurt?"

Behind me, Holland scoffed.

"I'm fine," I said, wiping my face. "It's just loud."

Sirens.

I flinched.

"We should go back to the hotel. It sounds like they found someone dead," Willa said.

"Dead. Drained of blood," Thierry said darkly.

I quivered, turning towards Holland. "I have to get out of here, I'm sorry."

He stepped forward, tilting my chin up and making me look at him. It helped me focus on his words, rather than the noise and commotion saturating the air. "Text me, if you'd like. I'll always respond."

I nodded, a stray tear running down my face as the sirens grew louder. Holland brushed it away, his eyes sad. I shook out my hands and crossed my arms over my chest before stepping back from him. Willa wrapped her arm around my shoulders. I covered my ears. She led me from the park.

It wasn't until we reached the gates that I realized Thierry hadn't joined us.

When I looked back, there was no sign of him or Holland.

CHAPTER
12

M y parents were angry.
    I sat on a bench in a small park across the street from Notre Dame with my headphones in, listening to their rage. Behind them, Indy sat on the couch, regretful that she'd called me while at their house for breakfast. She only wanted to show me the castle she made with waffle sticks, but my parents descended like wolves the moment they heard my voice.

I held my phone on my lap, only partially listening to all the reasons staying in Paris was a bad idea. I didn't have a job. My savings wouldn't last forever. I could be kidnapped, or pick-pocketed. My French was terrible. I didn't like to be alone. Was I even strong enough to get out of bed in the morning? What did I care about old buildings and croissants? On, and on, the list went. The longer they talked, the more ridiculous the reasoning became.

As I listened, I wondered if my parents didn't know me, or if I'd strayed so far from who I really was that I was unrecognizable. How long had I spent struggling to come up for air, drowning over and over again?

Pigeons skittered across the path in front of me, unbothered by all the people walking around them. I watched them and my mind wandered to the instance in the park yesterday. My stomach soured. Willa and I found the news article much later in the evening. A nineteen-year-old girl was murdered in the middle of the day, found with small stab wounds on her throat. Officials said the girl died of blood loss, though there was hardly a drop on her. The words in the article haunted me all night, coupled with Thierry's strange choice of words: the girl had been *drained of blood.*

I thought it was even more strange that it happened in the middle of the day, and no one noticed a thing. Willa, Thierry, and I lay in the park for hours and we hadn't seen her or heard anything. One minute she was alive, and the next she was dead.

In the background of the video call, Indy stuck her tongue out and tried to lick her own nose. I covered my snort of amusement just before my mom asked me if I had anything to say for myself.

"Actually," I said, sitting back and crossing my arms. "I'm starving. I wonder where I can get a good cheeseburger in France."

Indy burst into laughter.

"Not now, Lucinda," Dad snapped.

Indy said something in retort. Dad yelled at her while Mom scolded me for my attitude. I'd never said anything so brave to my parents before. I always responded to their accusations with a passive nod or a couple of tears when they turned their backs.

A couple of days in Paris and I already felt different... stronger... more passionate about what I wanted. I wanted to stay here. I was determined to figure out how.

I looked up when someone sat next to me on the bench. Willa. She offered me a weak, tired smile, and held out a cup of coffee. I took it, barely tilting my phone toward her to reveal the chaos on the screen. She laughed into her hands and leaned back on the bench.

She wore a purple scarf today, and a white jumpsuit. Her hair was pulled up into a high ponytail; she wore hoop earrings and golden bracelets. They jingled as she pulled a book out of her bag and put her earphones in to read. I reached over to tilt her book and take in the cover.

I muted my parents. "How much sex is in that book?"

Willa laughed. "A lot. Last night, I read a scene where he tied her up with her own panties and made her-"

"Adalyn!" My mom yelled, snatching my attention. "Are you even listening?"

"Hardly," I responded, shrugging.

Her face turned red. "You need to come home and patch things up with Donna. She's heartbroken."

I winced at the mention of her name. "Frankly, I don't give a shit about Donna, Mom."

In the background, Indy fist-pumped the air. She dropped her hands and batted her lashes when Dad spun to glare at her. I covered my laugh with a cough.

"Adalyn-" Mom started again.

"I want to make something very clear," I interrupted, watching her eyes widen. "I have no intention of ever speaking to Donna again. I loved her and she left me in front of everyone we've ever known."

My mom glared. "You're being childish."

"Whatever helps you sleep at night."

She huffed. "When are you coming home?"

I shook my head. "I am going to stay in Paris. Or, I'll go to London, or Rome, or Athens - but I will not come back until I'm ready."

"And what about money?" She sneered in response.

"I have a lot in savings. And when it runs out, I'll work."

My mom's scoff hurt more than her anger. "But Donna-" she started again.

"I have to go," I said. "I'm going to find a cheeseburger."

I ended the call without letting her say anything else.

Willa pulled out her earbuds and glanced at me. "We could walk to *Le Choupinet*? They have a great cheeseburger."

"Sold."

We gathered our things and started toward the restaurant.

"So, Thierry called last night," Willa said.

I raised an eyebrow.

"He wanted to apologize for his behavior. Work is stressing him out, and his sister is in town. Well, he didn't mean what he said, or how he acted."

"Did he apologize to me or you?" I said.

Willa sighed. "To both of us."

"Look," I stopped and turned to face her. "I know we don't know each other, and this may be bold of me to say, but I don't like the way he treats you. I like you and I want to be your friend, but I won't let you stay in a toxic relationship."

Willa stiffened, her eyes wide. I worried she would run or yell. Instead, she stepped forward and wrapped her arms around me.

"Thank you," she whispered.

I hugged her back for a prolonged moment. She pulled back and nodded. I straightened, and we kept walking.

"Do you love her?" Willa asked quietly.

My throat dried out. I couldn't stop the shiver of discomfort that shot down my spine. "No, I don't think so."

"I don't think I love my fiancé either," Willa said.

"Have you heard from him?"

"He calls every day. I haven't answered since he threatened to drag me home." Willa gulped. "I'll have to answer him soon."

I laced my arm through hers. "Not right now."

Willa smiled. "No. Right now, we're getting cheeseburgers."

"They better be good," I laughed.

An hour later, we ate cheeseburgers... and they were delicious. I tried not to moan as I bit into mine.

"Do you think you'll see Holland again?" Willa asked.

"I hope so."

"He's very pretty," Willa said, raising her glass of champagne.

I blushed, immediately thinking of the gold of his eyes and the delicate pink of his lips. Perfectly kissable. I shook my head to myself. I needed to get to know him better before I thought about kissing him.

Even though I thought about it every time I looked at his mouth.

"Want to go to London?" Willa asked suddenly.

"What? Why?" I jolted in surprise.

She shrugged. "Just for a day or two. I've never been. It's only like a two-hour train ride."

If I wasn't in Paris... if I hadn't been left at the altar... if my life wasn't teetering on the edge of devastation... I would have said no. Except, all of those things were true, and I didn't feel like the sad version of myself I knew so well.

I felt like someone new. Someone bright.

I beamed. "Let's go."

CHAPTER 13

L ondon felt sexier than Paris.

Paris was full of sensual charm. It was delicate. It drew me in and held me in a warm embrace. The lights were soft and the world felt like it stood still. I spent four days in the city, but it felt like minutes of fresh air and freedom.

London was fast, loud, and bright. It moved at the speed of light and glittered in a thousand different colors. After less than six hours in London, I longed to let go. I gulped down a glass of prosecco and reached for another slice of prosciutto and potato pizza. Willa danced a little in her seat as she gnawed on her slice.

We arrived in London and hit the ground running. Willa booked us a hotel room near the London Eye for a few nights and we bought tickets to see a show tonight - Moulin Rouge. While we changed, we chatted about what else we wanted to do while we were here. All the classics, of course - Big Ben, Westminster Abbey, St. Paul's Cathedral. Willa wanted to go dancing. I wanted to go to the National Gallery.

I'd never done anything like this before. I wasn't impulsive, and I hated making decisions.

And yet I rode the high of spontaneity.

I was avoiding real life. I thought Willa was too.

Her fiancé knew she was in Paris. He threatened to tear her out of the world and life she found on her own. At the same time, my family wanted me to come home and get back together with the woman I hadn't loved in a long time.

We'd deal with it all later. Tonight, we would eat, drink, go watch a musical, and forget about every bad thing in our lives.

Willa sat back in her chair, staring up at the ceiling for a long moment before taking a breath.

"Everything okay?" I asked, lowering my glass.

Willa offered me a gentle smile. "I'm in love with Thierry."

I sucked in a breath.

Willa shook her head and slumped over her pizza plate. "He doesn't know, of course. Men never do." She took a long drink of her prosecco. "I didn't come to Paris to fall in love. I came to run away from it."

I raised my glass of prosecco in a false toast, taking a sip. "Do you love your fiancé?" I asked.

Willa paused. I watched realization dawn on her face. Her eyes found mine, and she shook her head. "I don't think I've ever loved him," she admitted.

"Then you're not running from love, you're running from being trapped," I said. "Will you tell Thierry?"

"Not yet. Maybe never. I always pick the wrong ones." She whispered the last sentence, sadness filling her face. She opened her mouth to say something else, but our server returned. I was quiet while Willa ordered us another round of drinks.

The server sauntered off, and I turned to Willa. "What is Thierry's problem with Holland?"

I hadn't planned to ask about this tonight, but she'd brought up Thierry, and the question tumbled out before I could stop it. Thierry acted strangely whenever Holland appeared, like he was threatened by him. The whole thing was very unsettling.

Willa didn't seem surprised. Perhaps she'd been waiting for me to bring this up. "You like him, don't you?"

Across the restaurant, glass shattered. A loud table whooped with laughter. I flinched from the noises and dug my nails into my thighs. "I hardly know him," I admitted. "But I like the way he makes me feel."

Willa's eyes widened. "How does he make you feel?"

I sucked in a breath. "Warm. Safe."

Willa seemed sad, dropping her gaze. She hadn't answered my original question. The server returned with more prosecco. I reached for mine immediately. The buzz of alcohol overrode the hum of life around me - and I needed extra courage.

"Please answer me," I said.

"I can't," she said sharply. "I know it's frustrating and confusing, and I hope it'll make sense soon, but I literally can't tell you."

I slumped back in my chair. When I spoke, my voice came out colder than I intended. "If I asked Holland, would he answer me?"

"I don't know him well enough to know," Willa said. "Please don't hate me."

I shook my head, forcing my disappointment down my throat. I took a few more bites of my pizza, the silence stretching between Willa and me. She ate slowly, glancing at me every couple of seconds.

I straightened. "I don't hate you, Willa. Let's go to the musical, yeah?"

Hours later, I stumbled after Willa through dimmed London streets. We laughed hysterically, our joy echoing through the night.

It was after ten in the evening, and the last of the sunlight was dying as we skipped along the streets back to our hotel. The streets had quieted, people few and far between. Our laughter echoed off the surrounding buildings. My whole body felt feverish from all the alcohol I consumed. My mind still spun after the loud music and flashing lights from the musical. I clung to Willa, unsure whether I was holding her up or vice versa.

"Hang on," she cackled. "My shoe hurts, I gotta sit."

Snickering, I dragged her to the nearest bench. She plopped down, pulling me down next to her. Willa leaned over to tug off her tennis shoe and shake it out. I leaned back and gazed up at the darkening sky through the trees. The last of my alcohol buzz was wearing off, and I was acutely aware of every aching muscle in my body.

It was strange to think that this morning I'd woken up in Paris, and now I frolicked around London with a girl who could be my best friend... and I was happy.

I was happy.

The realization sank into me like cold water. Chills erupted over my skin as I stared up at the trees. *Happy.*

Happy.

Happy.

Happy.

I brushed away my tears, unsure how to explain to Willa that I cried because this was the first time I'd been happy in... a long time. I wasn't sure how long. Too long.

Willa finished fixing her shoe. She stood and rocked back and forth on her heels. For a moment, I wasn't sure whether she'd remain standing straight. I reached for her instinctively, both of us dissolving into giggles. She pulled me to my feet and started toward our hotel.

We only made it a few steps before Willa's laughter fell silent. My friend stiffened, her hand wrapping around my wrist and holding me close to her. Confused, I looked into the twilight where her eyes fixed on two figures in the shadows. A man and woman stood against a tree in what seemed like an intimate embrace. The woman's back was against the tree; his arms were around her and his face was buried in her shoulder. Except, she wasn't holding him in return. Her arms hung limp at her sides, and her knees bent like her legs weren't strong enough to hold her weight anymore.

Panic flooded into my veins. A lump formed in my throat, making it hard to breathe. I stared at the grotesque positioning of the couple, dread seeping into me. It wasn't right. None of this was right.

"We need to go," Willa muttered.

"We need to call the police," I told her.

She shook her head, squeezing my arm and taking a slow step back. "No, we need to go."

"Willa?" I shook my head frantically. "She needs help."

Willa's eyes burned into mine. She gripped both of my shoulders and turned me to face her. Her voice was barely a whisper. "She is already dead. We need to go, or we will be too."

I believed her. "Okay."

"Dead is such a... dirty word."

I spun towards the foreign voice. The man stood only a few

feet away from us. With every second, London grew darker. The stranger's face was dark and shadowed. A thick liquid dripped down his mouth and chin - at first, I thought it was chocolate.

Then he stepped beneath a streetlight the moment it flicked on.

It wasn't chocolate.

It was blood. Blood on his face, and his chest, and his hands.

Behind him, the woman lay crumpled and forgotten on the ground. Willa clutched my wrist, taking a single step in front of me. A scream built and caught in my throat, cutting off my air. I clutched my stomach and tugged on Willa. Every muscle in my body screamed for us to *run*.

"We don't want trouble," Willa said. "We were just leaving."

The strange man hummed deeply. His eyes flicked up and down Willa, then over to me. He licked blood off his lips. "I'm still hungry."

He took another step forward. Consumed by terror, I wrenched free of Willa in an attempt to run. My head spun from holding my breath; I stumbled and fell. Willa only straightened, stepping in front of the man with an indignant huff. As I pushed myself to my feet, I watched Willa unwrap her black scarf and tilt her chin up.

"We are already spoken for," Willa snarled.

The man clenched his jaw, displeased. He nodded and took a step back. Blood leaked from his mouth when he spoke with a sneer. "You are brave. Not all of us are honorable."

He disappeared into thin air.

Another scream built in my chest. Willa turned towards me, her eyes wide. I sobbed once when she helped me from the ground, wiping the dirt from my pants. I trembled so badly I couldn't see straight. Willa wrapped one arm around my torso, holding me upright as we walked.

The man was covered in blood.

The woman...

I spun around. If there was any chance we could help the woman on the ground, we had to. When I looked at the tree where she'd fallen, there was no one there.

"Come on, Addie." Willa tugged me along.

I shook my head. "I don't understand."

"I know, sweetie. You will," Willa said.

I wrung out my hands, letting Willa guide me toward our hotel once more. I couldn't stop picturing the blood on his face... on his lips... dripping from his mouth as he talked. There was blood *in* his mouth.

"Was he drinking it?" I whispered, my voice cracking.

Willa said nothing.

The rest of the walk to the hotel was a blur. I thought I spent it crying; the hotel receptionist must have been concerned when Willa ushered us through the lobby. When we made it to the room, she sat me on the edge of the bed and immediately started a shower. I stared at her when she returned. She said something about a shower to help me calm down.

I wasn't listening. Willa wasn't wearing her scarf. There was a mark on her neck. I stood, catching her arm to look closer. I found two little circular wounds on her throat, red and swollen. When she realized what I'd seen, Willa pulled back with wide eyes.

"What happened?" I asked.

"Addie," she started. "There are things you don't know."

"Explain them," I snapped. Then I shook my head. "You know what, I don't want to know."

She opened her mouth again. White noise pulsed through my ears, growing louder and louder the more Willa tried to talk to me. I took a slow step back, retreating to the bathroom. I think she called my name, but I'd already locked the bathroom door. I undressed, intending to get in the shower, only to hesitate when my phone clattered to the ground from my pocket.

I sank after it, resting my head on the wall.

Thierry said the girl in the park was drained of blood.

As soon as the thought echoed through me, I felt sick. I barely made it to the toilet before vomiting. I was sure the man had drunk the woman's blood tonight. Was that what happened to the girl in Paris too?

What kind of monster drank human blood?

I vomited again.

Willa knocked on the door, asking if I was okay. I didn't respond. I slumped against the wall and picked my phone up off the floor.

I hovered over Indy's name for a moment, desperate for someone to talk to that wouldn't lie to me. Only, there was no rational way for me to explain any of this to my sister. I couldn't even explain it to myself. She probably wouldn't believe me anyway. I scrolled through my contacts, desperate for anyone to talk to.

I hesitated on Donna's name.

I pressed the green button, waiting. My heart leaped into my throat. A tear burned down my cheek.

"Hello?" Her voice came through the line.

Instead of comfort and safety at the sound of her voice, I found revulsion.

I ended the call. Immediately, she tried to call back. I declined it, wiping my face. This time, I found a different name. Instead of calling, I texted.

I don't believe in impossible things.

Holland's answer came immediately. **What sorts of impossible things? True love? Vampires?**

I sniffled, pulling my knees to my chest.

All of it.

Are you okay?

I sucked in a breath, staring at the screen for a long moment. Twice, I typed out that I was fine, only to delete it. I turned off my phone.

CHAPTER 14

The next morning, when Willa asked if I was okay, I told her I wanted to see Westminster Abbey and the Tower of London. She gaped at me. When she asked if I was sure, I encouraged her to add whatever she wanted to our list. Her jaw was still on the floor when I got out of bed to do my makeup and get dressed.

I ignored her while we got ready. Willa watched me the entire time, waiting for me to say something. I didn't want to hear any more lies or excuses. By the time I showered and came out of the bathroom last night, Willa was already asleep - curled up on her side of the bed. She left a note on my pillow to wake her up if I wanted to talk.

I did not wake her up.

Things that didn't make sense were piling up.

The dead girl at the park - drained of blood. Wounds on Willa's neck. A man with blood in his mouth. Thierry's strange behavior towards Holland.

Willa knew something I didn't.

I couldn't bear any more lies, not today. I wanted to visit tourist attractions and eat good food without worrying about ghosts and blood. I didn't want to think about what that man looked like with blood leaking down his jaw. While I tied my shoes, I shook my head. I drank too much champagne yesterday; it was a dream.

Holland asked if I believed in true love or vampires.

I didn't.

I always believed in what I could see, but what if what was in front of my eyes didn't make any sense?

Willa asked if I wanted to go to the London Eye today too. I forced a smile as I followed her out of the hotel room. She opened the map on her phone. I finally turned mine back on. I'd considered leaving it behind altogether, but wanted to take pictures of my time in London. When the screen lit up, I paused and looked at the text on the screen - it was from a couple of hours ago.

I stopped by your hotel to see if you were okay, but you weren't there. Are you alright?

Adalyn?

I swallowed, texting Holland back with shaky hands.

I'm fine. I'm in London with Willa.

To my surprise, his response was again immediate.

I realized a few hours later that showing up at your hotel could have been considered creepy and overbearing. I apologize.

I resisted the urge to smile and glanced up to make sure I was one step behind Willa. She chattered about making it to the Underground stop. I didn't respond.

I'm sorry I worried you. There are some... weird things going on, and I was overwhelmed.

What kinds of weird things?

I pursed my lips. **I'll be back in Paris in a few days. Can we talk then?**

Of course.

I tucked my phone back in my pocket, finally catching up to Willa.

Willa and I laughed as we sank onto the bench. My thighs burned after climbing the stairs at the Tower of London. Willa handed me a water bottle from her backpack. I gulped it down without hesitation, desperate for relief. She kicked off her shoes, much to the dismay of passing tourists who grimaced at her like she spit on them.

"I am made to be carted around in a carriage and told I'm a good girl," Willa whined.

I snorted. "I didn't need to know about your praise kink."

She burst into laughter, barely able to keep from spraying water as she took another drink. "Please, that's the mildest one. I also like biting."

I covered my ears, laughing.

Willa reached up to tie her thick curls into a hair tie. My eyes lingered on the pink scarf she wore today, perfectly positioned on her neck. I resisted the urge to pull on it to see if the wounds I'd seen last night were real.

Or perhaps it was better for me to think it was all a dream.

I reminded myself everything was fine. Neither of us said anything about last night at all today. I wanted to keep it that way.

Willa reached for her shoes. "Sunset at the London Eye?"

I nodded.

It had been a long day of exploring London. We hit everything on the list, and more. We stopped and investigated anything that caught our interest. To end the day, Willa wanted to drink champagne and sit on the London Eye while we watched the city turn gold.

Some part of me was nervous to be out too late, afraid to stumble across another nightmare. But, Willa wanted to return to Paris tomorrow afternoon, so I thought we might as well soak in as much of London as possible.

Exploring today had me thinking about going beyond Paris. I could go to Spain or Italy or Greece, even. I had fallen in love with this feeling of being free.

My family seemed convinced I would come home soon with my tail between my legs. The longer I was here, the more I understood how utterly unhappy I had been at home. I lived in a too-expensive apartment, worked a job I didn't enjoy, and tried to love a woman who shut me out long before she actually left. I hated Phoenix - the dirt, the heat, and the people. I never realized how drained I felt just existing in that life.

Now, I was thousands of miles away from the place I grew up and everyone I'd ever known, and I'd never felt more like myself. I wondered how long I could keep this up. Would I get lonely? Was this enough?

Again with the question marks. I wasn't sure I knew myself well enough to have an answer.

"Willa?" I asked quietly.

She hummed in response, tying her shoe.

"Would you stay, if you could?"

"What do you mean?"

I crossed my arms over my chest. "I guess I'm asking if you're going home, eventually, to your parents, your job, your fiancé."

Willa shrugged. "He has a good job, a big house, and he went to Harvard. I could be happy."

"You don't sound convinced."

She shrugged. "Going home to him is the easy option. He's all I've ever known." She looked up. "Will you go home?"

"I don't know. I have nothing there, but my family seems to think that I can't, or won't, do this."

Willa was quiet, watching tourists frolic by us. She turned towards me with wide eyes. "I think you should give it a shot with Holland."

I started in surprise. "What?"

"He's infatuated with you, and you seem to like him a lot. Fuck what Thierry thinks, fuck what I think. You should try it. Besides, if anything is going to keep us here, it might as well be pretty boys."

I watched my friend, confused. Finally, I nodded. "Okay, I will."

"Good." She sat back.

Neither of us said anything else. After resting for a few more minutes, Willa and I set off with renewed ambition.

CHAPTER 15

Our excursion to London made me wonder about what could be next. After we returned to Paris, Willa disappeared to visit Thierry. I stayed in my hotel room, laying on the bed and scrolling through my laptop. Half the time, I took notes about what it would take for me to move abroad. When I needed a break from that, I researched other cities I could easily take trips to from Paris. There were so many to choose from.

My phone rang.

I reached for it, smiling when I saw Indy's name on the screen. I propped up the phone on the pillow and answered her video call.

"Where have you been?" Indy yelled as soon as the call started.

"In London," I said passively, reaching for my notebook to scribble information on how and where to find an apartment in Paris.

Indy squealed and demanded I tell her all about it. I grinned and set down my pen. I left out the strange and unexplainable details, instead focusing on the tourist attractions and the alcohol. Indy clapped her hands together and cheered when I laughed about some funny story or another.

She fell quiet after a while. I paused. "What's wrong?"

There were tears in her eyes. "You look happy."

I stiffened, pursing my lips. "Yeah, I think I am."

"I hate that it's not here, at home, but it's great to see you smile," Indy said.

"Thanks." I resisted the urge to cry and wished I could hug my sister. "How are Mom and Dad?"

Indy rolled her eyes. "Mom is having breakfast with Donna's mother almost every day. They're acting like the world is over."

I snorted. "Are they trying to decide how many goats I'm worth?"

"Three, at least," Indy teased

I laughed. I paused when a text appeared on my screen, one I didn't realize I'd been waiting for with bated breath.

Can't decide whether to ask to take you to breakfast or dinner tomorrow. Thoughts?

A blush crept over my cheeks, and I picked up my phone to respond to Holland.

Dinner if you plan to kiss me. Breakfast if you don't.

As soon as the text sent, my breath caught and I nearly choked. I prayed it wasn't too bold.

His response was instant.

Dinner it is. I'll pick you up at 7.

See you then.

"Yo! Addie! Where'd you go?" Indy yelled on the phone.

"Sorry, texting a friend," I said. "She wants to go out tomorrow."

"Look at you with friends, running away to London. You may be worth four goats."

We burst into laughter.

Hours later, Willa texted me asking if I wanted to go clubbing with her and Thierry. Every ounce of me wanted to say no. I wasn't one for clubbing, or any loud, crowded place - but I was determined to continue my search for happiness. I wanted to know if I had what it took to never go home again and if staying here would be worth it.

So, I put on a knee-length black dress, curled my hair, and joined my friend at Thierry's crepe restaurant for dinner. He was working the last minutes of his shift when we arrived, sitting down at our table halfway through our meal.

"Not eating?" I asked when he leaned over to kiss Willa on the cheek.

He glanced up at me. "No, I'm good."

I nodded, cutting into my pesto crepe.

Thierry couldn't keep his hands off Willa throughout dinner. Whatever anonymity had been between them seemed to be gone now. Willa giggled into his shoulder. He traced circles on her wrists. I paid extra attention to my crepes and champagne.

After dinner, we took the metro to a club across town. I tried not to flinch at the loud music and smell of smoke as we walked inside. I failed. Willa and Thierry immediately moved onto the dance floor, leaving me near the bar. I watched them go, immediately wanting to rush toward the exit. Instead, I fumbled through ordering a club soda and stood in a lonely corner. I wasn't sure how long I stood there, alone, staring at the rest of the room in bewilderment.

In hindsight, I should not have agreed to go clubbing.

The music was so loud I could barely hear myself think. Flashing lights and smoke filled the air; it made my vision blur. Strangers ground their hips and tongues together on the dance floor. I felt nauseous. My hands were sweaty. I stared down at the plastic cup in my hand; the liquid sloshed around on the inside and made me dizzy. My stomach flipped and I surveyed the room again.

There was too much going on. I couldn't focus. My eyes crossed while I searched for Willa and Thierry. They'd seemingly disappeared into thin air. Shaking, I pulled out my phone to text her, only to discover I didn't have service inside. I swore. I took a few brave steps out of my corner, tossing my full drink in the trash.

There had to be a bathroom here somewhere. It might be quieter in there, perhaps a little brighter. If I was lucky, the water would be cold and I could run it over my wrists until my heart stopped racing. I could sit safely in there until Willa found me.

I kept one hand on the sticky wall as I found my way around the room - one step at a time. Twice, someone bumped into me from the dance floor. I flinched away from the unwanted touch, feeling it linger on my skin like bleach. I made it around the corner, into a hallway I hoped would lead to the bathroom. It was entirely dark for a moment before my eyes adjusted, but I could hear the deliberate moaning from further down.

"Oh, no," I groaned.

Once I could see through the dark, my eyes widened. The couple in the dark was Willa and Thierry. His pants hung down around his knees and her legs were wrapped around his bare waist. That wasn't what caught my attention. It was the blood leaking down Willa's exposed chest, and Thierry's mouth attached to her neck. The scene was shockingly similar to the one in the London park, except I saw every inch of them.

He was biting her. His teeth had broken skin. She moaned as if it was pleasurable when she should have been screaming.

"Willa," I squeaked, the noise escaping me as I took a step back.

Willa's eyes opened, horror flashing on her face as she recognized me. "Thierry," she placed her hands on his chest and nudged his shoulder. "Addie!"

I took another step back, my whole body coiling when Thierry raised his head. Willa's blood stained his mouth and dripped down his chin. The sight of him was worse than I imagined. Instead of the gentle face I recognized, black veins raised under Thierry's eyes, which seemed bloodshot.

He had fangs.

He had fangs.

As I stared in disgust and horror, the fangs retracted and the veins faded. Thierry returned to normal. "Addie!" He called.

I stumbled backward when he stepped away from Willa, turning away to pull up his pants. Willa adjusted her skirt, taking a single step towards me and holding both hands up like I was a spooked animal.

I ran.

I ignored the bodies I bumped into, shoving people out of the way as I ran. I worried I would be sick mid-step. Behind me, I heard Willa and Thierry calling my name. I ran faster, desperate to get away from them, winding through the crowd so I would be harder to find.

The bouncer stared at me in bewilderment when I shoved my way outside. I ignored him. It was raining. It splattered against my face and I slipped on the wet ground, landing on one knee. I pushed myself up and ran into the rain. I skidded around every corner I could find, my vision blurred from the rain and my tears.

For a while, I heard Willa and Thierry calling my name. Eventually, they fell quiet as I kept running...

and running...

and running.

I fell to my knees next to the Seine when I physically couldn't take another step.

Thierry... his mouth on Willa's neck... so much blood. I didn't understand why Willa hadn't been screaming. Why hadn't she been screaming?

Why hadn't the girl in London screamed?

The girl in the park was drained of blood.

Two perfect incisions on Willa's neck.

Pieces of the puzzle clicked into place as I cried over the Seine, my chest convulsing. My heart screamed one answer, but my mind said that was impossible.

It was impossible, wasn't it?

God, there had been so much blood.

I buried my face in my hands.

"Addie!" I spun towards the voice, whimpering when I saw Thierry step under the streetlight. He was soaking wet, his hair falling in his face. Willa wasn't with him. "You'll catch your death out here."

Panic and terror flooded every inch of me, like a coiled spring. I scrambled back, despite my spinning vision and burning chest. "Go away!"

"I just want to take you back to the hotel," Thierry said. He appeared human.

I knew what I saw in the club. I didn't understand it, but I knew.

"I can get back myself," I said, pushing myself to my feet. My legs shook underneath me and I hadn't quite caught my breath yet. My dress was soaking wet, clinging to my legs uncomfortably. The sensation made me want to scream. "Go away, Thierry. Please, go away!"

Thierry opened his mouth to say something else, but something dark flashed across his face. He stopped in his tracks, staring at something behind me. "Addie, everything is fine. Come back with me," he said cautiously.

I turned to look at whatever made him so uncomfortable.

Holland.

CHAPTER
16

I whispered his name. Holland's eyes found mine, and the world seemed to fall quiet. Unable to keep standing, I dropped to my knees and clutched my stomach with a sob. Thierry made a noise behind me and I inched away from him, glancing between the mysterious stranger who always seemed to appear from nowhere and the one I thought might be a demon.

"This doesn't involve you, Holland," Thierry said, his voice dark.

Holland paid no attention to Thierry. He watched me. "Adalyn, are you alright?"

"Addie, don't." Thierry's voice was desperate.

I couldn't look at him. I only stared at Holland. He blinked rain out of his eyes, watching only me. He seemed... worried. Angry? I wasn't sure. I didn't know where he'd come from or how he'd found me. The hair on the back of my neck stood up as I watched him, just as afraid of him as I was of Thierry. Thierry took another step forward. I felt myself panicking and shutting down. I worried I would pass out if I tried to run anymore. "No, I'm not alright," I said. "I'm scared."

Holland walked forward, holding out his hand. I didn't hesitate to take it. Chills rolled through me when I realized how cold his skin felt - as cold as the rain pouring over us. My legs visibly shook beneath me as Holland helped me back up; I worried they would give out. I'd never run so far in my life. How had Thierry followed me? And where was Willa?

"You should go," Holland said to Thierry. "I'll take care of her."

"Like hell you will," Thierry snarled.

Snarled. Like an animal.

I turned to face him again, my back to Holland's front... and there they were again. His fangs. Thierry bared his teeth like he was something more than human. A hysterical sob escaped me. My knees nearly went out from under me. Holland's arm remained around my waist; he was the only thing holding me up.

Thierry didn't come any closer to Holland. He stopped a dozen feet away, his face frozen in a grotesque snarl, as if he didn't dare approach further.

Like he was afraid of Holland.

I found comfort in the thought for a moment, sinking into the man holding me. Then, I realized the only thing a monster would be afraid of was another monster. I whimpered, looking down at Holland's icy hands holding me close to him. Every cell in my body screamed for me to not look up.

I looked up.

What I saw on Holland's face was the same villainy reflected in Thierry's. The veins under his eyes were black and there was a bright red rim around his honey irises. He had *fangs*.

"No," I cried, wrenching myself free. "No, no, no. *God*, no!"

"Adalyn." Holland took a step after me after I'd stumbled back several feet. I watched his eyes widen. He paused, holding up both hands in surrender. I watched his face return to normal, and I wanted to melt back into his arms. "My dear, everything is okay," he breathed.

No. No. No.

Everything was not okay.

I looked between Holland and Thierry. Thierry still had fangs and those horrible black veins under his eyes. Holland appeared perfectly human, but he wasn't, was he? I was soaking wet, my clothes and hair clinging to my skin and creating an uncomfortable cage. My heart pulsed in my throat and I couldn't catch my breath.

"Everything is okay," Holland said again, lowering himself to one knee and holding out his hand. He did not try to come closer to me.

Out of the corner of my eye, I saw Thierry rush forward. His arms were outstretched, reaching for me. Terror spiked as I focused on his hands - his monster hands trying to catch me. I screamed and turned to run.

I didn't see how close I was to the edge of the river.

Holland called my name.

Everything went black when I hit the water.

I awoke to sunlight on my face.

I opened my eyes, basking in the warmth for less than a moment before I realized I didn't know where I was. I lay on an enormous bed in front of an open window and a balcony overlooking a garden. Sitting up quickly, I took in the sight of the studio apartment with a dirty kitchen, an acoustic guitar in the corner, and Holland sitting on a red velvet couch.

Holland.

He glanced up from the book he was reading when I moved. Images flashed through my mind of black veins and fangs - impossible things. The instant I moved my legs, my whole body ached and I nearly gasped at the pain. I ran. I ran from monsters.

I fell in the Seine.

I shivered at the memory of water rushing around me in complete darkness.

"What happened?" I breathed, scared of his answer.

"What do you remember?" Holland closed the book and set it down next to him.

I shook my head, squeezing my eyes shut. I didn't want to remember. "I don't know."

"Adalyn," he said, firmer this time. "Tell me why you ran from Thierry."

I reached up to place my hands over my ears, as if it would block out what I had seen. I sobbed once, scratching my hands down the sides of my face when I sat up. When I opened my eyes again, Holland stood in front of me, reaching for my hands and pulling them from my face. I almost wrenched away. Almost. His eyes were full of concern, devoid of the monstrousness I'd seen the night before.

"We were at a club," I whispered. "I can't - I don't do well in environments like that. So, I was trying to find a restroom to hide in. I turned the corner and I saw Thierry and Willa." I cleared my throat, worried I would be sick. "He was - biting her, I think. There was blood."

Holland didn't seem surprised. In fact, his shoulders slumped and he looked a little sad. My stomach flipped. I struggled again to catch my breath. He moved away from me, crossing the room and grabbing a bottle of water from the fridge. I appreciated the cold on my hands when he gave it to me.

"I ran. He followed. I ran for a long time. I don't know where

Willa went, but Thierry was there," I tried to sort through the fragmented pieces. My head pounded. "And then there was you."

I watched Holland, thinking of the first time he looked at me at the Palais Garnier - like he wanted to consume my body and soul. On our midnight date, the homeless man called him a *creature*. And last night, he had fangs. *Fangs*.

"What the hell are you?" I breathed.

Holland's eyes softened. "Adalyn," he started.

"Please, answer me." I moved back, pulling the blankets with me. "I'm so confused, I don't understand. Please, tell me what I saw."

Holland sighed. "My sweet girl, if I answer your question, everything you know about this world is going to change. Do you want that?"

I stared at him. No, I didn't want the world to change. I hated change. But, there was a persistent image stuck in my mind of my sweet, charming Holland with fangs that made him a demon. I thought of the dead girls in the parks - drained of blood. I knew what I wanted to say to explain all of this - one single, impossible word. One word and it would all make sense, but I couldn't say it. I couldn't possibly believe it.

"Please," I said.

Holland's gaze held mine. As I stared at him, I watched the rim around his irises turn bright red. The veins under his eyes turned black and seemed to crackle under his skin. A scream built in my throat. I pulled my knees to my chest. Holland let his lips part ever so slightly, revealing the truth of what I'd seen. He had two razor-sharp fangs on the top of his mouth.

"I am a vampire, Adalyn."

CHAPTER 17

L aughter bubbled up inside me. I buried my face in the blankets bundled over my knees, muffling my laughter. My nails dug into the duvet as my laughter turned to cries.

This couldn't be real.

The word *vampire* echoed in my head.

Willa asked me if I believed in the supernatural. When I saw her with Thierry's fangs in her throat, she hadn't been scared. She seemed delighted.

I sobbed until my lungs ached.

When I looked up, Holland was still there. He wasn't a figment of my imagination; he was real. He looked... well, he looked like a vampire. Holland watched me, his eyes sad while he waited for me to come back to myself. My chest heaved with sobs. My hands trembled as I reached for the water bottle I'd dropped in my frantic scramble backward.

Willa knew.

Somehow, my friend knew about this strange truth long before I could have guessed it. She knew what Thierry was. I wondered if she knew what Holland was too. Thierry wanted me to stay away from Holland, but they were the same kind of demon.

Vampire.

I wiped my eyes frantically. My face was soaking wet. Holland pulled a handkerchief from his shirt pocket, holding it out hesitantly. I glanced between his face and the handkerchief, my heart skipping a beat. I reached out to take it. My fingers brushed his; he felt cool. Dead. Impossible.

I wiped my face, trembling while I drank some water. I jumped, despite myself, when Holland stood off the edge of the bed. When he turned back to me, he appeared normal. A strand of sandy hair fell into his face and his eyes seemed eternally sad.

"Would you live forever if you were a monster?" I whispered. It was what he'd asked me at midnight. Holland sucked in a deep breath. I swore his bottom lip quivered.

It wasn't possible that the boy in front of me, made of sunshine and molten gold, could be a monster. I stood out of bed, acutely aware I wore clothes that weren't mine - an oversized t-shirt that barely covered my hips, and socks that were too large. I ignored the discomfort for a moment and crossed the room to stand in front of Holland. He tensed, his brow furrowing. Another tear trailed down my cheek. I watched his hand hover at his side as he resisted the urge to wipe my tears away.

No, he wasn't a monster.

He couldn't be.

I took another step closer, reaching up to place my hand on his cheek. His eyes drooped. "Show me again," I breathed.

Holland paused. "Adalyn."

I repeated myself, rubbing my thumb over his cheek.

The veins under Holland's eyes rippled and changed to black. He blinked, and red rimmed his eyes. Fear shot through me. I forced myself to stay standing in front of him - to keep touching him. I lifted my fingers, tracing my index over the black veins, lifted slightly from the rest of his skin. Holland never looked away, his eyes searching for my reaction.

I shook my head. "It's not possible."

His lip quirked up in an almost smile. "I can assure you that it is."

I stepped away from him, shaking out my hands and breathing in shakily. I walked back to the bed, sitting before my knees went out from under me. When I looked at Holland again, his eyes were golden and warm and entirely human. My heart beat so hard I couldn't catch my breath. I placed my hand on my chest, reaching for the water bottle again.

"How did you know where I was?" I asked.

Holland motioned for the window. "We're only a few blocks away from where you ended up. I was here, at home, and I heard you scream."

"And in the Tuileries?"

Holland smiled. "I was looking for you."

"Why?"

"Because I am entranced by the girl who danced with me at the opera house," he answered.

"Me?"

Holland smiled. "Of course, you."

I wrinkled my nose. I wanted to let myself feel the butterflies in my stomach, but I had more pressing questions.

"And what about Thierry?" I asked.

Annoyance flashed across Holland's face. "What about him?"

"Would he have hurt me?"

"I don't know," Holland said. I watched him as he moved to sit on the edge of the bed opposite me.

"He seemed... afraid of you," I said cautiously.

Holland scoffed. "He should be."

"Should I?"

Pain flashed on his face and he shook his head. "No, god, no. I don't want to hurt you, Adalyn. I never intended for you to know about any of this. Truthfully, I never expected to see you again."

His words hurt more than I expected. I took another sip of water, letting out a long breath. "Why not?"

"An eternal existence is a lonely one."

"So, it's true, then? You'll live forever?" My voice quivered.

"We don't have to talk about that," Holland said. "I don't want to overwhelm you further."

There were so many stories of vampires, and each of them was a little different from the rest. Obviously, Holland could go out in the sun - I'd watched the daylight glitter in his eyes. What about mirrors, garlic, holy water, or wooden stakes? A million questions rose to the tip of my tongue.

He was right, though. I was overwhelmed and exhausted. I needed to check in with Willa and let her know I was okay. I was full of questions for her too. How long had she known about what Thierry was? Did he hurt her? What did she know about Holland? I leaned down, rubbing my burning eyes.

"What time is it?" I asked, dragging my fingers through my hair.

"Barely noon."

"Fuck," I groaned. "I'm so tired. I'm not convinced I'm not dreaming."

"You can rest here, or I can take you back to your hotel?" Holland offered.

"Where's my phone?"

He stood and crossed the room, lifting it from the coffee table. I took it daintily when he offered. There were two dozen calls from Willa and three times as many texts. I flinched back from a text from my mother, saying Donna brought over more of my

97

things. Indy asked me to check in. I texted her back with a couple of pictures I took a few days ago, telling her everything was fine. I supposed saying I discovered vampires over text wasn't the best idea.

I texted Willa telling her I was safe and fine. I did not tell her where I was. Holland's offer to take me back to the hotel was tempting, but my stomach flipped at the thought of seeing Thierry there. I was convinced he would have hurt me if Holland hadn't appeared.

"Can I stay for a while?" I asked.

Holland nodded. "Of course. What do you need? A shower? Anything to eat?"

I stared at him, warmed by his attention. He seemed genuinely concerned, his eyes wide and hands fidgeting at his sides. "I want to sleep, if that's okay."

Holland took a step back. "Windows open or closed?"

"Closed, please."

He pulled the curtains shut. "I'll be on the couch. Let me know if you need anything."

I didn't know what else to say to the vampire.

CHAPTER
18

Vampire.

Holland was a vampire.

I lived in a world where vampires existed.

I woke from my nap a couple of hours later to a note on my pillow from Holland. He'd gone to find me something to eat. I still wasn't sure I wanted to be awake, so I lay back in his bed and stared at the ceiling. If I ever imagined myself in Holland's bed, it certainly wasn't like this.

First, I would be wearing fewer clothes. Second, he would be here too. And third, I wouldn't be contemplating the existence of vampires.

The longer I lay alone, the faster my heart raced. My palms felt sweaty. Outside, cars honked and people yelled - striking sounds of everyday life. I flinched each time, shaking my head to rid myself of the noise. I sat out of bed, finding the dress I wore the night before. It was dry and hanging over a chair in the kitchen. I changed quickly, worried Holland would walk through the door while I changed. I trembled, wringing out my hands before pulling on my shoes.

I had to get out of here. I needed time to think about this without laying in a stranger's bed - a vampire's bed.

I gulped down the rest of my water, tossing the bottle in the recycle bin. I tucked my phone in my pocket, peering through the closed curtains. It was the middle of the afternoon, and the sun was at its highest. I turned and surveyed the apartment again. It was charmingly simple, quiet, and cozy. The perfect place to spend a lot of time with a boy made of sunshine. I wrapped my arms around myself, shivering when I left.

I shut the door after myself, hoping it would be okay to remain unlocked for a while. Holland's apartment was on the third floor, the stairs creaked with each downward step. I worried I would run into him mid-escape and he'd be angry with me. I walked faster.

Once outside, I used my phone to navigate back to the hotel. Thankfully, my hotel key card and Navigo pass were still in my pocket. I prayed they worked. My steps were uneven. I skidded around every person and weaved through crowds, darting down the stairs at the nearest metro station.

I hoped he wouldn't be angry.

I sat on the metro train, rubbing my face in my hands. I liked Holland. I liked his smile and how he made me feel, but I still couldn't wrap my head around the reality that he was something more than human. Vampire. The word felt wrong on my tongue. I tried not to think about it. I needed a shower, something to eat, and to call Indy.

One thing at a time, I reminded myself. First, I needed to get back to the hotel.

By the time I did, I was seconds away from being sick. My hand shook as I unlocked my door, stumbling inside and slamming it behind me. I barely made it to the bathroom before I dropped to my knees and vomited up everything in my stomach, and then some, my whole body convulsing.

When I finished, I sank to the ground and rested my head against the wall. My phone buzzed in my pocket. I pulled it out. It was Willa.

Are you back? Can we talk?

I dropped the phone to the ground, letting out a long breath. I didn't have the strength to talk to her - not yet. *One step at a time*, I reminded myself for the thousandth time. Shaking, I stood and limped across the bathroom to start the shower. The shower breathed some life back into me. It stopped the incessant shivering. I scrubbed my skin until it was red and raw, but finally felt clean.

When I was dressed, I texted Willa back.

Are you alone?

Her response came a few minutes later. **Yes, Thierry is working.**

I told her to come over, and her knock sounded on the door seconds later. I opened the door, peering into the hall behind her cautiously. It was only her. My friend swooped into the room, gripping my shoulders and looking me over like she expected me to be banged and bruised. My eyes fixed on the blue scarf she wore today. It covered a vampire bite, I realized. Thierry's bite.

"You're okay? Holland didn't hurt you? God, Thierry made it sound like-" Willa was frantic.

I pulled away and locked the door behind us. "No, Holland didn't hurt me."

Willa's eyes filled with tears.

"You have some explaining to do," I said coldly.

She nodded rapidly, moving to sit on the edge of the bed. "I found out the day I ditched you at Shakespeare and Company. We came back here to, uh, get frisky. Well, it turns out sex and blood are similar aphrodisiacs for vampires."

"Did he hurt you?"

Willa gulped. "No, he didn't."

I shivered. "Did you know about Holland too?"

"Thierry told me when we left you in the Tuileries," Willa said.

I rubbed my palms on my leggings. I thought about curling up in bed and forgetting about all of this. I could wake up tomorrow and it would all be a distant dream. No vampires. No blood. No lying best friends. I didn't want any of this.

"Thierry isn't dangerous," Willa said, reaching for me. I flinched away. Hurt flashed across her face; she didn't try again. "But Holland might be."

"You don't know Holland," I snapped.

"And you do?"

My shoulders slumped. I shook my head. "I know it looked an awful lot like Thierry wanted to hurt me, and Holland didn't."

To my surprise, Willa didn't defend Thierry. She hadn't been there; she didn't see what I did. Thierry looked... deadly, unhinged. He didn't even sound like himself. Willa's lack of defense made me wonder whether she'd seen that part of him too. "Do you hate me?"

I scoffed. "Of course not. This is just, well, it's a lot." I lay back on the bed. "Why does Thierry say Holland is dangerous?"

"He doesn't give a reason," Willa said.

I hummed, tapping my fingers on my stomach. "Vampires."

"Vampires," she echoed.

I shook my head, my voice breaking. "It's just, I can't-"

Willa reached up to pull at her scarf. She revealed two perfect bite fang marks on her throat. They were red and swollen. My stomach flipped. That was damning evidence to prove this was really happening. There were vampires in Paris.

In London too. The man in the park, with blood on his face.

"Does it hurt?" I grimaced.

"Only for a second." Willa blushed bright red. I raised an eyebrow. "Then, it's quite wonderful."

I groaned, shaking my head and wringing out my hands. Too much. Too much. Too much. I needed a break. "I'm starving. Want to get some food?"

Willa looked relieved. "We're okay?"

"We're okay," I echoed. "I don't want to see Thierry today, though."

"I understand."

CHAPTER
19

Thierry called Willa while we walked to the Champ de Mars to watch the Eiffel Tower sparkle. She gave me an apologetic frown as she answered. Through the phone, Thierry sounded worried. He asked if she'd heard from me yet. The sound of his voice sent shocks through me - too calm, too cool; it was the opposite of how he sounded the other night when he begged me to follow him instead of Holland. I crossed my arms over my torso. Willa told him we were together and we'd be back later. I narrowed my eyes when he demanded she come back to the hotel. Willa glanced at me. I shook my head. Vampire or not, he didn't have any reason to speak to her so rudely.

She hung up after telling him to be patient.

"Willa," I started.

"I know," she said. "I shouldn't let him act like that. He's just worried."

I shrugged. I was halfway into telling Willa I wasn't sure I'd see Holland again when I saw him sitting in the grass. He wore a black sweater and blue jeans. He held a sketchbook in one hand and a pencil in the other. An unopened bottle of champagne sat on the blanket next to him. I grabbed Willa's arm instinctively. We both stopped in our tracks when Holland looked up from his book. His eyes roamed over me, like he was worried I was hurt. When he saw I wasn't, his face spread into a soft smile.

"I'll give him credit for that," Willa said. "Do you want me to go?"

"No, stay," I breathed, gripping her arm harder.

Every part of me wanted to run. But, when Willa took a step toward Holland, I followed.

He stood from his blanket when we approached. He paid no attention to Willa, his eyes fixed solely on me. "You could have told me you wanted to leave," he said quietly. He sounded hurt.

"I'm sorry. Sometimes, I run." I lowered my eyes. "I needed to breathe."

"I understand."

I gulped, shaking out my hands and motioning to Willa. "You've met Willa, right?"

Holland held his hand out first, flashing a dazzling smile that threatened to knock me off my feet. "Pleasure to see you again, Willa. You're Thierry's girl, yes?" Willa's eyes widened with relief, recognizing something comforting in Holland's words. She took Holland's hand shyly. Holland motioned for his blanket. "Please, join me, it's almost time."

Willa and I exchanged a look. She smiled at me, then at Holland, before sitting on one corner of the blanket. Holland turned to me again, inclining his chin.

"What are you doing here?" I asked.

"Watching the Eiffel Tower," he said.

"Haven't you seen it before?" I tilted my head.

He shrugged. "Doesn't mean it's any less beautiful."

I let myself smile back at him, but didn't take his hand when he offered it. I sat on my own, wrapping my arms around my chest. Holland lowered himself onto the blanket, his eyes never straying from me. I glanced at Willa again. She seemed entirely relaxed. She'd known about vampires longer than me; she was not afraid of what Holland was. Holland shrugged out of his sweater, offering it to me. I took it, letting my hand brush against his. He sucked in a breath. The look he gave me was almost desperate.

He opened his mouth to say something, but the Eiffel Tower went dark for half a second. Then it erupted in glittering lights. The crowd cheered. Willa laughed. I looked away from Holland to beam up at the extraordinary sight. Willa reached over to squeeze my hand. I bumped my shoulder up against hers.

I wanted to see beautiful things like this for the rest of my life.

Around us, people danced. Couples kissed. Families cheered. I watched them all, smiling. Everyone seemed so... happy. I yelped when Willa pulled me up to dance with her. I laughed at our fumbling movements, skipping around the grass with her while the entire world glittered.

The tower went dark again and returned to normal. I stumbled into Willa, laughing as we returned to Holland's blanket. My eyes found Holland's again. He watched me intently, his eyes wide with wonder.

"I want to stay here forever," Willa said.

"Why don't you?" Holland asked, his eyes on me. I gulped.

She paused. "I have a whole life in the states. A family, a fiancé, a career."

"You could have that here," Holland countered. "All of that, and be happy."

She stared at him for a moment. "You're right."

Holland paused, tilting his head. "Thierry, how kind of you to join us."

I tensed, the blood draining from my face as I stared over

Holland's shoulder. Sure enough, the blonde vampire emerged from the crowd. His eyes were full of rage. Shock and anger flashed on Willa's face when she stood up.

"What are you doing here?" She snapped when Thierry approached her. I watched him wrap his hand around her arm. Willa pulled back in indignance. "I told you I'd be back later."

"I was worried." When he looked at her, the rage faded, replaced with something like concern. Or... possession. I shifted uncomfortably.

Willa crossed her arms, shaking her head. "I'm not doing this with you, Thierry. I don't do alpha male bullshit. I'm a grown woman having a nice night with my friend." Thierry opened his mouth to argue. Willa wasn't done. "If this happens again, we are done. This is your last warning."

Thierry's eyes widened. He stepped back, his eyes flicking to Holland, then to me. I tensed, sinking into myself. Thierry reached forward to place his hand on Willa's cheek. Willa leaned into his touch, despite her anger. "I am sorry, my love. I will listen in the future. We should go, Addie too."

Willa shook her head. "Addie is fine."

Something dark crossed Thierry's face. "My love," he started.

"You heard the girl," Holland said, standing off the blanket. I whimpered, clenching my hands at my sides. Too much. Too much. Too much. "Adalyn is fine. She is safe."

Willa sighed, stepping in front of Thierry. "Why don't we all ask Addie what she wants to do?"

Everyone turned to me. My heart stuttered. I nearly choked on my saliva, crushed under the weight of everyone's attention. Thierry's lip curled in fury. Willa winked at me and tilted her head towards Holland.

And Holland...

He looked hopeful.

I stared at him for a moment, waiting for anything I should be afraid of. There was nothing. He looked warm. He looked safe. I wrapped his sweater closer around my shoulders, trying to stop shivering. I wasn't even cold - just nervous.

I turned to Willa when I spoke, too afraid to look at Thierry behind her. "I'm gonna stay."

Willa beamed at me. "Text me when you get back tonight." She turned to Thierry, looping her arm through his. "Let's go."

Thierry had another idea. I flinched back when he took a few steps towards me. Holland stepped in front of him, gripping his arm with a low, inhuman growl. My stomach flipped.

"Mine," Holland hissed.

Thierry yanked his arm back from Holland's grip. He looked between me and the vampire and smirked. "She's not, is she? Careful, Holland, many of us would kill for one like her."

"Thierry!" Willa snapped, stomping her foot. "What the fuck?"

He stepped back, letting Willa grab onto him.

Willa turned to me again. "Text me," she repeated. "And send me your location if you go anywhere else."

"I will," I whispered, praying I hadn't made the wrong decision.

Then they were gone, and I was alone with Holland.

CHAPTER 20

"Holland," I asked quietly when he sat on the blanket next to me. "Should I be scared?"

"Of me?" He clarified. I nodded. "Never." My shoulders slumped. "Of this world you've been brought into? Yes."

I laughed once. "That doesn't make me feel any better."

"Champagne?" He offered with a boyish smile, motioning to the untouched bottle.

"Please."

Holland reached into the basket next to him, pulling out two champagne flutes. He handed me one. Again, I let our fingers touch. Chills spread down my spine. Holland paused, watching me for a moment before reaching for the champagne bottle. I jumped when he popped the cork, barely making it to a flute before it spilled over. I laughed, sipping away the foam. Holland smiled as he filled both glasses, clinking his against mine.

"Thank you for staying," he said. "Why did you?"

I sucked in a deep breath, taking a sip of the champagne. "Because every part of me is telling me to run."

"I won't stop you if you do," Holland said. "For what it's worth, I hope you don't."

I rubbed my hands on my pants again. "Is this real?"

"I'm afraid so."

Another drink. "What's Thierry's problem?" I paused. "Should I be worried about Willa?"

Holland leaned back to rest on one of his elbows, taking a slow drink of champagne. "No, you should not be worried about Willa. He won't hurt her." I sighed in relief. "He's a new vampire, impulsive, possessive. He feels threatened."

"By you?" I swallowed.

Holland took a deep breath. "I'm going to preface this next statement by saying I would never do anything to hurt you, Adalyn. I would worship the ground beneath your feet if you'd let me." My eyes widened; butterflies erupted in my stomach. He held my gaze. "But, I am not a vampire you want to make an enemy of."

I raised an eyebrow. I should have been scared. I should have walked away and gone back to my hotel to forget about all of this. I didn't move. Instead, I stretched out on the blanket and gazed at the Eiffel Tower again - standing proud against the night sky.

"What are you thinking?" Holland asked.

I turned back to him. Despite everything I should have been doing, I melted. "I'm thinking that I have a million questions. And I'm hoping you have the time to answer them all."

Holland smiled. "For you? I have all the time in the world." I finished my champagne and held it out to him to refill. He did, his eyes never leaving mine. "Whenever you're ready, my dearest."

I took another sip and pulled his sweater tighter around my chest. Taking a few deep breaths, I watched the Eiffel Tower glow. I dug my nails into the palm of my free hand as I gained my bearings.

"How old are you?"

Holland hummed. "I was born in 1834. I died when I was twenty-five."

I shivered. I couldn't look at him again, not yet. I needed the courage to keep asking questions.

"So, technically, you're dead?"

"Yes. You have to die to become a vampire."

I whimpered, pulling my knees to my chest. "But, your heart beats."

"Slower than yours, but yes."

I turned to him, shocked by the sadness on his face. "Can I feel it?"

Holland nodded.

I moved closer, setting my champagne flute down and kneeling next to Holland. He leaned back on his hands, moving slowly like he was afraid to startle me. I paused, licking my lips.

"Show me again," I whispered.

He blinked, and black veins rippled beneath his eyes. The red rim appeared, stark against the honey gold. I sucked in a deep breath and reached forward to trace the veins on his face. His lips parted. My eyes dropped to take in the sight of two, perfectly sharp fangs in his mouth.

Holland was a vampire.

It was impossible, and yet right in front of me.

I trailed my hand down to rest on his chest and closed my eyes. I blocked out the rest of the world, focusing only on the faint beating against my hand. It was soft and slow, but it was there.

"I don't understand," I breathed, sniffling.

Holland placed his hand over mine. "You don't have to, at least not tonight. Maybe not ever if you don't want to."

"Okay," I said, wiping a tear.

"What other questions do you have?" Holland asked, distracting me from the fear creeping into me.

I thought about pulling my hand from his chest. His hand tightened on mine. I stayed where I was. "How many vampires are there?"

Holland shrugged. "Thousands. Tens of thousands. A lot."

"You don't burn in the sun." My mouth felt dry, like cotton.

"No."

"Holy water?"

"Drinkable." Holland almost smiled.

"Garlic bread?"

"A great addition to spaghetti."

I laughed once, brushing another stray tear.

"Wooden stakes?"

"Deadly."

"Oh," I paused.

Holland shrugged, unbothered by my question. "Fire will also do the trick, if you were thinking about it."

My stomach flipped and I shook my head. "Will you really live forever?"

"Unless I find myself at the business end of a stake, yes."

I sucked in a breath. "When you told me about your family," I trailed off.

Holland's shoulders slumped. "My parents were both dead before I died." He cleared his throat and said, "my sister lives in Rome."

I stiffened, my brow furrowing as I looked at him. Holland blinked up at me. His hand tightened on mine again, like he sensed my desire to bolt.

"How did you die?" I whispered.

"I drowned."

I winced, hating the memories that coursed through me. I changed the subject. "And you drink human blood?"

Holland inclined his chin. "Yes."

I pulled my hand from his chest then, sitting back and returning to sitting with my knees near my chest. I didn't miss the fall of Holland's face for half a second before he composed himself.

"Keep going," he coaxed gently.

I stiffened. "The girl in the park. The one drained of blood." Holland inclined his chin, waiting for what I was afraid I already knew the answer to. "Did you kill her?"

"Yes."

I flinched.

"It was an accident. I try to be very careful."

My head spun. My breath caught and I wrapped my arms around my knees.

"We don't have to talk about this," Holland said. "We can talk about anything you'd like. Or, not at all."

I rested my chin on my knees. I wasn't sure when I started talking, but as soon as I did, I couldn't stop. Holland listened while I told him what happened in London, about the girl in the park and the man, the vampire, with blood on his face. No details were spared, and I detailed what happened at the club - the sight of Thierry's teeth in Willa's throat and how terrified I'd been. I told him I couldn't breathe, and I wanted to run.

He said nothing.

The Eiffel Tower erupted in a billion glittering lights. The vampire next to me stood and held out his hand.

If I took his hand, I would choose to step into a world I didn't understand. I would choose to believe in vampires, no matter how scared I felt. If I took Holland's hand, I couldn't ever go back.

If I didn't, everything could go back to normal. I could

convince myself this never happened. Perhaps I would go home after all. I could feel safe again.

Except, with Holland's eyes on me, I felt brave. And warm. And safe.

I took his hand.

Holland pulled me to my feet. My chest pressed against his and my eyes widened. I placed one hand on his arm and gripped his hand with the other. Holland took a tentative step forward. I took one back.

And while the tower glittered, we danced.

He told me he would worship the ground I walked on. I was tempted to let him.

The Eiffel Tower fell dark.

My heart fell.

"I should get you back to your hotel," Holland said, his face inches from mine.

His cheeks were pink from the night air and his eyes seemed slightly tired. He looked perfectly... kissable. "Sure," I said.

Neither of us moved.

"How long will you be in Paris?" He asked.

"As long as I have a reason to be," I responded. Holland's lips parted and he tilted his chin up ever so slightly, closer to me. I swallowed. My gaze trailed from his eyes, down to his mouth. I watched him lick his lips. I wasn't sure who leaned forward first, but my breath caught when he was a hair's breadth away. "Holland," I breathed.

"Yes?"

"Give me a reason to stay."

He kissed me.

CHAPTER
21

Holland's kiss felt like coming up for air after drowning for years. His lips pressed against mine daintily at first. I forgot I'd just discovered a dark truth about the world. I forgot he was supposed to be dangerous. He tasted like champagne and chocolate. A small gasp escaped me as he leaned forward, his fingers tracing my jaw.

And nothing else mattered.

I deepened our kiss. His lips were just as soft against mine as I imagined they would be. His touch was delicate, but there was something else behind it, something desperate - something I longed to become familiar with. I grabbed the collar of Holland's shirt and coaxed him closer. Silently, I asked for a little *more*. He obliged.

His tongue traced mine slowly once, twice, three times. Then, it was less of a kiss and more like being consumed. Holland's hands wound in my hair, pulling me against him. I whined into our kiss, clinging to him desperately. One of Holland's hands fell to my hip, carefully pulling me closer. He lowered himself to one knee, holding me effortlessly as I pressed against him. Together, we fell against the blanket. A gasp escaped Holland; it was music to my ears.

Someone in the park whistled. Another person cheered.

Holland pulled back, and I swore he blushed. I grinned up at him, laughing once.

"We should get back," he sighed.

"Okay." I did not move. I didn't want to.

"One more." He leaned down again, kissing me deeply. I relaxed beneath him. I could have spent forever beneath his mouth.

One more kiss turned into five. Then ten. Holland kissed me endlessly. He kissed my mouth, my cheeks, my jaw, my throat. He kissed me until I was breathless, and then he kissed me more.

Eventually, he stopped when most of the Champ de Mars had emptied. Holland sat up, drawing me with him. A cool breeze rustled through my hair. I shivered, blinking up at the dark sky. Holland leaned forward, placing another kiss on my jaw. When I lowered my eyes, he kissed my mouth.

Together, we gathered up the blanket and threw out the trash at the nearest garbage bin. Every few steps, Holland stopped me to kiss me again. I lost myself in him every time.

In the middle of the street.

On the metro.

In a quiet alleyway.

Outside the hotel.

In the elevator.

Holland kissed my shoulder as I fumbled with the hotel room door. I pushed it open, hesitating only a moment before stepping back to invite him in. His eyes darkened and he crossed the threshold, his hands cupping my face and pulling me in for another kiss. I gasped when he pushed his sweater over my shoulders, nipping at my jaw like I was the sweetest dessert.

I clung to Holland as I walked backward until my legs touched the bed. Holland's hands found the bottom of my shirt, gripping the fabric. I paused, realizing what was about to happen, and my hand fell to stop his movement.

Holland stopped, his eyes searching mine. My heart pounded.

"I'm sorry," I said. "I'm not ready for this."

Holland's eyes softened. He released the bottom of my shirt and pressed delicate kisses to each of my cheeks. "Don't apologize. Do you want me to leave?"

I opened my mouth a few times. I didn't have an answer. I didn't want him gone, but I also wasn't sure I wanted him in my bed in any capacity - not yet.

Fuck, I wished I knew that before I invited him in.

I expected him to be annoyed at my denial. Holland only smiled and kissed the palm of my hand. "How about tomorrow? I'll pick you up at noon?"

"Okay," I breathed. A tear dripped down my face.

Holland brushed it away. He stepped forward, kissing both of my cheeks quickly. His mouth covered mine. I jolted in surprise. His arm wound around my waist, holding me tight.

Then he pulled away, bowing low and taking a few steps back. I watched him leave, closing the door behind him. The elevator dinged. He was gone.

"Fuck," I swore, dragging my nails through my hair. I sobbed once.

In the last five years, I only slept with one person. One person with a very different anatomy than Holland. I'd been with a man before, my first boyfriend. It had been so long. I didn't know what I was doing.

Holland wasn't even angry with me. He smiled and kissed me again. He promised to pick me up tomorrow.

I pulled out my phone to text Willa.

Are you here?

I only waited a moment before her response came. **Yeah. You back?**

I sucked in a breath. **Have time to talk? Need advice.**

A minute later, Willa knocked on my door. I moved to open it, hands shaking.

"Hey," Willa said immediately. She wore pink pajamas and there were socks wrapped in her hair. "Are you okay? Did he hurt you?"

"God, no," I whispered, sitting down on the edge of my bed.

"Then, why are you crying?" Willa sat next to me, taking my hand.

I turned to face her, straightening my shoulders. "I'm attracted to him," I started.

"Well, duh, have you seen him?" She snorted.

I laughed once, shaking my head. "No, I mean. I was engaged to a woman, and now-"

Recognition flashed on Willa's face. "Have you ever had sex with a man?"

I nodded. "I was eighteen, so it's been six years."

"Okay, so what happened? Is he mad?"

"No." I buried my face in my hands, laughing at the absurdity of the situation. "He's picking me up tomorrow at noon. He was a perfect gentleman. God, I didn't even think."

Willa laughed. "Should I get a banana and teach you?"

We both burst into hysterical laughter.

"I know how to give a blowjob, Willa," I said.

"So, if you know what you're doing, and you're sure Holland won't hurt you or pressure you into anything you don't want, what's the problem?"

I opened and closed my mouth, straightening in surprise. There wasn't a problem. I was nervous because I didn't expect to be so attracted to him. Truthfully, I wanted to touch him, taste him, feel him. Willa smiled at me knowingly. I huffed, wringing out my hands. "I need you to tell me what you know."

"About what?"

"Vampires, and," I cleared my throat. "Intimacy with vampires."

"Okay, the biggest thing you need to know is that bloodlust and sexual desire are extremely similar for vampires," Willa started. "Thierry can't, uh, he can't always control himself. I don't ask him to, not anymore. They're stronger than humans, and faster too. Thierry is super careful, but I have to remind him sometimes - I'm breakable."

"How are you okay with this?" I interrupted her, my chest constricting. "How am I okay with this?"

"It's hard to deny what we've seen with our own eyes," Willa said, shrugging. "I think it makes the world a little more exciting."

I let out a long breath, laying back on my pillows. I swore and shook my head.

Two weeks ago, I was getting married. I was in a toxic relationship with a woman I hadn't loved in a long time. Now, I was in Paris talking about vampire sex because I was absurdly attracted to one.

"Another thing," I said. I'd been too nervous to ask Holland about it earlier in the evening, even if he would have answered. "About something Thierry said."

Willa sucked in her breath like she expected my question.

"What did he mean when he said I wasn't Holland's?"

She sighed. "From what Thierry has told me, vampires are very possessive over their humans, when they have them. Basically, if they bite you, you belong to them and no other vampire can touch you. Until then, you're technically fair game."

I wrinkled my nose. My stomach churned. "That's disgusting."

She almost laughed.

I reached for her hand, squeezing it. "Willa, tell me what Thierry tells you about Holland."

"Just that he's dangerous and much older than he looks. Apparently, the older the vampire, the stronger, faster, and more deadly they are."

"He doesn't feel dangerous. And he's almost two hundred," I said blandly.

Willa's eyes could have popped out of her head. "Really? He told you that?"

I shrugged. "I asked. He answered."

Willa softened and nodded, almost to herself. "I told you I thought you should go for it, even while I knew what he was. I still think you should."

I turned to face my friend. "I need Thierry to back off. I'm not scared of Holland, but I'm scared of him."

Hurt flashed on her face, accompanied by understanding. "I'll take care of it." Willa lay back on the bed next to me, both of us staring at the ceiling. "My mother called me today," she said after a while of silence. "She threatened to cut off all my bank accounts if I don't come home. I'm not ready to choose between my life at home and Paris."

My bottom lip quivered. "You can't leave. We haven't found ourselves yet."

"I know. But I can't stay here with no money."

"Did you tell Thierry?" I asked.

She shook her head. "No. He doesn't know a thing. My mother and my fiancé are both threatening me. I'm worried one of them will come here."

"We'll figure it out," I told her. "Besides, you have a hot vampire boyfriend to kick ass if you need him to."

She wiped her tears. I wasn't sure how, but I would help her if I could. Willa was my friend. She wanted to be happy, and free, just as much as I did.

"Tell me more about your time with Holland," she sniffled.

I blushed and told her everything.

CHAPTER

22

I met Holland outside at noon.

He wore a dark blue button-up and his hair fell into his face. Sunglasses covered his eyes, and he carried a messenger bag. I blushed immediately, glancing back inside the hotel lobby where Willa waited. She waved expectantly before wrapping her cardigan around her waist and retreating. I crossed the street to meet Holland.

As I approached, he pulled a single red rose out of the bag and held it out to me.

"Where are we going?" I asked after thanking him, bringing the rose to my nose to breathe in the smell.

Holland held out his arm. "Just a short walk away if you're up for it?"

"Of course."

I looped my arm through his and let him lead the way up the hill. As we passed through a busy roundabout of cafes and restaurants, I alternated between watching Holland and watching my surroundings. I noticed his hand felt especially cold against my forearm, and his cheeks seemed paler than usual. Holland kept walking, pointing out a cute dog wearing a pink bow. I grinned. The sun was out in full force today, hot on my face and skin. Holland's hand on my arm was a cool relief.

We walked for nearly a mile before he beckoned me through the gates of the Luxembourg Gardens. I walked a step behind him, sweat beading on my forehead.

Holland fell back, holding onto me and leading me toward a patch of shade beneath a row of trees. He pulled a water bottle out of his messenger bag, offering it to me. My shoulders slumped in relief as I took it.

"I didn't expect it to be so warm today. We'll find a place in the shade for today's activities," Holland said.

I smiled. "That sounds great. What are we doing?"

Holland patted his bag. "It's a surprise."

I took another sip of water. "Are we there yet?"

"Yes, let's find a place to sit." Holland offered me his hand. I took it.

"How are you so cold all the time?" I asked.

"Technically, I'm dead, Adalyn." My lips parted in shock. For half a second, I thought I might have upset him. Then his lips spread into a smile and he raised my hand to his mouth, pressing a kiss to my knuckles. I smiled softly, taking a step closer to him as we followed the paths through the trees. "You're taking this remarkably well," Holland said.

I tilted my head. "You'd prefer a hysterical mess?"

He squeezed my hand, rolling his eyes. "No, I enjoy your smile."

"It's easy for me to believe in what I can see," I told him honestly.

We found a grassy spot in the shade. Holland pulled a thin blanket out of his bag, laying it over the grass and motioning for me to sit. I did. He sat across from me. My eyes widened when he pulled out two small canvases, a dozen paintbrushes, and several small bottles of acrylic paint. Once everything was spread out over the blanket, Holland grinned at me.

"We're painting?"

He nodded.

I chose a thin paintbrush and green paint. Holland grabbed a thick brush and a pink. I stretched out on the blanket, kicking off my shoes and brushing grass off my bare legs. I didn't miss Holland's lingering gaze on my thighs and his thick gulp. Before he saw how brightly I blushed, I turned away. I took off my sunglasses, setting them next to me as I dipped my brush in paint and smeared it across the canvas.

While I painted, I thought about how it felt to be kissed by Holland. Intense, all-consuming, like my whole body was on fire and he was the only thing that could quench the flames. I glanced at him twice; he remained focused intently on whatever he painted. Once, he bit his bottom lip, and I swore my stomach did somersaults. He'd also taken off his sunglasses. His brow furrowed while he focused.

I swore quietly, returning to the trees I painted and trying to ignore the quivers in my heart. It had been a long time since I'd been this attracted to a man, it was unfamiliar yet entirely welcome.

I rolled from my stomach to rest on one elbow. "What are you working on?" I asked him.

Holland raised an eyebrow. "A secret. What are you working on?"

I held up my terrible tree. A smile spread across his face as he took in my awful painting. "I never said I was good at this," I told him.

"No, it's spectacular."

"Liar."

Holland laughed. "Yeah, I'm totally lying."

"Okay, your turn," I said, pointing to his canvas.

He shook his head.

"Why not?" I sat up, sitting cross-legged.

Holland set his canvas behind him, smiling. "I'm not finished."

I wrinkled my nose. "Not fair, I showed you my shitty tree."

"I didn't ask to see your tree," he countered.

"Fine," I said, crossing my arms. Holland laughed as I rolled away from him, pretending to hide my canvas from him. When I looked back, he'd picked up his canvas and was dipping a small brush in a bit of red paint. I watched him paint for a moment, his eyes dark and focused. I smiled, crossing my ankles as I worked to make my tree look less like a green blob and more like a plant.

I glanced at Holland again, watching as he mixed red and brown on his canvas. He chewed on his bottom lip, narrowing his eyes and reaching for a new, tiny brush. He dragged it across the canvas swiftly, nodding to himself and repeating the movement.

"You're staring," he said quietly, barely glancing up at me. A smile teased the corner of his mouth.

"You're nice to look at," I responded bravely.

Holland raised his gaze, smiling. "Thank you. Paint your tree, I'm almost finished."

I lay back on the blanket with a dramatic sigh. "My tree is bad. It's not getting any better."

He chuckled, mostly focused on his painting. I rolled onto my back, sighing at the sunlight peeking through the trees. It stretched across my face. I tilted my chin up, sighing into the warmth. I heard Holland gasp and clear his throat. When I turned to him, he stared down at his painting, black veins rippled under his eyes. He blinked a few times and they faded. He didn't look back at me.

I sat up again, dipping my fingers in paint and tracing them over my leg. I drew circles around the bare skin, mimicking the leaves and ferns tattooed up my left leg. I drew pink flowers, green ones, and a single red one. This was much more fun than struggling with my canvas tree. My hands were covered in paint in moments. I didn't care. I followed the shadows on my leg, creating art where there had been none.

"Fuck," Holland murmured.

When I looked up at him to see what was wrong, he watched me with wide eyes. I paused mid-flower, blinking in confusion.

"What?" I breathed.

Holland tossed his canvas to the side. I looked after it to see what it was, but he moved forward and kissed me before I could. Shock rolled through me. My paint-covered hands fluttered at my sides before he grabbed them and placed them on his chest - practically begging me to touch him. I clutched the collar of his shirt when his tongue found mine hungrily. Holland pulled me onto his lap. Paint smeared all over his clothes, and mine. He invaded all of my senses; he tasted sweet like chocolate and orange.

Holland's hands dipped beneath the fabric of my shirt. I whined at the feeling of his cold skin against mine, leaning further into him. Paint smeared on his face and in his hair. He kissed down my jaw, his tongue leaving wet trails down my skin. I let my head fall back.

Holland stilled with his lips on my throat. I started in surprise when he leaned back. Black veins rippled under his eyes as he squeezed them shut. His lips parted to reveal his fangs and his hands tightened on my hips.

"I'm sorry," he whispered.

I pursed my lips, reaching up to brush his hair off his forehead, smearing pink paint on him while I did. I leaned forward and pressed my lips against his again. Holland whimpered. His returning kiss was slow and shy. He kissed me only once before he pulled back again.

"Open your eyes, Holland," I said quietly. He did. They were red-rimmed and desperate. "I'm not afraid of you."

He laughed once, shaking his head. "Adalyn," he started. "Do you have any idea what's going through my mind right now?"

"Tell me."

Holland let out a long breath. I watched his gaze drop from my eyes to my throat. He shook his head again, clearing his throat. Instead of answering me, he lifted me off his lap and stood away from the blanket. I sat, slightly deflated, watching him clench his hands at his sides.

He took a few steps away from me, growling quietly. I stood, following him, barefoot. I caught his arm, turning him to face me.

"Tell me, Holland," I repeated.

He spun towards me. I stumbled back against a tree I hadn't realized was so close. Holland took a dangerous step forward, placing both of his hands on either side of my head. "I'm caught between desperately wanting to fuck you and make you bleed for me. You're not ready for either of those things yet, so please, a moment," he hissed.

I gasped at his words, looking up at the vampire above me. Holland looked angry; I didn't know whether it was with me or not. He didn't move away from where he trapped me against the tree. I placed my hand on his chest. I was sure he felt it shake against him. Still, Holland's eyes closed in relief.

"I'm not afraid of you," I repeated.

He laughed once. "You should be."

"You haven't given me a reason to be," I said.

He shook his head, stepping back and clearing his throat. "I have to go, Adalyn. I'll find you tomorrow?"

He didn't wait for me to answer; he walked away quickly, leaving me with a racing pulse and a lump in my throat. I watched him go and resisted the urge to run after him.

Shoulders slumping, I stood off the tree and returned to our blanket. I picked up Holland's canvas from where he'd discarded it, eyes wide with shock.

He painted me.

A happier, brighter version of me, smiling and sitting on a swing. It was incredibly lifelike for being done so quickly. I wondered if that was how Holland saw me - full of sunshine. My heart warmed at the thought. I watched where he'd disappeared, frowning.

I packed up and walked back to the hotel alone.

CHAPTER 23

"I don't know how you're not in love with him yet," Willa said, setting Holland's painting down on my bed. "That's incredible."

Shaking my head, I laughed once. I'd showered and gotten ready to go to dinner with Willa and Thierry after Holland left me in the Luxembourg Gardens. I thought about texting him and asking if he was alright, but I was too scared to upset him.

My phone rang before I could respond to Willa. I answered Indy's video call, setting her on the nightstand so she could see me and Willa sitting on the bed.

My sister seemed flustered, grumbling to herself until she saw the call went through. She smiled weakly. "Hey!"

"What's wrong?" I asked.

"Shitty day at work, wanted to call you before I passed out in bed," Indy responded. "Hi, Willa!"

"Hey, kid," Willa called.

"What are you two up to tonight?" Indy asked.

"Going to dinner with Willa's boy toy," I said.

Indy paused. "So, I take it you're not coming home tomorrow?"

My stomach flipped when I remembered my plane home was supposed to be tomorrow afternoon. I exchanged a glance with Willa, who shifted nervously.

"No," I said. "I am not coming home tomorrow."

"When, then?" Indy sounded angry. I wasn't sure where her change in attitude came from. She was excited for me just days ago.

I shrugged. "I'm not done in Paris."

"Come on, Addie. This isn't like you. You hate being away from home for too long."

I cleared my throat, still trying to catch up. "Well, I hadn't planned on coming home at all."

Indy hung up the phone.

I stared at the phone in disbelief, glancing up at Willa. She looked as shocked as I felt, her eyes wide and mouth hanging open. I didn't even have time to process my sister's aggression because there was a knock on my door. Mind reeling, I waved for Willa to answer it. I assumed it was Thierry, ready to take us to dinner.

"Oh, hi!" Willa squeaked.

I glanced up passively, my breath catching when I saw Holland in the hallway, wearing all black. His hair was mussed and his brows crinkled. He looked between me and Willa nervously, his brows furrowing.

"I'll be in my room," Willa said, slipping past Holland and darting across the hallway.

"It's not tomorrow yet," I said.

Holland stepped inside, closing the door behind him. "I'm sorry about earlier."

"Which part?" I inclined my chin and raised an eyebrow.

"All of it." Holland stared down at his feet. "For getting carried away. For leaving you there."

"I'm not upset about the first part," I said.

Holland shrugged. "I am."

"Okay."

"I came to ask for another chance, but it seems like you're busy, so-"

"We were just going to get dinner," I interrupted. "It's not important."

Holland glanced between me and the door, letting out a long breath. "Thierry is here to pick you up."

I shook my head. "Give me a reason not to care."

He did not hesitate. He crossed the room and held my face in both of his hands while he kissed me. I melted immediately, stepping into him. I reached up to tug his hands off my face, feeling too claustrophobic. He hardly noticed, one arm winding around my waist and the other tangling in my hair. I took a single step back, my calves hitting the bed. Holland followed, his tongue dancing with mine.

I placed my hand on his chest. He pulled back. "I should tell them I'm not going," I whispered.

Holland grinned, tilting his head slightly. "Thierry heard you. There's no need."

I smiled. "Fascinating."

He stepped back and took a deep breath. "Are you hungry? We could go to my apartment - I'll cook."

I took his hand. "Sounds great."

I sat in Holland's window seat, watching the sunset over Paris while he stood in the kitchen. The entire apartment smelled delicious, full of warm seasonings and a sandalwood candle. I sipped my wine, turning to watch Holland cook. He wore an apron over his black clothes and seemed much more relaxed than he had earlier today.

"Can I ask you something?" I stood from the window seat, walking barefoot across the floor.

"Only if you try this," Holland responded, turning and offering me a spoonful of the soup he made.

I blew on it carefully before taking it in my mouth. It was rich, creamy, and warmed my soul. "That's delicious."

He grinned, reaching to take a sip from his wine glass. "Thank you. What's your question?"

"So, depending on the movie-" I started.

Holland rolled his eyes. "Oh, this will be good."

I laughed when he turned to face me. "How do you eat food? If technically, you're," I trailed off.

Holland stepped forward, kissing me once. "Dead is not a bad word, my dear," he said, returning to chopping carrots and celery to add to the soup. "My body functions similar to a human's. I'm cold because my heart beats slower than yours, and while food like this no longer offers me any nutrition, it's still delicious."

I leaned against the counter, watching him swipe the vegetables into the simmering broth. Holland added shredded chicken and covered the pot before side-stepping to kiss me again. I watched, awestruck when he moved away. He refilled both of our wine glasses, stirred the soup, and put the garlic bread in the oven.

"Are there any other vampire things I should know?" I asked.

Holland thought for a moment. "We cry blood."

I started in surprise. "Seriously? Does it hurt?"

He shook his head. "It feels no different than human tears, it's just messier."

I returned to my window seat, smiling at the golden sun over Paris. I sighed, leaning out the window for a breath of the cool fall breeze. Holland came up behind me, wrapping both arms around my torso. I sat back into him, resting my head on his chest.

"I like having you here," he said. "I like you."

I smiled into the sunshine.

Holland kissed my shoulder. "Why are you in Paris, Adalyn?"

I tensed. "You've asked me that before."

"Give me the actual answer this time. What are you running from?"

I sucked in a deep breath, letting my eyes slip closed while he kissed my shoulder. My heart pounded in my throat.

"My fiancé, ex-fiancé I guess, left me at the altar," I started. Holland paused for half a second before continuing his slow, repetitive kiss. "And I think I ran because of that, but also because I was living a life I didn't want. A dead-end job in a city I hated, you know the cliche."

Holland hummed.

"I wanted a breath of fresh air," I whispered.

"Should I be worried about your ex-fiancé's attention?" Holland asked.

"No," I said. "I don't expect to ever hear from her again. And, I think I fell out of love with her a long time ago."

"Her?"

I gulped, turning my head slightly towards him. My stomach twinged. "Yeah. Is that a problem?"

He smiled, a small blush on his cheeks. "Of course not." He leaned forward to kiss my cheek, then my mouth.

I turned to face him, wrapping both arms around his shoulders to kiss him deeply. Holland groaned into the kiss. Chills spread through me at the noise. I kissed him harder, desperate for him to do it again. Holland's tongue found mine, slowly at first. He pulled me closer, and it was more like being consumed. I hummed into his kiss, feeling like my whole body was on fire.

Holland gripped my hips and lifted me off the window seat. I clung to him, smiling into his kiss at the lack of balance. A couple of steps back and we fell onto the bed. I straddled Holland's hips, running my hands up his chest. His hands roamed beneath my shirt, sending shivers of cold through the fire that caught within me.

This time, when he tensed and paused, I sat up to watch him squeeze his eyes shut. Black veins rippled across his face as he took a couple of deep breaths.

"I'm sorry," I said.

Holland opened his red-rimmed eyes, sighing miserably. "Why would you be sorry?"

I watched his fangs flash in his mouth while he talked. "I don't mean to make you uncomfortable."

Holland sat up quickly, wrapping one arm around my waist to keep me from tilting backward. "You know why I feel like this, Adalyn?" he whispered.

I shook my head.

"Because you are irresistible," he growled. "Because you smell like sunshine and taste like heaven. I feel like this because I want you so badly I can't control myself."

"Oh," I breathed.

Holland fell back on the mattress with a huff. I traced my hand up his chest, my fingers lightly grazing his collarbone. Holland took a deep, shaky breath.

"I need to stir dinner." He opened his eyes, the last of the red fading from them. "And perhaps take a cold shower."

I blushed.

CHAPTER 24

I thought about kissing Holland throughout dinner. I watched him talk about going to culinary school, but my attention was focused on his pink, swollen lips instead of what he said. He sat across the table from me, like he was trying to put space between us.

I didn't want space between us. In fact, I wanted nothing between us at all.

It had been such a long time since I wanted someone this much. I thought about his hands on my skin and lost track of everything else, wondering how much better it might be if I let him have me. His mouth on mine was delectable, but I wanted it elsewhere - everywhere.

I helped him clean the dishes, resisting the urge to grab him and kiss him while my hands were covered in soapy water. It fell dark outside and Holland replaced the overhead light with a couple more candles and a small lamp. He offered me another glass of wine, leading me over to the couch to relax. I let out a long breath, watching him sit down and lounge back.

I paused and frowned, looking between him and the glass of red in my hand.

"What is it?" Holland asked, adjusting a pillow next to him for me to sit comfortably.

I set the wine glass down on the coffee table. Holland's brow furrowed and he tilted his head in confusion. Instead of sitting down next to him, I carefully straddled his lap. His golden eyes widened. Before I could hesitate any more, I leaned down to kiss him.

He jolted in surprise; his arms wound around me to pull me into a deeper kiss. I gasped at how tightly he held onto my hips and used that pressure to determine how hard I kissed him. This time, I swiped my tongue over his first, practically begging him for more. Holland whined. A gust of wind blew in from outside, extinguishing a couple of candles.

Holland sighed and made the slightest move to go fix them. I held onto him, shaking my head. He melted. I kissed down his jaw, over his throat, listening to his small gasps of pleasure. I flicked my tongue on his collarbone before returning to his mouth with a sigh.

My stomach flipped when I pushed my hips harder against him. He was hard beneath his jeans, pressing into me. The sensation was unfamiliar. Tentatively, I rocked my hips against his. Holland's hands tightened on my hips, coaxing the movement out of me again with a deep groan.

"Adalyn," he started.

I shook my head, sitting up to watch him drop his head against the back of the couch. "Don't pull away from me again," I breathed. "Please, Holland."

He opened his eyes. They were red-rimmed and filled with desire. I raised my hand, placing it on his cheek and leaning down to kiss him - fangs and all. Holland whined, his hands grazing my thighs. He kissed me so slowly that I thought I would cry from desperation.

He pulled back, his eyes searching mine. "You're sure?"

"Yes."

When he kissed me again, he kissed me like a starving man. I whimpered in surprise, clinging to him as he pulled me closer. I placed one hand on the wall behind him to hold myself up, grinding my hips against his while he kissed me like it was all he'd ever thought about. Holland leaned forward to kiss my throat, his hands fiddling with the buttons on my blouse. I sat back to watch him undo them. His tongue flicked over his teeth and his eyes darkened before leaning forward to kiss my chest.

I shrugged out of my shirt, letting my head fall back as Holland left wet tongue marks over my breasts. I gasped in shock when he reached behind me and snapped my bra clasp with an easy flick of his wrist. The bra fell off, and he glanced up for permission again. I nodded, whining at the feeling of his tongue on my nipples.

"Fuck," Holland murmured, dragging his tongue between my cleavage. He leaned up to kiss my mouth again, standing. I yelped in surprise, wrapping my legs around his waist. Our kiss did not break until he reached the bed, lowering me to lie on the mattress. I watched with wide eyes as he pulled his shirt over his head.

My mouth felt dry as I dragged my eyes over his sun-kissed, chiseled chest. I stared at his hands as he undid his belt and the buttons of his jeans. When he wore only boxers, he returned to me, laying on the mattress next to me and pulling my body against his. He felt warmer than he normally did. I welcomed the sensation, kissing over his chest, his neck, his face, his mouth.

"I'm going to ask one more time if you're sure," he breathed against me.

"Yes, I'm sure," I responded immediately. "Please, Holland."

Holland reached up, tilting my chin up and holding me in place. "You should save your begging. You'll need it later."

Oh.

Holland winked, rolling me onto my back and nestling himself between my thighs. My whole body tingled as he kissed down my chest, stopping to swirl his tongue around each nipple. He kissed me hungrily, covering every part of me in his touch. I trembled beneath him, unable to stay still. Holland looped his fingers beneath the edge of my pants, glancing up for permission. I granted it. I lifted my hips for him to strip me bare, watching his eyes widen. Black veins darkened beneath his eyes and he licked his lips. Then it faded and he was my Holland again, leaning down to kiss my mouth.

"You're fucking perfect," he whispered against my lips. I blushed, my heart squeezing.

I couldn't respond. His hand trailed down my hip and up the inside of my thighs, sending shocks of lightning through me. Holland sat up, watching my lips part as his fingers found where I was hottest for him. I whimpered when he touched me.

"Keep your eyes open," he growled. "I want to see what I do to you."

I did as he asked, gasping aloud as he swirled his fingers around my clit. Holland raised his hand to his mouth. I watched in shock as he dragged his tongue along his fingers before lowering them back to me. I was already wet for him, quivering in antic-ipation.

I almost closed my eyes again when he pushed one finger inside of me. A short growl from him made me open them again. I whined deeply as he pumped his finger in and out before adding a second. His thumb traced over my clit while he moved his fingers. Waves of pleasure rolled through me. I reached for him, longing for more. Holland kissed me deeply without ceasing the movement of his hand. I rocked my hips up to meet his hand. He chuckled, kissing down my chest and stomach until he lay between my thighs.

I gasped when he pulled his hand from me, only to yelp when he replaced it with his tongue. Holland's groan sent vibrations through me as he buried his face between my thighs. Immediately, I grasped the sheets on either side of me, feeling every swirl and flick of his tongue against me. He gripped my hips while he worked, licking and sucking until I thought I'd scream.

His hand joined his mouth, pushing two fingers into me. Heat built in my stomach at the added sensation. Holland's pleasure was merciless.

I came beneath his tongue, seeing stars.

Holland raised his head only after I'd collapsed onto the mattress. He pressed a kiss to each of my thighs before standing. I watched him tiredly as he crossed the room to close the windows. I blushed brightly.

He returned to the bed, kissing me softly. "When you come again, I want you to say my name. And no one else gets to hear that except for me."

"Again?" I shivered.

Holland smirked. "Of course."

He settled himself between my thighs again. I watched, in shock, as he dragged his tongue up the full length of me, groaning deeply. I let my head fall against the mattress, gasping and moaning. He moved faster this time, his tongue and fingers in perfect unison as he coaxed my tired body toward another orgasm.

When I came again, I called his name into the galaxy I found myself lost in.

I saw stars when Holland kissed my face, both of my cheeks, and then my mouth. I tasted myself on his tongue, sighing into him. He lay next to me and reached down to pull the blanket over us.

"What about you?" I asked quietly.

"That's enough for now," he responded, kissing my cheek.
I whined.
He laughed. "Eager?"
"Yes." I pouted. I wasn't sure I could hold my eyes open.
"Get some rest, Adalyn."

CHAPTER
25

I woke in the middle of the night to the feeling of Holland getting out of bed. My eyes drooped as I watched him cross the room to the kitchen. He opened the fridge, filling the room with dim light. I rolled onto my stomach, prepared to ask him for water when he knelt to open the bottom drawer of the fridge and pull out a wine bottle. He didn't bother with a glass, instead unscrewing the top and tilting it straight back. A bead of liquid leaked down his jaw, glinting red in the refrigerator light. I realized, with a sinking feeling, that it wasn't wine he was drinking.

It was blood.

Holland swallowed thickly, setting the bottle on the counter and letting his head fall. He let out a long breath of relief. He wiped the blood from his jaw. I paused, remembering what he'd said earlier. Human food offered him no nutrients. So, while I'd eaten my fill throughout the evening - he had nothing. My heart sank at the realization. Holland lifted the bottle again, tilting it back further this time.

I sat up, holding the blanket around my bare chest. Holland paused at my movement, his eyes widening as he lowered the bottle.

"Sorry to wake you," he said. He reached up to wipe his mouth nervously.

"It's fine," I replied, running my fingers through my hair. "You don't have to do that, you know. Hide, I mean. Wait until I'm asleep to-"

"I know," Holland interrupted. "It's a habit. I'm sorry." He set the bottle on the counter, lifted a glass of water, and rinsed out his mouth before returning to the bed. Before he sat down, he popped a small piece of chocolate in his mouth before leaning forward to kiss me.

I sighed as he sank into bed next to me, his kiss deepening. He tasted like chocolate and orange; his hand was cold as he brushed my hair out of my face to kiss me harder, deeper.

A blush crept over my cheeks when Holland pushed the blanket off, nudging me back against the pillows so I lay bare beneath him. I resisted the urge to cover my stomach with my hands. As if he sensed my concern, Holland leaned down and kissed my breasts and stomach, leaving wet trails behind him.

"Say yes, Adalyn," Holland whispered, nipping at my jaw. His tongue dragged down my throat. I whined, chills running over my skin as he kissed lower. He closed his mouth over my nipple, sucking lightly before blowing on the wet skin.

"Yes," I gasped. "Please."

Holland moaned as he repeated his movement on the opposite side of my chest, swirling his tongue over my nipple. His eyes flicked up to watch me writhe beneath him, desperate for more - whatever he was willing to give.

I sat up, pulling him with me and bringing his mouth back to mine. His gasps echoed through the room like music as I traced my hand down his chest and over the front of his boxers. Holland whined into our kiss as I felt him hard and heavy in the palm of my hand. I dragged my tongue along his lower lip, biting softly and listening to him growl.

Without breaking our kiss, I pushed his boxers over his hips. Holland nudged my hands away, falling back against the mattress as he stripped naked. I placed my hand on his chest, keeping him from returning and running my eyes over his naked body.

It had been a long time since I'd been with a man. At times, I wondered if I'd ever be with one again.

The sight of Holland naked beneath me had me practically trembling with desire. I licked my lips before lowering myself to leave wet kisses down his chest and stomach. I paused only a moment before taking his length in my hand and dragging my tongue up the underside. Holland whined, his head falling back against the pillows. I repeated the movement before taking him fully in my mouth. I slid my mouth down as far as I could go, humming as I pulled back.

"Fucking hell," Holland gasped. "Open your eyes."

I did as he asked, holding his gaze as I pleased him. Black veins rippled beneath Holland's eyes and he groaned, shaking his head to blink them away. I lifted my head, swirling my tongue around the tip and letting saliva trail down his length.

"Don't," I whispered.

Holland paused, watching me. The veins on his face darkened, his eyes rimmed with red. I covered his mouth with mine. His tongue slipped past my lips as he melted into me. I took his length in one hand, pumping him and relishing in his soft moans.

Holland lifted his hand to close around my throat gently, tilting my chin up so I'd look at him. "I want you so desperately," he whispered.

"Then take me," I challenged quietly.

Holland's eyes darkened, and he sat up, his mouth claiming mine with renewed fervor. I yelped in surprise as he pushed me back against the mattress, nestling himself between my thighs. Holland was everywhere all at once, kissing and touching every inch and curve of my body. His tongue left wet trails over my stomach, his fingers dug into my thighs. When he glanced up at me before burying his face between my legs, his eyes were redder than I'd ever seen them. I went limp with pleasure beneath his tongue.

"Open your eyes, Adalyn," Holland growled in warning. I hadn't realized I closed them. "Watch me."

I nodded, chest heaving as the waves of pleasure grew within me. I watched Holland's hands tighten on either side of my thighs. He lowered his head again, consuming me like I was his last meal. His tongue pressed hard against my clit, rubbing perfect circles. He glanced up, likely checking that I was still watching. His hum of approval shot through me like fireworks.

I kept watching, my whole body beginning to tremble when Holland took two of his fingers in his mouth, coating them in saliva. His eyes met mine as he pushed one into me, then two. I whined at the sensation, my mouth falling open.

"Beautiful," he whispered. I let my head fall back on the mattress. Holland chuckled, lowering his mouth to rejoin his hands. Before his tongue touched me again, he spoke again. "Come for me and I promise I'll fuck you."

"Please," I gasped.

Holland's tongue took me to the moon and back. Even as I came with a cry, he clung to me harder, moving his tongue faster against me until I called his name. He moved up my body, tilting my chin to kiss me. His hips pressed against mine.

"You're so pretty when you come," he murmured. "And even prettier when you blush like that."

I smiled, kissing him softly.

Holland paused. "I can get a condom if you want, but vampires can't procreate."

I pulled him back down to me. "Don't leave," I breathed.

Holland smiled, shifting his hips. His kiss was breathtaking as he pushed forward. I dug my nails into his biceps, gasping as he filled me. He thrust into me once, twice, three times. I watched him as he did, his eyes squeezing shut from pleasure. He bit down on his bottom lip, his fangs drawing blood. Curious, I pulled him back down to kiss me. Holland's blood coated my tongue, my mouth muffling his moan.

His blood tasted metallic, smooth, and satisfying. I felt him adjust over me, his hips pausing their slow, torturous movements. Holland lifted his head, watching me writhe.

"You promised you'd fuck me," I whined.

He smirked, licking blood off his lips. "I did, didn't I?"

"Yes," I breathed.

Holland sat up, tracing his hands over my sides before gripping my hips. "Then hold on tight."

I barely had a moment to prepare before he slammed into me hard and fast. The world spun around me; I clung to the sheets on either side of me for some semblance of reality. Holland growled deeply, clinging to me as he fucked me. His eyes never left mine. Each time mine fluttered, he clicked his tongue in disappointment, drawing my attention back to him.

I dropped my hand between my thighs where we met, gasping at the added contact.

"Good girl," Holland said.

I yelped when he leaned forward to kiss me, thrusting into me deeper. I arched into him, wrapping both legs around his hips in a desperate attempt to keep him close. I touched myself faster, finding it harder and harder to keep my eyes open and on the vampire above me.

Holland reached up, brushing my hair out of my face before

closing his hand around my throat. His eyes searched mine for permission. I gave it, letting my eyes roll back.

"Come for me, Adalyn," he demanded. I whined as the knot built tighter and tighter in my stomach. Holland's hand tightened around my throat, his thrusts coming faster and sloppier. "Now," he snapped. "Come now."

The world shattered.

I was vaguely aware of Holland's orgasm, and the delicious sound of him calling my name. I clung to him until he rolled off to lay next to me.

Everything was quiet for a while.

CHAPTER 26

I stepped out of the bathroom wrapped in a towel, brushing out my wet hair. Holland sat at the dining room table, leaning over a sketchbook. Next to him, there was a mug of thick red liquid I tried not to look too hard at. Across from him, though, a cup of coffee and a croissant sat waiting for me.

The warmth in my heart was startling. I straightened, watching him for a moment and resisting the urge to gather my things and bolt. This felt safe. This felt like home. That was ridiculous - I hardly knew him.

I swallowed my bewilderment and crossed the room, tracing my hand up Holland's back and leaning forward to kiss his cheek. He hummed into my touch, closing his sketchbook before I could see it, leaning back to smile at me.

"Sleep well?" He murmured. I'd left him in bed to shower, thinking he was sound asleep. I supposed I couldn't sneak around a vampire's apartment.

"Exceptionally," I said, kissing his cheek again. I moved to kiss him on the mouth, shocked when he paused, tilting his head back slightly. I blinked. Holland reached back to tap his mug. He was drinking blood, which meant he tasted like it too. I kissed his cheek harder this time and basked in the sound of his cheerful hum.

I sat down across from him, pulling my phone from my purse hanging on the chair. There was a text from Willa a few minutes ago.

Are you staying with Holland today?

My fingers hovered over the keyboard as I glanced up at the vampire across from me. He'd opened the sketchbook again, his brow furrowed in concentration. I watched him for a moment. Despite the fire alarms in my mind, I leaned into the warm feeling of sitting in his apartment with him.

I didn't come to Paris to fall in love.

So why did I feel like one wrong move and I'd fall hard?

"What are you brooding about?" Holland asked, not glancing up.

I almost asked him to take me back to the hotel. Almost. Instead, I took a sip of my coffee. "What do you want to do today?" I asked.

Now, his eyes melted like honey. He closed the book, sitting back in his chair. "Anything in Paris you haven't seen yet? Or I can throw you into my bed and never let you leave."

I blushed crimson. Holland's eyes darkened and he sat back, lifting his mug to take a long drink. The red stained his lips. I watched him lick it away.

A vampire.

Holland was a vampire.

And I wanted to fall into his bed over and over again.

I opened my mouth to answer him when my phone rang. It was Indy.

I straightened before answering her FaceTime, trying to position it so she couldn't see much of the background to realize I was in someone's apartment instead of my hotel room.

"I wanted to call and apologize," Indy said. She sat on her couch with a long groan. Her hair was in a messy knot on top of her head and her makeup was smudged under her eyes.

"For what?" I asked. I wanted to hear her say it.

"I shouldn't have reacted the way I did about you not coming home," Indy admitted. "I was surprised."

"I don't understand why everyone is so shocked," I muttered.

Indy shrugged. "Because it's you, Addie."

I flinched. "What's that supposed to mean?"

Across the table, Holland frowned. I tried not to let my gaze linger on him, not wanting to invite any questions from my sister.

Indy let out a long breath and sank into the cushions of her couch. "Well, it's just - you have a comfort zone, and you never leave it. I've never once seen you do anything that could be construed as mildly shocking. Except for this, of course."

Holland sat up, closing his sketchbook and reaching for his glass of water. I fumbled with a response to Indy while he drank, crossing the room too quickly for me to set the phone down. Shock crossed Indy's face when he appeared behind me, wrapping one arm around my waist and smiling into the camera.

"Adalyn has to go," he hummed, kissing my cheek as he reached forward to end the call. He set my phone on the table in front of us.

"I'm not as pathetic as she makes me sound," I mumbled.

Holland tilted my chin up. The rest of the world faded as I stared up at him. "I don't think you're pathetic, my dear." I shrugged. "I think you were sad for a long time. I think you're sad right now, and you're learning how not to be."

I closed my eyes when he kissed me. A single tear escaped, searing my skin as it trailed down my cheek. Holland brushed it away, cupping my face in his hands as he kissed me again... and again... and again. I leaned into him, opening my mouth to his tongue and my heart to the sunshine that he was made of. Holland tasted slightly metallic, which I realized with a shiver, was from the blood he drank. Still, when his hands dragged up my sides, pushing open the towel I wore so I was bare to him, I let my head fall back and he leaned down to kiss my throat.

My sister's words floated through my mind. I'd never done anything even remotely shocking.

Well, now I planned to let an actual vampire have his way with me.

Holland gripped my hips, lifting me like I weighed nothing to sit on the edge of the table. He stepped forward, lowering his mouth to my chest, flicking his tongue over my nipples. I whined and spread my legs for him to step between them.

"You're fucking intoxicating," he murmured against my skin.

When he glanced up to watch me gasp, his eyes burned red. The sight sent shivers of delight through me. Holland placed his hand on my chest, gently nudging me back so I lay on the dining room table. I didn't see him move, but felt his tongue swipe up my core. My cry of delight echoed through his apartment. Holland hummed deeply as he consumed me, gripping my hips and holding me down - prey to his tongue.

I reached down hesitantly, tangling my fingers in his hair for something to hold on to. The whimper he released was permission enough to keep holding on. I pulled him impossibly closer, frantic for more. Holland paused, licking his fingers before pushing one, then two inside of me. He watched me writhe at the novel sensation, the veins under his eyes rippling.

"Mine," he whispered so quietly I wondered if I heard him properly. It only took another moment or two of his tongue flicking against me for me to see a million stars.

I still reeled from my orgasm when Holland pulled me off the edge of the dining table, turning me over quickly. The rustle of fabric and the clink of his belt as it hit the floor sent chills down my spine. I felt his hard length press between my thighs and my mouth watered.

Before he bent me over the table, his lips brushed my ear. "I'm going to fuck you until you scream."

My knees nearly went out from under me. "Please do."

I bent over the table, yelping when he didn't wait a moment before pushing into me. My whole body ignited, glowing like a sunrise as Holland dug his fingers into my hips. With each thrust, I felt myself unraveling into a million strands of daylight.

I wanted to feel like this every moment for the rest of my life - on the edge of something extraordinary.

Holland growled. I glanced up. I saw him in the window reflection. His head fell back as he fucked me, his mouth parted to reveal perfectly sharp fangs. His eyes were closed, but I knew they were the deepest of reds. He looked entirely inhuman; the sight made me quiver with desire.

"Holland," I whispered. His eyes opened. "I want to come again, please."

A smirk spread across his face. His thrusts slowed, deepening as he leaned down to kiss my shoulder. "Anything for you," he said.

His hand dropped between my thighs, touching me where I throbbed for him. My eyes fluttered at the added sensation and I dug my nails into the wood of the table. Holland traced soft circles over my clit, his thrusts slow and torturous. I felt the moment he changed his mind; his free hand holding my hip tighter. He slid his hand up my back, tangling his fingers in my hair and pulling back.

Oh, god. Yes.

My cries filled the room like a rising crescendo as he fucked me again, hard and impossibly fast. The knot built in my stomach again, hot and bright.

"You're fucking dripping for me," Holland snarled. "Do you like how I make you feel?" I nodded frantically. His hand tightened in my hair. "Use your words, Adalyn."

I opened my eyes, watching him through the window reflection. I could hardly breathe, the knot in my stomach was so tight I thought I might explode. "You make me feel alive," I whispered just before my orgasm crashed through me.

Holland kept thrusting through my orgasm. When he pulled away, my legs gave out. He caught me easily, smiling as he kissed my cheek and lifted me in his arms. I kissed his shoulder dreamily as he carried me to the bed, laying me back and moving over me.

This time, when he pushed inside me, it was slow and delicate. He peppered kisses over my face and jaw. I wrapped my legs around his waist, smiling into his affection. He felt warm against me and his mouth felt like home.

We spent the rest of the day in his bed.

CHAPTER 27

"Tell me about your engagement," Holland said as he offered me a mug full of hot chocolate.

I paused, eyeing him nervously as I took my mug. Holland sat on the couch next to me, glancing out at the dying light of Paris.

"Why?" I asked stiffly.

"Call me curious."

I sucked in a deep breath. I tugged the fleece blanket over my waist and tucked one arm underneath it. I thought about brushing him off and changing the subject, only to remind myself I didn't want to run anymore.

"I was with her for five years," I said. Immediately, my voice cracked. "I proposed a year ago and we were supposed to get married six days before I met you."

Holland inclined his chin, sipping his hot chocolate. "Do you love her?"

I shook my head, staring out the window. A cool breeze whispered through the apartment, blowing out a candle and sending chills down my bare skin. I wore only one of Holland's shirts and my underwear.

"No," I admitted. "I haven't loved her in a long time."

Holland hummed. "And the girl on the phone this morning?"

"My younger sister, Indy," I said. "She's not normally so condescending."

Holland raised an eyebrow. "Why are you sad, Adalyn?"

I jolted at his question. "You keep saying I'm sad," I whispered. "I'm not sure I know any different."

Holland frowned. He stood, taking a couple of steps around the coffee table to sit behind me. I moved so my back rested against his chest, letting out a long breath. He leaned down to murmur in my ear. "That weight on your chest? The dull ache in your heart? That's sadness, Adalyn."

My breath caught. I considered pulling away. As if he anticipated my escape, Holland's arm wound around my waist and held me against him. I rested against his chest and listened to the sound of his breathing.

"I think it's always been there," I said finally.

"I don't believe that."

I scoffed. "You barely know me."

Holland kissed my shoulder. "I know enough." My bottom lip quivered. "I know your laugh sounds like sunshine and your smile could set the world on fire. I know you read Peter Pan as a child and wanted to live forever - sad children don't wish for eternal life. I know the taste of your mouth and the smell of your shampoo. Do you know what would make you happy?"

I couldn't respond. My heart felt heavier than ever. I shook my head, staring out the window.

Holland didn't ask any more questions. He held me as the sun set.

I woke up in his bed again the next morning. I blinked up at the ceiling. Holland slept next to me, his breathing deep and even. Rolling toward him, warmth built in my chest as I took in the sight of his hair falling into his face. His bare chest was smooth and golden in the early morning light. My eyes trailed down to the blanket around his waist, barely covering the bare rest of him.

An idea formed in my mind and I inched forward, pressing a slow kiss to Holland's shoulder. Then, another to his chest. On the third kiss, Holland's breath caught, and I knew he was awake. I peered up at him. He kept his eyes closed and remained perfectly still. I blushed deeply, licking my lips and continuing my kisses. With each one, I moved lower. I flicked my tongue over his skin when I kissed him, watching goosebumps spread over his stomach. Again, and again, and again, I kissed him lower. I pushed the blanket down over his hips, exposing his bare waist and hard length.

Again, I glanced up. Holland hadn't moved, but his lip quirked up in the smallest of smiles. I laughed softly. Then, I dragged my tongue up his length and took him in my mouth. Finally, Holland gasped and his hands tightened on the sheets on either side of him.

I moaned when I took him as deeply as I could, sliding my hand up behind my mouth when I did. When I looked up again, Holland's eyes were open. Black veins rippled beneath his eyes and I could see his fangs in his mouth. I flicked my tongue over the tip and closed my mouth over him again.

"Fuck, you look amazing with my cock in your mouth," Holland gasped.

I whimpered.

Holland's sounds of pleasure spurred me on as I licked and sucked. With each swipe of my tongue, he lost himself a little more. I gazed up at the vampire above me. His chest heaved and he tilted his head back into the pillow. I flicked my tongue against the base of him, humming in approval when he gasped and writhed beneath me.

"Adalyn, please," he whispered.

I lifted my mouth, licking the taste of him off my mouth. "Say it again."

He whispered my name again as I covered him with my mouth - up and down and up and down. Holland rolled his hips up to meet my mouth, unable to keep still. When I glanced up again, I caught sight of Holland's fangs again. Chills shot through me. I wrapped my hand around him to follow the movement of my mouth and immediately knew I'd made the right choice. Holland's breath caught. One of his hands tangled in my hair, subtly guiding the movements of my mouth. He whispered *yes* over and over again.

"Just like that, baby, please-" Holland broke off as his orgasm crashed through him.

I licked my lips as I sat up, running my tongue along him one last time. Holland quivered as he came down from his high.

"Please wake me up like that every day you're in my bed," Holland gasped, turning to smile lazily at me. I watched his fangs retract and the black veins fade from his face. I reached for the towel next to the bed from the night before, handing it to him so he could clean himself up.

I lay on his chest when he was finished, smiling softly. "I've been avoiding real life in your bed," I murmured.

Holland lifted an eyebrow. "I'm aware."

"For two days," I added.

Holland nodded.

I rolled onto my back. "I have to call my sister. And respond to Willa."

"Do you want to do either of those things?" Holland asked, standing out of bed. He crossed the room to the kitchen, pulling out a dark wine bottle.

"No," I said honestly.

"So, don't."

I sat up to watch him pop open the bottle and pour the contents into a wine glass. I tried to ignore the thick red liquid, but my eyes lingered as Holland brought it to his mouth.

"I'm not sure it's that easy," I said.

"Sure it is." Holland grinned. "Answer the calls, or go to *L'Atelier des Lumières* with me today."

I paused, blushing. I pulled the blanket up to my chest. "What's that?"

"An art exhibit," Holland said simply. He leaned against the kitchen table, taking another sip from his wine glass. His lips were bright pink from the liquid in his glass. My eyes trailed down his entirely bare body, unable to help myself. "Eyes up here, beautiful. Do you want to go or not?"

I laughed, burying my face in the pillow in embarrassment before grinning at him. "Can we stop at my hotel so I can change?"

Holland beamed.

CHAPTER
28

Holland offered me a piece of chocolate on our walk back to my hotel. It was a lovely day out and I was in no mood to deal with the loud, overwhelming metro. Holland didn't question my request to walk. Besides, it was only a mile or so.

"Do you always carry candy?" I asked while I unwrapped it.

Holland hummed, popping a piece in his mouth. "Yes, I do."

I raised an eyebrow, linking my arm through his. "You like snacks, or?"

He glanced over at me and sighed. "It hides the taste of blood."

I lowered my eyes. "Sorry."

Holland kissed my knuckles. "I keep waiting for something about all of this to freak you out."

"The walk to the hotel or the pretty vampire on my arm?" I teased.

Holland shook his head with a soft smile. "The vampires. Spending time with me. Not answering your sister. Any of it."

My smile faded and I stared at the ground for a while. "I don't know why it's not."

Holland opened his mouth to say something else, pausing. He stopped mid-step, tightening his grip and pulling me close to him. I followed his gaze, startled.

Across the street, Willa and Thierry stood at an ice cream cart. Another woman stood with them, a tall blonde. She laughed and reached over to nudge Willa, who smiled and bit into her ice cream.

"We need to go," Holland murmured.

"Why?"

I wasn't sure whether it was his words or mine that caught Thierry's attention. He looked up from handing the other blonde girl her ice cream, his expression darkening. Willa followed his gaze and beamed.

"Addie!" She waved, bouncing on her tiptoes.

Holland swore under his breath, gripping my arm as we approached the other group. His reaction sent my stomach flipping, and I glanced at him. His eyes were fixed on Thierry and the blonde on his arm, who looked remarkably similar to him. Willa said Thierry's sister was in town - surely that was her.

"I was wondering where you were," Willa said through her teeth when we met in the middle of the sidewalk.

"My, my, if it isn't Holland Hawthorne," the blonde spoke up. She flashed a smile, revealing two perfectly sharp fangs. Holland's hesitation made more sense. Her eyes flicked from him to me. "And aren't you pretty?"

I held out my hand. "I'm Addie."

She took it. She didn't introduce herself, instead glancing up at Holland. "Oh, I bet she's sweet like cotton candy."

The growl that came from Holland was inhuman. I wasn't sure whether to be afraid of him or the vampire woman.

Willa groaned and tossed her hands in the air. My eyes caught on something red on her wrist. I reached for her, starting in surprise when Holland's grip on my arm didn't loosen. I caught Willa's hand, turning her wrist over to reveal a swollen bite mark. Willa swallowed nervously.

"And she's a perfect snack," the blonde vampire laughed.

Horror sank into me. The vampires saw Willa as a snack. Willa pulled her hands back from me and crossed them behind her back. She plastered a perfect smile on her face. "What are you two up to?"

I glanced at Holland. His attention remained fixed on the other vampires. I stumbled over my words. "Uh, an art exhibit, I think."

"*L'Atelier des Lumières,*" Holland said coldly.

"Oh, right, it's like a light digital art show thing," Willa stuttered. "Text me later?"

"You got it." I forced a smile.

Willa grabbed Thierry's hand and dragged him off. The blonde vampire followed them reluctantly.

I spun towards Holland with a gasp. "Sweet like cotton candy?" I squeaked.

"We should go," Holland said. His eyes were dark.

"Holland," I whispered.

He didn't answer, instead pulling me along. My heart pounded so hard and fast I couldn't breathe. At some point, Holland was the only thing holding me up and keeping me placing one foot after the other. I focused entirely on the feeling of his hand on my arm, the vampire's words echoing in my mind.

Sweet like cotton candy.

Sweet like cotton candy.

She bet I tasted sweet.

She was talking about the taste of my blood.

I worried I might be sick.

Holland took the key from my shaking hand, scanning it on my hotel room door. I whimpered when he pushed it open. Holland finally released me and I stumbled into the room, wrapping my arms around my torso and sinking to the ground.

"Sweet like cotton candy?" I gasped out. Holland sat on the edge of the bed, his shoulders slumping. "Holland," I whispered. "I need you to answer me. Was she talking about-" I trailed off.

"The taste of your blood, yes."

"Fuck," I swore, shaking out my hands. I whimpered his name again, placing one hand on my chest as I tried to catch my breath.

Holland moved to kneel in front of me, taking both of my hands in his. "Adalyn, I know you're scared but I need you to breathe."

I shook my head, trying to pull my hands away so I could curl into myself. Holland didn't budge, holding my hands tighter. I couldn't focus. The only thing I could think about was the taste of my blood... and vampires... black veins and fangs... the marks on Willa's skin... the dead girl in the park. Images flashed in my mind so quickly I couldn't make sense of them. I felt dizzy.

Vampires. I had sex with a vampire. I was in Paris on my honeymoon, dancing at sunset with a vampire.

Vampire.

Holland.

I was wet.

Warm water poured over my face as I blinked out of my panicked stupor. I spluttered in surprise; I stood in the shower. Holland stood in front of me, his hands gripping my forearms to hold me up. Water splashed on his face and soaked into the pretty red shirt he wore.

"Oh," I whispered.

"I've got you," he breathed.

"So about that freak out," I said, my voice breaking.

Holland laughed once, shaking his head. I focused on his hands on my arms and forced myself to focus on the feeling of his fingers pressing into my skin. Real. Warm. Safe. My breathing slowed. Holland matched his breath to mine, and that was all I needed. I took a deep breath.

"Are you okay now?" He asked.

I met his eyes. "Do you think about the taste of my blood?"

Holland swallowed. His eyes flicked from my eyes to my throat, confirming my answer before he said anything at all. "Of course I do," he murmured. "Adalyn, I will never touch you without your explicit permission, especially with that."

I reached up to place my hands on Holland's wet cheeks. "Show me."

He blinked and his eyes rimmed with red. Black veins slithered beneath his eyes. I ran my thumbs over his skin. Holland was real. He wouldn't hurt me. Everything was okay. I took a deep breath and felt my heart rate slow.

"I'm sorry your only clothes are wet," I said, dropping my hands to his shoulders.

Holland blinked again and his face returned to normal, soft and glowing. He leaned down until his mouth was only a breath away from mine.

When he kissed me, my fear melted away.

CHAPTER
29

Holland left a few hours later after his clothes had mostly dried. I felt awful sending him out in damp clothes, but he was insistent that he had errands to run. Once he was gone, I wondered what those things were - especially considering we were supposed to go to the art exhibit.

I sat down on the edge of my bed, blinking through memories of Holland's voice, his hands, his body, his *tongue.* I blew out a long breath.

What the hell was I doing?

I wasn't here for a relationship. I wasn't here for any kind of... relation with anyone. When I got on the plane to come to Paris, I was determined to find myself. Some part of me had forgotten who I was. I had no idea what I liked to do, or what made me happy. I wasn't sure if I'd ever known.

I was running from an engagement that ended in flames.

I wasn't sure I wanted another person in my life like that.

So, why was I so damn desperate for Holland to call me again?

I fell back on the mattress, trying to hold on to how it felt to waltz with him in the Palais Garnier.

Free.

Exhilarating.

Warm.

There was a knock at my door, and I swore. I padded over to answer it, letting a frantic Willa barrel into my room.

"Are you hurt?" She yowled.

"No?" I tilted my head.

I flinched when Willa grabbed me, turning my wrists over to inspect my forearms. Then, she reached up and pushed my hair out of the way. Her brow furrowed when she realized there weren't any marks on me. Her fear faded into surprise and she stood straight. My eyes roamed to the bite marks on her wrists, finding three perfect sets overlapping, like her vampires hadn't bothered to heal her wounds before causing more.

Silently, I pulled her into my room and sat her on the edge of my bed. She stared, dazed, while I pulled a first aid kit out of my backpack.

"He didn't hurt you?" She breathed while I knelt in front of her. I shook my head. "Thierry was so convinced."

"I'm fine," I muttered, taking off her bracelets so I could clean her wounds.

"He didn't drink from you?"

I winced. "No."

Willa seemed genuinely shocked. "And you had sex?"

I tilted my head. "Not that it's any of your business, but yes. What's the problem?"

Willa sobered. "Thierry told me vampires can't control their bloodlust during sex. Every time we," she trailed off. "And then, he kept talking about how much I should be worried about you after you left with Holland."

I crossed my arms. "Willa, what's Thierry's problem? Because from where I'm standing, Holland has given me no reason to be afraid of him, but Thierry is looking awfully dangerous, and I'm getting really fucking sick of this conversation."

"I don't know, okay?" Willa snapped. "Every time I ask, I get some cryptic, bullshit answer about how he's dangerous, not a vampire to be messed with, blah blah blah."

"Until he gives a real answer, I don't want to hear it. I am safe with Holland."

"Until you're not."

I stared at my friend for a long moment, dragging my tongue over my teeth. My anger bubbled at the surface, barely contained. "I've had a lot of people telling me what I should and shouldn't be feeling lately. So, either take a step back and restart this conversation or please let me be today."

Tears welled in Willa's eyes. Shock poured through me. She clutched her chest. "My mom and fiancé are on their way."

Nothing else mattered.

Willa sank to the ground in front of me. Tears dripped down her face, staining her skin with mascara. When her head fell back with a deep cry, I was shocked to see more bright red and swollen bite marks peeking out from beneath her scarf.

"Can we move hotels?" I asked, taking her hand.

She shook her head. "They'd find me."

"We could leave the country?"

Willa stared at me. "Would you do that for me?"

I shrugged. "If your safety was at stake, of course."

Willa squeezed my hand. "My dad, and my fiancé, come from old money. They can make things happen."

I moved to sit next to her. "What about Thierry? I feel like vampire trumps oil tycoon."

She sniffled, curling into me like I was the only piece of safety she had. I held one of her hands in both of mine, desperately trying to come up with some sort of plan to save my friend.

"They would kill him," she whispered.

Chills spread through me.

I sat back. "What about Holland?" Willa jolted in surprise. "Thierry seems convinced Holland is dangerous. Do you think he's dangerous enough to stand against your family?"

"Would he?" Willa's voice cracked, telling me all I needed to know. Yes, Holland was powerful enough to handle this.

"He would if I asked him to."

Willa wiped her face. "We keep Holland as a last resort, okay?"

"How long until they get here?"

She checked her phone. "Five hours. I'm supposed to meet them at the hotel."

"Fuck that," I said. "They want you so badly, they can come get you."

It took another hour to calm Willa down and convince her to rest while we waited for her family to arrive. She napped in my bed while I showered and called Holland.

"Miss me already?" He answered, his voice warm and charming.

"I have questions," I responded, closing the door to the bathroom and shutting myself inside so I wouldn't bother Willa.

"You sound serious," Holland said.

"First, I want an honest answer for why Thierry keeps convincing Willa you're going to hurt me," I started.

Holland rustled on the other end of the line and let out a long breath. "Adalyn-" he started.

"Please," I interrupted.

"There is a tale in the vampire world, a story about a vampire so bloodthirsty he stained the streets red with the blood of his victims. I'll spare you the gory details. My love, that vampire is me."

I shivered, unsure how to feel about the thought of Holland killing people. "How long ago?" I whispered.

"A hundred years or so."

I clutched my stomach, wondering if I would be sick from shock. "Holland," I whispered. "Do you still kill people?"

"I try not to," he answered me honestly. "But I'm not perfect."

"So, when you told me-" I started.

He interrupted. "You're safe with me, Adalyn. I swear it."

I was silent.

"Are you alright?" Holland asked in a voice barely above a whisper.

"I think Willa is in trouble," I told him, shaking off my nausea.

"She has Thierry." Holland's response was colder than I expected.

"She doesn't. She said something about her father and fiancé killing him if they found out," I said.

Holland was quiet for so long that I worried he'd hung up. "What's Willa's last name?"

I opened my mouth a few times. "Bennett, I think."

Holland cleared his throat. "You have no reason to be afraid of me, Adalyn. Please believe me."

"Okay," I breathed.

The line went dead.

I swiped past a dozen texts from Indy, unable to focus on her. I needed to figure out how to help Willa out of this. I needed to know if I needed to be afraid of Holland. Most of all, I had to find Thierry and tell him to stop tearing Willa to shreds.

Right on cue, someone knocked on the hotel room door.

I walked out, glancing over at where Willa snored softly. I opened the door, my eyes finding Thierry. Anger coursed through me and I snatched my key before stepping outside and locking my friend in the room.

"She's resting," I said coldly.

Thierry dragged his tongue over his teeth. "My sister is hungry."

"I don't care," I snapped. "There's a whole city out there." My stomach twinged as I thought of some innocent victim.

Thierry's eyes darkened. "Where's Holland?"

"He's not here," I admitted, my heart skipping a beat.

Thierry stepped closer. "Perhaps I'm hungry," he growled lowly.

I jutted out my chin in indignance, clinging to the last of my bravery. "Willa's family is coming to take her home."

"So?" Thierry hummed.

I paused. "You don't care?"

"I'll find another snack. Maybe you." Again, he stepped closer. He placed his hands on either side of the wall behind me, trapping me beneath him. My heart raced.

"Oh, I would suggest stepping away from her."

Holland.

Fury flashed on Thierry's face and he immediately let his hands fall. I whimpered softly, my eyes flicking to see my vampire standing at the top of the stairs. He wore a black silk shirt, his hands crossed behind his back while he waited for Thierry to retreat. He blinked and the red appeared around his eyes for half a second before fading.

"What a pretty toy you have, Hawthorne. It would be a shame if something happened," Thierry huffed.

Holland chuckled. "Go ahead, try. We'll see how you enjoy having your spine outside your body."

My stomach flipped. For the first time, even without the fangs and red eyes, Holland looked entirely like a vampire - dangerous and as deadly as the night. And he was here for me.

"I'm here for Willa," Thierry said.

I met Holland's gaze over Thierry's shoulder, shaking my head. He inclined his chin and licked his lips. "No," he growled simply.

"Excuse me?" Thierry fumbled.

Holland walked forward, stepping around Thierry to stand in front of me. Thierry flinched back like he'd been burned. "From what I saw of Willa earlier today, you're one bite shy of draining her dry. Let the girl rest."

Thierry stormed off without another word.

I trembled, sinking against the wall. Holland reached for my room key, opened the door, and motioned for me to step in first.

"How did you get here so fast?" I whispered.

"I would move heaven and hell to make sure you're safe," he replied. His eyes found Willa when she sat up in bed. "Especially from people like her family."

Willa's shoulders slumped.

Holland shut the door behind us. His hand brushed my wrist. The smallest touch brought me comfort and my bottom lip quivered.

"So, you know?" Willa said quietly.

"That your father killed your brother and called it a fishing accident? Oh, I'm aware," Holland said. My eyes widened. "Will that happen to you if you go back with them?"

Willa swallowed. "Yes, I think so."

"Wait, what?" I gasped out.

Holland crossed the room, holding out his hands. Willa whimpered, offering her arms to him. He grimaced as he took in the bite marks on her arms and her neck. "Is this all of them?" He asked.

Willa shook her head without making eye contact.

I yelped when Holland lifted his hand and bit onto his palm, drawing blood. "Thierry will be furious," he said, holding his hand out to Willa. "At least this will stop the pain."

I watched her lower her mouth to Holland's hand. Despite my confusion and concern, something else soured in my veins. I felt disconnected, on the edge of something they understood and I didn't.

Jealousy.

I jolted in surprise, shaking my head and hugging myself. Holland pulled his hand back from Willa. Her skin was smooth like the bite marks never existed.

My eyes widened.

Holland moved away from her, crossing the room. I stood, stoic, when he kissed my forehead. His brow furrowed in concern. "Have you eaten today?"

I shook my head, realizing I felt tired and a little dizzy.

"I should find Thierry and get ready," Willa said.

Holland turned towards her. "It's best you don't find Thierry without me. I'm going to get you both something to eat. Stay here." He returned to me, tilting my chin up. "Please, stay here."

I agreed.

Then he was gone.

CHAPTER
30

I helped Willa get ready to meet her family. She hardly touched the food Holland brought back for us. He didn't stay long, only kissing my cheek and telling me he had things to take care of.

While we waited, Willa's hands shook so badly she couldn't hold her own eyeliner. I dried her face and did it for her, watching as she put on hoop earrings, several rings, and bracelets, including her engagement ring. I knew the moment her family landed. She tensed, turning her phone off and staring at herself in the mirror.

I ignored more messages from Indy. In some of them, she apologized for what she said. In others, she raged over me not answering. A good portion of them demanded to know who Holland was.

While I sat and helped Willa, I realized I was never going to make my own decisions with my family screaming over my shoulder and telling me I couldn't do this. Once, I thought Indy was exempt from that. I thought I trusted my sister. But, she was just as angry and degrading as my parents. I knew I shouldn't hold it against them; they didn't know any version of me other than the one who floundered every day, cursed to never catch a breath of fresh air.

I worried I wasn't capable of the change I wanted. What did my family see that I couldn't?

I rubbed my burning eyes and shook away the thoughts. Willa wiped her hands on her jeans. Her eyes welled again; she blinked until the tears faded.

"We could still go," I offered.

She shook her head. "They'd burn this city down to find me."

I walked forward and wrapped my arms around her. She jolted in surprise, resting her head on my shoulder a moment later. I rarely enjoyed being this close to another person, especially touching them, but I also couldn't stand the sight of her trembling. Willa always seemed larger than life, overjoyed with every moment she spent alive. Sitting next to me, she seemed small - broken. If this was the life she ran from, I would run with her forever.

We both jumped when a loud knock resounded on my door. Willa sank back in terror. I walked over, swinging the door open, prepared to try and prevent her family from getting into the room.

It was Thierry.

I stepped back, letting him in and watching as Willa threw herself into his arms with a dry sob. I melted a little when I saw Holland standing in the hall behind Thierry.

He looked exhausted, more pale than usual. My eyes met his, and I resisted the urge to curl into myself, overwhelmed by the gravity of this situation and the reality that Holland was danger-ous. Holland tilted his head in confusion, slipping past me into the room.

"What are you doing here?" Willa asked Thierry.

"Saving your life," Holland said, sounding bored. "You're going with Thierry."

"What? No, I have to be here," Willa protested.

"So you can make sure your fiancé doesn't hurt anyone, right?" Holland tilted his head. He hardly seemed like himself - darker, angrier. "I think I have it handled." His eyes flicked up to me. "You're going to stay here."

"What? No," I gasped out, reaching for Willa.

She took Thierry's hand, glancing between me and Holland. Holland placed his hand over the doorway, keeping me inside.

"Go, now," Holland snapped at Thierry and Willa.

"Holland-" I started.

When Willa and Thierry were in the elevator, Holland shook his head. "Please don't ask me to put you in danger," he murmured.

"Danger?" I squeaked.

Holland wrapped his arm around me and closed the door behind us. "My dear, Willa's father got away with murder, and I assume that dud of a fiancé of hers has too. If anything happens while you're there-" he trailed off, shaking his head. "I will help Willa because she's important to you, but I can't let you come with us."

"Please," I whispered.

He shook his head. "I'll never ask you for anything again. Do this for me. Stay here."

I stepped back. "Don't let them take her."

"I won't."

Holland kissed me deeply, only once.

The door slammed behind him.

I felt sick.

The world turned hazy as I paced around my room. I stopped every few steps, placing my hand over my mouth and worrying I'd be sick. As soon as the nausea faded, I kept pacing.

I respected Holland. I appreciated his concern. So, I would do as he asked. But, god, I was scared.

I never knew about Willa's family. I never knew how much danger she was in by being here. She must have been terrified. I sobbed once, shaking out my hands and sitting on the edge of the bed.

Outside, there was a loud *crack*.

My blood ran cold.

Another one.

Gunfire.

No.

I lost my mind, darting towards the door. I didn't bother with the elevator, seeing red as I ran down the stairs frantically. As I rushed through the lobby and onto the street, I barely noticed the receptionist's horror.

Blood.

There was so much blood.

I stumbled to a stop, taking in the scene in front of me. Willa writhed in Thierry's arms, blubbering hysterically as she tried to pull from him. Thierry's eyes were wide and red.

Next, my eyes found Holland.

He leaned into a man twice his size - much taller and wide like a bear. I wasn't sure how I knew, but everything in me screamed that he was Willa's terrifying fiancé. The man's smile was fading into something like horror. Blood splattered at his feet, covering his hands. A scream built in my throat when I realized the blood was Holland's.

Holland released the man and took a slow, wavering step backward. His hand fell to his stomach. I saw the gun, held in the larger man's hand. It had been pressed against Holland's stomach.

"God, no!" Willa cried. "Duncan, please, stop, stop, stop."

I looked at Thierry, whose eyes found mine as he struggled to hold on to a hysterical Willa. He shook his head.

Holland looked down at the wound oozing blood, nodding once. His eyes darkened, black veins rippling beneath his skin.

The other man's smile faded.

"Wrong move, my friend," Holland said. When he spoke, blood dripped from his mouth and his voice sounded raspy.

"Holland, no, please," Willa cried, trying to escape where Thierry held her against his chest. "God, please."

Holland tilted his head towards her, blood leaking from the corner of his mouth. For a moment, I thought he'd listen.

He didn't know I was here, not yet.

"Fucking demon," the man, Duncan, spat.

Holland spun towards him.

Duncan fired the gun again, only this time Holland knocked his hand back. The bullet fired straight into the air. Duncan went white. In a frantic attempt to gain the upper hand, he brought the handle down towards Holland's head.

I hardly saw my vampire move.

Duncan fell to the ground without a noise.

Willa screamed.

I felt frozen.

There was blood on his neck. Blood spread on Holland's shirt. Blood on Holland's face... on his mouth. Willa's screams echoed through the streets - she withered in Thierry's arms. He held her up, his arms wrapped around her torso. I could hardly hear her, though, my eyes were permanently fixed on Holland. Or, rather, on the nightmare Holland had become.

He stared down at Duncan's body for a moment before stepping back slowly. He wavered slightly, placing a hand on his chest and falling to one knee. A small part of me wanted to run to him and another was broken by the sob that escaped him.

The rest of me wanted to run.

"Addie," Thierry's voice broke through the white noise. "Help him, the bullet didn't come out."

I shook my head, taking a step back.

"Hold Willa, I'll help him," Thierry cried. The blonde vampire was wide-eyed and horrified. Willa still screamed and pointed at the dead body on the ground, lost to the rest of us. My ears rang. A glance back at Holland and I watched him clutch his chest, coughing wetly. "Addie, damn it, look at me," Thierry begged.

Another step back.

Two.

Three.

Blood on Holland's mouth. A dead man in the middle of the street.

"Addie!"

When Thierry yelled my name again, Holland raised his head. His eyes met mine, wide with pain, shock, and something else.

I didn't wait to see what it was.

I turned on my heel and ran.

I still didn't know Paris well enough to know where I was going. I put every ounce of myself into each step. I needed to get away from there. This was a nightmare. I skidded around corners and tried to remember how Holland's hands felt on my skin - safe. How was the Holland that made me scream his name in the dark the same one who tore the throat out of someone twice his size?

Eventually, I ran up to Notre Dame, sobbing as I stumbled up to the cathedral. I had run nearly a mile. My lungs *burned*, the world spinning around me. I almost slumped against the massive wall, until a dark image flashed in my mind, giving me extra incentive to keep running.

Holland killed that man.

Without a thought. Probably without remorse.

I veered left at the Seine, pushing myself to run along the side of the river. My chest heaved. I worried I would pass out. I ran. Tears blurred my vision, so I wasn't sure where I ran. Twice, I tripped over an out-of-place cobblestone, cutting my knees when I fell. Once, I crashed into a trash can. Still, I ran.

Until I couldn't possibly run anymore.

I fell to my knees at the edge of the Seine and vomited on the stone. Pushing myself backward, I clutched my stomach and struggled to take another deep breath.

"Are you alright?"

I turned to see a woman in a black cloak and red-bottomed heels. She moved with the night, tilting her head as she approached me.

"I'm fine," I lied, heaving. "Training too hard."

"You're bleeding," she hummed. "It smells sweet."

Like cotton candy.

My knees were scraped. I recognized the burn, sucking in a breath. I raised my head, prepared to tell the woman I was fine. Instead, I recognized her from earlier - the vampire who looked like Thierry. His sister. Red rims formed around her eyes and the dark veins on her face. She smirked, dragging her tongue over her teeth. My whole body trembled as I pushed myself to my feet, prepared to run.

"I was just leaving," I said. Little black dots flooded my vision.

"Are you sure?" She smiled sweetly. "I can walk you back to your place. Thierry would never forgive me if I left you alone out here."

"I'm fine," I insisted, harder this time.

I turned away from the vampire behind me. As soon as I took a step, she stood in front of me again. My body coiled in terror.

"I wonder if you taste as delicious as your friend," she giggled. I barely had time to blink before she descended.

"I'm fine," I insisted, harder this time.

I turned away from the vampire behind me. As soon as I took

a step, she stood in front of me again. I barely had time to blink before she descended.

And there was pain.

It was impossible to pinpoint where the pain came from; it radiated through every vein in my body. I opened my eyes from cringing back, only to discover the only thing keeping me standing was her mouth attached to my neck. I felt my flesh tear beneath her teeth, warm blood spilling down my chest like molasses. A scream stuck in my throat. I couldn't move, couldn't make a noise.

The world blurred and seemed to move slower. I felt faint.

I wanted Holland.

My chest ached as I tried to gasp for breath. The pain pulled at me harder and faster. I think my eyes slipped closed.

Until it all stopped.

The murky world came into crystal focus as my knees hit the ground. I barely opened my eyes quick enough to throw my hands out and catch myself. Blood splattered on the ground in front of me. I realized it was mine at the same moment the woman began to beg.

I lifted my head to watch her fall to her knees, my blood staining her mouth. Tears of blood stained her face as she looked up at a shadow in front of her, something more impossibly terrifying.

Holland.

He stood with his back to me, so I couldn't see his face. I wasn't sure whether to be scared or relieved that he had shown up - saved me.

I reached up to touch my aching throat. With a quiet cry, I realized the vampire woman had torn through my skin, leaving a large wound - wide and bleeding. Blood poured down the front of my chest, warm and sticky. The sensation made my skin crawl.

"Mine," Holland's voice was as dark as the night, entirely inhuman.

"I didn't know she was yours. She didn't smell like you," the vampire woman sobbed. Holland knelt in front of her. "Please, Holland, I would never touch another vampire's-"

She didn't get to finish.

Holland moved forward suddenly. I never saw where the weapon came from, only that there was a piece of wood sticking out of her chest a moment later. Her mouth fell open in shock, her skin turning a horrific, ashy gray.

She fell back into the river with a resounding splash.

Everything was quiet.

I held my breath as Holland stood and turned. He was covered in blood. It stained his face, hands, and chest. A bullet hole was burned through the center of his shirt, also saturated with blood - I wasn't sure how much of it was his.

Holland knelt without coming any closer. Every part of me wanted to run. The world spun faster and faster around me and I couldn't breathe, let alone see straight.

"You're losing a lot of blood, Adalyn. Will you let me help you?" Holland's voice sounded distorted.

I wasn't sure if I responded to him. I wanted to.

I blinked down at my hands - covered in blood. My blood. I was still bleeding.

Another blink and the world moved slower.

"Holland," I whispered.

A third and I felt like I was drowning.

I was twelve years old again, at the moment I thought I was going to die. Water rushed around me, my sister's frantic screams and gurgles echoing in my ears. My ears felt like they would explode. Everything was in slow motion.

Holland moved forward, his arms closing around me like wings. I closed my eyes.

CHAPTER
31

N one of the TV shows or movies really depicted how terrifying it felt to wake up after a vampire bite. Immediately after opening my eyes, I felt the pain that pulsed from the wound on my throat. I didn't dare turn my head, too afraid of the sensation to follow. The rest of my body felt stiff and tired. I blinked up at the ceiling, recognizing Holland's apartment.

I watched Holland kill someone. Two people.

Icy fear sank into me and I shivered. The tense muscles caused quick fireworks of pain to shoot from my neck. My mouth felt like cotton and my lips tasted like blood - mine, my bottom lip was split open. Even breathing felt heavy.

Unsure how much I could handle, I moved my fingers first, tapping them on the bed next to me. I was covered in a soft blanket. When my fingers moved without resistance, I clenched my hand. Then, I dragged it up slowly to touch my stomach and my chest. My fingers stopped at the edge of a bandage on my neck, a thick wad of gauze and a sticky cover that made my skin itch.

Pushing myself into a sitting position, I took in the empty apartment. Early morning sunlight peeked through the curtains, so faint it was gray.

"Holland?" I called. My voice broke.

Silence.

My whole body vibrated with exhaustion and fear as I pushed myself out of bed. I was barefoot and wearing one of Holland's shirts. It fit snugly and smelled like chocolate and... safety. The hardwood felt cold beneath my feet. My head spun and I paused halfway to the kitchen to catch my breath. I made the last few steps to the fridge, reaching for a water bottle.

The door opened.

I almost dropped the water bottle, falling back into the fridge, startled. The sudden movement caused me to gasp in pain. My eyes watered. Holland's eyes widened, like he hadn't expected me to be awake, let alone in the kitchen. He appeared impossibly human in a black t-shirt and blue jeans, not a speck of blood anywhere on him. There was a brown bag in one of his arms; I recognized a carton of eggs sticking out the top.

"Hi," he said carefully, closing and locking the door behind him. "Are you alright?"

I opened my mouth to tell him I was fine. Then, I felt the pain, and the hunger, and the exhaustion, and the fear. My eyes filled with tears and I tried to turn and shake them away. A couple escaped anyway. I held my breath while Holland crept into the kitchen, setting his bag down on the dining room table.

"I have some ibuprofen, I think," he murmured, unpacking the bag. I wiped my tears, too cowardly to turn and face him. He opened a couple of cabinets, humming to himself. "Are you hungry? You lost a lot of blood, so I went and got some food to help - some steak, and eggs, uh, and some iron tablets. I wasn't sure what you'd want. I can make some tea. Perhaps some hot chocolate-"

"Holland," I interrupted.

He snapped his mouth shut.

Wincing, I turned towards him, letting him see me cry. Holland's golden eyes were wide with concern; his hands shook at his sides. A thousand words caught on my tongue.

I wanted to beg him to tell me last night wasn't real, to lie and say he hadn't killed anyone. For a moment, I thought I would scream. Next, I wanted to ask about Willa. Was her mom still here? Was Duncan dead? Where was Thierry? All of my questions and concerns died when I opened my mouth.

My shoulders slumped. "Ibuprofen sounds good," I rasped.

He opened the closest cabinet to him and pulled out a small bottle. I eyed him as he approached, holding out the medication. My gaze fell from his face to his hand - remembering how it looked covered in blood.

I shivered, taking it from him and inching backward. Thankfully, he took a step away from me. I reached for my water bottle with a shaky hand.

"I need you to say something," Holland blurted. "Because I expected you to scream, but you seem way too calm. And, I just - Adalyn, look at me."

I did.

Holland's eyes filled with tears of blood, red liquid pooling at the edges. I jolted in surprise at the sight. "I would never hurt you," he breathed. When the tear spilled over, I watched it stain his face red. "Please, believe me."

I swallowed thickly.

I had two options here.

If I didn't believe Holland, I could find my pants and shoes, leave this apartment, and never look back. Perhaps I would pack my things at the hotel and book the next flight back to Phoenix. I could return to my job, rent an apartment in the same complex as my sister, and drink red wine until I forgot all about the way Holland looked with blood on his face. In a couple of decades, this would all be nothing but a dream.

It was the easier option.

It was the resolution I wanted to want.

Instead, I believed him. I stood in the kitchen and stared into the eyes of a heartbroken vampire, contemplating my next move. I wanted to run.

Or, I could sit down and let him make me breakfast. I could step into his arms and kiss away the fear on his face... fall into his bed all over again... and never leave.

It came down to one thing - was this the life I wanted to live?

This wasn't what I came to Paris for. Two weeks ago, I would have laughed in the face of anyone who told me vampires existed.

Two weeks ago... I was getting married.

The realization hit me like a truck, on top of everything else. I'd been in Paris for a little over a week, which meant that fourteen days ago, I stood on an altar in front of everyone I'd ever known. They watched me break, and not one of them stood to catch me when I fell. My parents, my sister, my friends, her family... they all watched until the moment I knew Donna would never come down the aisle.

In the days that followed, I wondered how many of them knew before I did. How many of them waited for me to drown?

My heart raced in my chest as I stared at Holland. He waited for me to weigh my options, his brow furrowed with concern.

My shoulders slumped. "Breakfast sounds good."

Holland clutched his chest in relief. "Okay," he whispered.

I motioned to the stack of groceries. "I don't like steak. The eggs, I'll take. And, can I shower?"

Instinctively, I reached up to fiddle with the edge of the bandage on my neck.

Holland watched my movement, clearing his throat. "A bath might be better. I'll help you?"

I nodded.

Holland drew me a lavender-scented bubble bath and sat behind me while I rested in the water. His hands traced through my hair, brushing through the knots. I sat with my head in his hands and my eyes drooping.

"Adalyn," Holland started.

"I don't want to hear an apology, or an explanation, or anything about last night. I might break," I said.

He paused his massaging motion and took a deep breath. "Later?"

"Later," I echoed, sinking further into the water.

CHAPTER

32

fter I was clean and changed into one of Holland's flannels, he sat me on the couch with a cup of tea and a water bottle. He opened the window and the curtains, letting the morning light fill the apartment. I basked in the warm sunlight and pulled a blanket over my lap. Holland set some bread out on the table while he cracked eggs in a pan.

My phone rang.

I eyed it as it buzzed on the table, too tired to pick it up. Holland crossed the room, lifting it to offer it to me. I blinked, taking it with a shaky breath.

It was Indy.

I pressed the red button, resting my head back on the couch. Immediately the phone rang again. I sighed, thankful it wasn't a video call. I answered.

"Oh, my, fuck, you're alive!" Indy yelled.

"I'm alive," I echoed. My sister had no idea that there was weight behind those words. If Holland had been a minute later... I shook the thought away. Across the room, Holland glanced up. His eyes were sad.

"Where the hell have you been?" Indy's angry voice cut like knives.

"Around," I breathed. "With friends." I wasn't strong enough to offer her any more.

"Look," Indy said. "I'm sorry about what I said. But you have to understand-"

"No, you need to understand," I interrupted, wiping my face. "I don't want to spend the rest of my life being the broken girl at the altar. I have friends and I think there might be a life for me here. I know this isn't the version of me you're comfortable with, but it's time to get comfortable."

Indy was quiet for a moment. "You really don't plan to come home?"

"No," I said.

My sister hummed. "So, who was the guy?"

I knew she didn't believe me. I didn't have the energy to keep arguing. My head pounded. "A friend."

Across the room, Holland laughed once. I glanced up at him, unable to stop my soft smile.

"You're not going to give me anything? Is he actually a friend? A boyfriend? Fuck buddy?"

"Indy," I groaned.

"All three, perhaps?" Holland muttered across the room. Despite my current state, my heart warmed at his comment.

"I have to go," I told Indy. "I'm going to breakfast. I'll let you know I'm alive sometimes, but tell Mom and Dad I'm staying."

I hung up the phone, staring at it in my hand. Holland approached again, holding out two hands. I took them weakly, trying to ignore the pounding in my head as he hauled me to my feet. Holland led me to the dining table, holding out my chair. My shoulders slumped as I sank into the seat. Holland placed a plate and a cup in front of me. I stared at my eggs blankly. Holland returned to lay a blanket over my shoulders, lingering behind me and resting his hand on my shoulder.

"You need to eat," he said.

Hands shaking, I reached for my fork. "I'm going to break, Holland."

I looked up at him. My lips quivered. I felt myself falling apart - breaking.

Without a word, he leaned forward to kiss me.

I sobbed into his kiss, reaching up to wrap my arms around him - one around his neck and the other clutching the collar of his shirt. Holland tasted like hibiscus tea and his mouth was warm against mine.

Once, I asked him to give me a reason to stay.

Now, he was my only reason.

My family didn't believe I could do this. I wasn't sure I wanted this.

But Holland was made of sunshine and kissed me like I was his entire world. A vampire willing to kill to keep me safe.

Holland kissed me until I was breathless. His tongue traced mine while tears dripped down my face uncontrollably and I clung to him.

"As much as I would love to keep kissing you, the tears and the ghostly pallor don't really do it for me," Holland said, kissing my forehead. "Try and eat."

I laughed once, nodding and sinking into my chair. I took a few slow bites of eggs while he sat across from me, swirling his tea in his cup idly.

"There's something you should know," he said quietly. My stomach sank. I set down my fork. "I killed another vampire for you last night."

"I know," I breathed. My hand fell to my stomach. I worried, for a moment, I would be sick. My skin pricked with worry.

Holland blew out a long breath and shifted. "I would do anything for you. Including killing Thierry's sister."

I gulped. My heart beat faster. My hands felt clammy. I shivered like I was cold, despite the blanket and warm tea. My next words were barely a whisper. "Are you in trouble, Holland?"

He shrugged. "Hard to say. It's still early. It's easier not to say anything to Willa. I would hate for Thierry to find out from her."

I watched him for a long moment. "Thank you," I said. "For coming after me. For getting there on time."

Something sparkled in Holland's eyes. Something softer than the sunrise. "Anything for you."

I felt better after breakfast. Holland placed me back in front of the window for fresh air while he cleaned up after breakfast. I stared out the window.

"Hey, are you alright?" Holland asked, padding over.

I was crying again. "A long day, I guess."

He sat down next to me. "The day's just started, it's a new sun."

I wrinkled my nose and reached for his hand. "Can I ask you something?" I asked. I reached up to touch the bandage on my neck, unable to stop my quiver of discomfort. "It's not - always like that, is it?"

Holland flinched. "No, my love. That vampire wanted to kill you. It doesn't have to hurt at all."

My lips quivered. I buried my face in both of my hands, whimpering. "It hurts," I whispered.

"What does?" He leaned forward, brushing my hair out of my face.

I stared at him for a moment. No matter what I'd seen, or how scared I felt of Holland - one thing remained the same. He made me feel safe. Every ounce of me wanted to fall into his arms and cry until I had no more to give.

"Everything," I said.

"Let me see," Holland said.

I closed my eyes as he leaned forward, peeling the bandage off my neck. My stomach curdled at the thought of what the wound might look like. To my surprise, bloody tears welled in Holland's eyes. One dripped down his cheek.

"I can fix it," Holland whispered. Another tear ran down his face. I watched, fascinated, as the red tear stained his skin. His eyes met mine. "If you want me to."

"How?" I asked.

"Vampire blood heals all wounds," he said. "All it takes is one drop."

I watched one of his tears run down his lips. He waited for my answer, eyes wide with concern. The word 'no' formed on my tongue. But, everything hurt. Every breath I took felt labored. My heart ached. My head pounded. The gauze on my neck itched considerably. Relief sounded very appealing. Holland reached out, waiting patiently.

I kissed him.

Holland's blood tasted warm and metallic.

My lips paused against his while I tasted him on my tongue. Holland tilted his head back ever so slightly. My heart pounded in my throat as I kissed him again, raising one hand to cup the side of his face. A low whine escaped him. I shifted my weight hesitantly.

I paused again, pulling back as my neck tingled. I reached up, feeling only a jagged mark that faded even more as I touched it. Holland brushed my hair away, his brow furrowing as the last of the mark disappeared. I looked back at him. Tears of blood stained his gentle face. The sight was enough to shatter my heart. With a sigh, I kissed him again. Holland's arms wound around me, pulling me close. Another tear trailed over his mouth. I deepened our kiss, enjoying the metallic taste on my tongue.

"I'm sorry," he whispered against my lips.

I shook my head, carefully crawling forward to straddle his lap. Holland sat further back on the couch. His mouth moved against mine hesitantly. His hands shook on my hips. I brushed his hair off his forehead, tangling my fingers in it and kissing him harder.

Holland pulled his mouth from mine, shaking his head. "Adalyn-" he started. "You've had a long day."

"I know," I responded.

He sighed. "You should be afraid of me."

I kissed him again. "I am." He shivered and sobbed once. I watched tears drip down his face. My lips were a hair's breadth from his as I tilted my head forward. "I want you to take my fear away," I whispered.

Holland's grip on my hips tightened. "Fuck, this isn't the time." he breathed.

I flicked my tongue against his bottom lip. He responded to my kiss with a gasp. "Seems like you have all the time in the world," I said.

I slid off his lap, pressing kisses down his chest as I knelt in front of him. Holland's eyes widened, his lips parted, and I had him. The mark had disappeared from my neck. I felt stronger. I was terrified of what Holland could be, but I saw none of that now. I saw a boy with a smile like sunshine, whose kiss made me breathless. I wanted him, more than I'd ever wanted anything before. He leaned forward, lightly gripping my chin and tilting it up to smother my smile with a kiss.

"You look very pretty on your knees," he whispered. My eyes widened. "Stay right here."

Holland stepped away from me, crossing the room to the bathroom. I rested my hands on my knees.

Holland returned. He had wiped the blood off his face. He stopped one step out of the bathroom, his eyes darkening as he looked me over. I turned to face him, resting back on my heels with a smile. He pulled his shirt over his head, exposing his golden chest. Every ounce of me wanted to touch him. I stayed perfectly still. I wanted to find out what happened when I did as I was told. Holland kicked off his shoes.

My eyes followed his hands as he reached down to unbutton his jeans. My breath caught in my throat. Holland was left in only his boxers, and, god, he was already hard for me. I licked my lips eagerly.

Holland knelt in front of me. I hummed when his thumb traced my bottom lip. "You're sure you're okay?" he asked.

I nodded.

"Say it."

"I'm sure," I said, kissing him delicately. "Please fuck me, Holland."

He growled into the kiss, standing again. "All in good time."

Holland stripped naked, standing tall over me. I let my eyes trail down his body, sure he was a living god. My eyes flicked back up to his face and I swallowed thickly.

"Open your mouth, Adalyn," he said.

Fucking hell.

I held his gaze while I obeyed, sticking my tongue out. Holland gulped, taking a single step forward. I hummed when I felt the tip of his length rest against my tongue. I stayed where I was, watching, as he moved forward more - carefully pushing himself into my mouth. When I couldn't take anymore, I placed my hand on his hip to stop him. Holland eased up, reaching down to brush my hair out of my face. I whined deeply as he pulled back, thrusting into my mouth again. And again. And again.

I kept one hand on his hip, controlling the depth of his thrusts. I moaned around his length, watching his eyes widen. Delicious gasps escaped him. His thrusts faltered when he reached up to brush his hair out of his face with a desperate groan. I took control, wrapping my hand around him to follow the movements of my mouth. I flicked my tongue against his tip each time I pulled back, groaning when I took him as deep as I could.

Holland pulled away, his eyes wide as he gasped for air. I grinned up at him, standing. He stepped forward, covering my mouth with a frantic kiss. I melted into his touch, sighing as he snapped the clasp of my bra. In one fluid movement, Holland lifted me off the ground, tossing me back onto the mattress. I laughed, crawling further up the bed as he joined me.

He smiled when he kissed me again. "I want to taste you so badly," he said, his fingers tracing my core over my panties.

I rolled my hips up to meet his touch. Holland sat up, looping his fingers beneath the fabric of my panties and pulling them off without hesitation. I blinked, and he leaned down, gliding his tongue over where I throbbed for him. I gasped. One of my hands tangled in his hand air, and the other gripped the blankets. Holland wasted no time, licking and sucking all the right places. My orgasm built quickly, coaxed by the sensation of his tongue on my clit and his fingers pressing inside of me.

My cries echoed off every crevice in the apartment, growing more frantic as the knot tightened in my stomach. Holland sped up his fingers, and the whole world came crashing down around me.

"Fuck," he swore, sitting up and kissing his way up my torso as I quivered in the aftermath of my orgasm. "I can't wait to have you coming around my cock," he whispered in my ear, his tongue tracing over my throat.

"Please," I begged.

I opened my eyes when he sat up, kissing my cheek. His eyes

were red, and black veins adorned his face. Shivers ran down my spine as I brought him down to kiss me again. My nightmare. My vampire. My Holland.

Holland groaned into our kiss, adjusting himself to rest between my hips. His tongue traced along mine hungrily, like he couldn't get enough of me.

Holland pressed himself against my entrance, rubbing his tip over my clit. I whined into his mouth, tangling my fingers in his hair as I arched my hips towards him. I was slick with desire and he slid into me easily. His mouth fell from mine. An inhuman growl escaped him, sending chills through me. I stretched beneath him, dragging my tattooed leg up the side of his hip and wrapping it around him. He boosted himself up, watching me as I writhed, frantic for more friction.

"I'm going to ruin you," he whispered.

"Please," I said again.

Holland pulled his hips away, thrusting back into me tantalizingly slow. I gasped, my eyes rolling back in delight.

"That's my girl," he breathed.

He sat up, looping both of my legs over his arms and holding my hips down on the mattress. He thrust harder into me, faster, angling his hips to meet mine perfectly. I dragged my hands up my chest, then through my hair as I sobbed in delight. I dropped one hand between my thighs, shivering at Holland's growl of approval when I touched myself.

He leaned forward, releasing my legs and gripping the headboard. I yelped at the change in angle, wrapping my legs around his waist to keep my balance.

"God, Holland," I cried, feeling heat build in my stomach again.

"Yes," he whispered. "Say it again."

I did.

I looked up at him, eyes wide. He appeared as every bit the

monster he could be and yet I needed him just as much. He bared his fangs as his head fell back in pleasure while he fucked me. For half a second, I wondered how his fangs would feel in my throat. Holland leaned down, kissing me deeply and shattering my thoughts. I clung to him, trembling uncontrollably.

Holland's hand closed around my throat while he kissed me. "Come for me, Adalyn."

I didn't realize I was close enough to my high yet, but I tumbled over the edge nonetheless. Holland's thrusts turned frantic as he followed me into his own orgasm. His cries were music to my ears, the darkest symphony.

CHAPTER 33

" **A** re you sure you'll be alright?" Holland asked as we approached my hotel.

"I'll be fine," I said, eyeing the spot on the ground that had been covered in his blood the night before. I glanced at him again; there wasn't a mark on him, like last night never happened. Instinctively, I reached up to rub my neck - where there was no wound left. My fingers lingered on my skin and I shivered when I remembered how the tearing skin and oozing blood felt.

"Not very convincing," Holland said, squeezing my other hand and pulling my attention back to him.

"I'm sorry. I'm overwhelmed," I muttered.

"Do you want me to stay?"

I shook my head. "No, I need to shower and rest and talk to Willa. You're sure she's okay? What if Thierry's here?"

Holland turned me to face him. "Willa is upstairs arguing with her mother, who gave copious amounts of money to hide what happened to Willa's beast of an ex-fiancé." I flinched at his choice of words. Holland sobered. "I'm sorry, that was crude. Thierry is not here. I can stay if you're worried?"

I reached up and placed my hand on Holland's cheek. "You told me before we left that you don't feel well, and you're quite pale. I'm going to check on Willa, then try to get some rest. I'll see you tomorrow?"

Holland gave in. "Fine, tomorrow."

I accepted his soft kiss, resting my hand on his chest and counting his heartbeats. "Thank you," I said.

"For what?"

"For getting there on time."

Holland kissed me again. "Call me if you need me."

I watched him walk away, resisting the urge to cry. He looked back before turning the corner, motioning for me to go inside. I did.

I avoided eye contact with the receptionist when I passed her, knowing she'd seen what happened last night. She stared intently at me until I leaped into the elevator. I fumbled in my pocket and pulled out my phone and room key, counting to ten silently as the elevator took me to the third floor. When I got out, I contemplated which door to open, standing between mine and Willa's rooms.

I took a step towards my room, only to jump in surprise with Willa's door flung open. "I will be back this evening, Willa," a cold, hard voice said. "You better be packed, or your father will hear of your disobedience."

I blinked when a short, thin blonde woman stepped out of the room. She stared at me for a moment, her hot pink upper lip curled. Then she stepped past me and her heels clicked as she stormed down the stairs.

"Willa?" I called quietly. The door to her room was still open.

"Addie?" Her voice came soft and broken.

I rushed forward, forgetting about my need to shower and rest. I barely remembered to shut the door behind me. Willa sat on the edge of her bed. I wrapped my arms around her and pulled her against me. The sound of her sobs shattered my heart. Willa's whole body convulsed with the weight of her cries.

"I can't leave," she blubbered against me. "God, he'll kill me and no one will ever know."

I pulled back, shaking my head in confusion. "Willa, would your father-"

"Yes," she interrupted, her eyes wide. "No one will ever know what happened to Duncan either."

"Duncan?" I raised an eyebrow.

"My fiancé," she whispered. I remembered the sight of Holland's teeth on the big man's neck and shivered. He tried to take Willa away. Holland stopped him - because I asked him to. "I watched him die, and that was terrifying, but I feel nothing now. I might be glad he's dead."

I didn't know what to say.

"I should get packed," Willa murmured.

I shook my head, gripping both of her hands. "Tell me what I can do to help you. We could change countries. Find you somewhere else to stay. Anything."

Willa stared at me for a long moment and nodded. "I'm going to call Thierry and see if I can stay with him for a little while."

"Okay," I said. "Can I help?"

Willa's lips quivered. She took my hand. "Sure. I should get packing."

Willa's room was a mess, so packing her things was overwhelming. We didn't say much and instead focused on folding and stuffing her suitcases full. I tried not to worry about what Willa leaving Paris meant for me.

My family would never drag me home. They would be angry with me from afar, and would eventually stop trying. I wasn't expecting the thought to sting so much.

Willa stormed into my life at a moment I needed a friend the most. I leaned on her joy and positivity.

I was being selfish, thinking about myself when I should have been worrying about Willa. My shoulders slumped and I glanced across the room at where Willa stared down at her phone.

"You okay?" I asked, lowering the shirt I folded.

Her lip quivered. "I'm fine."

"Willa-" I started.

"I'm gonna shower and rest for a bit. Thierry will be here in an hour," she muttered.

I sat up, getting the hint that she wanted to be alone. "Sure," I said. I moved towards the door. "Call if you need me."

Willa said nothing else when I left. I tried not to panic while I cleaned my room and showered. I stared at myself in the mirror with wet hair that uncomfortably clung to my neck and shoulders. My eyes trailed to my throat. I reached up and traced where the horrible wound had been. I never saw it, but I didn't need to; I remembered the tearing and shredding of my skin as the vampire consumed me. I shivered.

I dressed quickly and sat on the edge of my bed, unsure what else to do. I wanted to be here if Willa needed me. Even as I thought about waiting for her, my eyes drooped with exhaustion. With a sigh, I lay back on the pillows, staring up at the ceiling. Thierry would be here soon. I could wait for his knock on her door, then I'd help her out of this hotel - hopefully, to somewhere her family would never find her.

My eyes slipped closed while I waited for Thierry.

I woke up to a loud pounding. For a second, I thought the echoing was inside my head. Until I jolted into reality and realized I'd fallen asleep. I checked the time and horror crept into me. I'd been asleep for more than an hour. Frantically, I leaped out of bed, stumbling towards the door and pulling it open.

Holland.

He looked pale as a ghost, and frantic.

"Fucking hell, there you are," he breathed. "Where's Willa?"

I blinked, still trying to wake up. I shook my head. "She should be in her room."

Holland swore. He spun towards the room across from me and I yelped when he kicked the door open.

Blood.

So much blood.

A scream built in my throat as I took in the sight of the puddle in the middle of Willa's room.

And Willa.

She sat on the ground, leaning against the bed. The wounds on her forearms were deep and gaping, blood oozing from both of them. All at once - I knew what she'd tried to do to escape her fate at home.

Holland darted into the room, falling to his knees in the blood next to Willa. "What the hell have you done?" He cried.

The blood splattered like a rain puddle. I didn't know humans had that much blood in them.

Willa's eyes flicked open. Her voice was barely a whisper. "Where's Thierry? He was supposed to be here."

Horror sank into Holland's face. He shook his head. "I don't know where he is. Was he supposed to be here?"

Willa didn't answer.

"Adalyn, I need a towel," Holland said.

I couldn't move.

My whole body vibrated and I couldn't see anything other than red.

"Adalyn, look at me."

I tried. I did. I felt like I was underwater. Everything moved in slow motion. Every sound was a hundred miles away. My head pounded, my heart raced.

Willa and I agreed not to talk about the things that hurt us because we were in Paris to find joy. I knew her mother threatened her. I knew she didn't want to go home.

I didn't know she would ever hurt herself.

"Willa, where's Thierry?" Holland's voice brought me back to reality. I blinked, staring at my bleeding friend with wide gashes in her arm.

She shook her head. "I'm tired."

"Fuck!" Holland yelled. "Willa, I can't help you. It has to be Thierry." He looked up at me. "A towel, a sheet, something to stop the bleeding. Please, Adalyn."

All at once, I could move again. My feet slipped beneath me as I ran for the bathroom, skidding through blood. I grabbed the first towel I saw off the rack, returning to hand it to Holland. He was drenched in Willa's blood, pressing the towel against her wounds to hold them shut. His eyes were blood red and the veins on his face darker than I'd ever seen them before.

"What about the hospital? An ambulance?" I squeaked.

"Where's her phone?" Holland ignored me. "Call Thierry. Keep calling until he answers."

I found her phone on the toilet in the bathroom. It was half-covered in blood. With shaking hands, I did as Holland asked, finding Thierry's number in her contacts and clicking on it. It rang... and rang... and rang... and went dead.

I tried again.

And again.

And again.

I dropped to my knees in a puddle of blood, sobbing as I tried again to call Thierry. Holland held onto Willa, trying to stop the bleeding.

"He's here," Holland said, his voice full of relief. "Open the door."

I slipped on blood again, barely catching myself as I moved to open the door. The instant I turned the handle, Thierry shoved into the room. The door hit me square in the forehead and I stumbled back with a gasp, but he paid no attention to me.

"What the hell happened?" He roared.

"We could ask you the same question," Holland snapped. "You were with her last."

"She was fine when I left," Thierry yelled, falling to his knees in front of Willa. I reached up to touch my throbbing forehead, whimpering. My fingers came away bloody and I felt dizzy. I closed the door again, sinking to the ground with a quiet sob. No one looked at me.

"I'm here, Willa," Thierry said, pulling her against him. Holland moved with him, keeping the towel on her gashed arms.

"I knew you'd come," Willa whispered. "I didn't want to go home. I want to stay here with you."

"You are with me." Thierry's brow furrowed. His eyes were red, his fangs shining as he spoke.

"Forever," Willa's voice was barely audible.

Thierry and Holland exchanged a look.

"Could she make it to the hospital?" Thierry asked.

Holland shook his head.

I sat up quickly, terror rushing through me. I think I said

something frantic, because Holland moved away from Thierry to wrap both arms around me. I reached for Willa, crying.

"She can't die," I repeated the same sentence over and over.

"Thierry is going to take care of her," Holland said firmly. "We need to go."

I made eye contact with Thierry. He seemed bewildered, looking between me and the limp girl Holland left in his arms. I tried to pull away from Holland again, but he was too strong to resist. He was... inhumanly strong. Willa's eyes didn't open. Was she breathing?

Willa... Willa... Willa.

Holland's hand covered my scream. I collapsed back into him when my vision blurred and went black.

I opened my eyes again at the slam of a door. My hotel room door. I was in Holland's arms covered in blood that wasn't mine. I tried to regain my footing; my shoes slipped on the ground.

Holland let me fall.

I slid and hit the ground. I whined in shock as Holland stumbled back into the door with a snarl. He dragged his hands down his face, smearing blood down his face.

"Holland?" I whispered, my stomach flipping. I moved towards him, freezing when he held up one hand. "Holland, what's happening?"

He didn't answer, snarling instead. I scrambled back with a weak whimper. The sight of Willa stuck in my head like a broken record as I looked up at my vampire. I was terrified. I didn't know if she was going to be okay. Holland blocked the door, and I couldn't get to her.

There was so much blood.

Holland sobbed once, sinking to the ground and slamming his hands onto it. I stared at Holland, made of fangs and blood. My stomach churned and my whole body trembled in terror.

"I need you to do something for me," Holland whispered, his voice broken and desperate.

I said nothing.

Holland's eyes opened. "I need you to leave, and go back to my apartment."

I shook my head. "I can't do that. I'm covered in blood. Willa is... God, what's wrong with Willa?"

"Adalyn, my dearest," Holland's voice was low and dark. I whimpered. "You aren't hearing me." He pulled his apartment key out of his pocket and tossed it across the floor. It left a bloody trail. "I'm telling you to *run*."

I trembled. "Holland," I whispered.

Holland took a deep breath, a tear dripping down his cheek. "Willa is going to be okay," Holland clenched his fists, slamming one on the ground again. "I promise you, but, my love, there's a lot of blood and... fuck, Adalyn, if you stay here, I may tear your throat out."

I froze.

He groaned, sobbing again. "And I don't want to do that, okay? So, please, take the key and *run*."

"Okay," I whispered. My hand closed around the key. "Will you let me out the door?"

"I'm going to try," Holland whispered. He moved away from the door, resting his head against the wall.

I stared at him for a moment longer, my bottom lip quivering. I pushed myself to my feet, unable to stop my whimper of terror. Holland looked at me again, desperation clear on his face.

"I don't want to hurt you," he whispered.

I nodded. "I know."

"Run fast, okay?"

I was more terrified of the scared expression on his face than I was of him. I hated that I made him feel like that - desperate, frantic, deadly. Holland squeezed his eyes shut, roaring in desperation. I took a single step towards the door. Holland did not move. Another step. I placed my hand on the door handle, turning it slowly. Holland remained stoic as a statue.

I opened the door.

His eyes opened.

Gone was any trace of the kind, warm person I enjoyed. Holland became a monster.

"Run, Adalyn," he snarled.

I ran.

CHAPTER
34

I made it outside before I saw Holland again. He appeared across the street, dripping blood and snarling like an animal. I stopped mid-step, shaking my head. I wanted to say his name. I wanted to run to him. I wanted him to kiss me until I was breathless.

Except, there was no warmth in the vampire across the street, no safety. No sign of the vampire I adored.

"Holland, I'm so tired," I whispered.

His only answer was a deep growl.

I sobbed once, taking a step back. Holland took a step forward to mimic mine. I shook my head. I didn't want to run.

But I did.

I skidded around a corner, nearly losing my balance and leaving a trail of splattered blood behind me. I ran as quickly as I could around the block. As I scrambled down into the metro station, I left bloody handprints on the railing. People leaped away from me, yelling about the incensed girl covered in blood. I slipped on the stairs twice, landing hard and bruising my hips, my knees, and my elbow.

I barely made it into a metro car before I saw Holland again, stumbling down the stairs. The doors closed, and the vampire roared. I hated what I saw in him - monstrousness, evil. As the train raced away, I swore Holland's eyes burned through me. I sank to the ground, sobbing hysterically, grateful it was the middle of the night and I was alone in this train car.

When I made it to the transfer station, I was still crying. I vomited in a trash can before stumbling onto the next metro car. I screamed in the train car. Finally, it pulled up to the stop right outside Holland's apartment. A couple of homeless people stared at me as I limped up the stairs. I clutched my stomach as it flipped.

I walked into the cool night air and waited to see Holland.

Everything was still for a moment. I took a few steps away from the metro station, turning in a slow circle.

There he was.

Holland leaned back on a bench, like he'd been waiting for me for a while. Willa's blood was splattered on his face like paint and dripped from his hair. I wondered how long he'd been there. I sucked in a deep breath and shook my head.

"Holland, please," I whispered.

He said nothing. His eyes followed me like a predator as I approached him - stopping just out of his reach. He licked his lips, likely tasting the blood on them. I reached up to wipe my tears, smearing blood across my face.

"Please don't make me run anymore," I begged.

Holland cleared his throat. A dark, haunting smile grew on his face. "Run, pretty Adalyn."

I sobbed.

Holland lunged for me. I scrambled back with a cry, shaking my head. I tripped over a garbage can. My yelp echoed through the empty street as I fell back. I never hit the ground, though. Holland gripped my arm, pulling me upright. For half a second, he looked like himself - like sunshine.

Then it faded, and he growled.

I wrenched away. Holland's hand left bruises on my arm from holding me so tightly. I scrambled in what I hoped was the direction of his apartment. I wasn't convinced getting there would keep me safe, but at least it was a destination. I cried while I ran. This time, Holland was one step behind me the entire way. I turned while we were on the stairs, letting him grab a hold of me. His hand closed around my upper arm and I spun, pushing him hard. Holland stumbled back to the bottom of the stairs, groaning in a crumpled mess on the ground.

"I'm so sorry," I cried.

I ran up the rest of the stairs, my hands trembling as I shoved the key into the lock. Holland's footsteps on the stairs. Holland snarling. Holland... Holland... Holland.

The door opened. I fell into the apartment. Holland reached the top of the stairs. I slammed the door shut, turning the lock right as he fell into it.

"Adalyn, open the door, my love. Everything is okay," Holland cried on the other side.

He didn't sound like Holland.

"No," I sobbed, dropping to my knees. "Holland, please."

I didn't even know what I was begging for.

Holland shook the handle so hard I thought the door would break. I heard him yell in the hallway. Glass shattered. I sobbed harder, scrambling back and covering my ears.

Then, quiet.

A knock on the door woke me in the morning. I was wrapped in a blanket, curled up in the corner of the couch because I couldn't stand the thought of laying in bed without Holland. I showered last night to wash off the blood after I was sure he was gone. I wore one of his snug t-shirts and my underwear.

I stared at the door when the knock sounded again, quieter this time.

"Adalyn?" Holland's voice was soft, tired. "Are you awake?"

I was too afraid to move. Every muscle in my body burned as I pulled the blanket tighter around me. I raised my hands, thinking about covering my ears again.

Holland could have broken the door down last night. I watched him kick Willa's door down to get inside, but he didn't do that here. He yelled outside the door for a while, then left entirely. I spent a long time thinking about that before sleep took over.

"Adalyn, it's me. I am completely in control. I will not hurt you. And, I'm fucking exhausted."

I covered my ears for a moment, sobbing silently. Holland called my name again. I couldn't keep listening to him beg. I stood slowly, crossing the room. I stopped in front of the door, staring at the handle. I felt coiled like a spring, ready to bolt.

"Adalyn," Holland spoke again. I whimpered. "I can hear you on the other end of the door. I know you're scared, but everything is okay."

"Holland," I whispered.

"I'm here, baby. I promise it's me."

I unlocked the door, immediately scrambling back. I made it

back to the couch and curled in the corner before the handle turned. Holland stepped through the door and I pulled my knees to my chest, quivering. He wore clean clothes, without a drop of blood left on him. His eyes were soft. Holland locked the door behind him. I watched his every step as he moved to sit on the edge of his bed.

"I'm sorry," he said, burying his face in his hands. "I'm so fucking sorry."

"Is Willa okay?" I asked quietly. "I tried to call her a few times last night. She didn't answer."

Holland shook his head. "Is that what you're worried about right now?"

"Please answer me." My voice cracked.

Holland rubbed his face and cracked his neck. "She's with Thierry. He'll take care of her."

"I don't know what that means," I cried.

Holland paused, falling back on his mattress. "It means she's dead, Adalyn."

My blood ran cold.

Holland sat up again. "It means she already lost too much blood to make it to the hospital. It means she succeeded in killing herself and we can only hope Thierry arrived in time to save her."

I stared at him, silent tears dripping down my face. I shook my head, standing off the couch and reaching for my shoes. "I have to go."

"Adalyn-" Holland stood to reach for me.

"No," I spun towards him, grabbing my phone and my wallet off the kitchen table. "I can't handle this, Holland. I'm not brave enough for this."

He gaped at me like I'd slapped him. Images flashed in my head as I remembered how it felt to run from him. Any trace of the monster I'd seen last night was gone, but I couldn't stop reliving it.

"I'm going to go find Willa," I said, taking another step back. "And then, I'm going home."

"Adalyn."

I shook my head, feeling my heart break. "I'm not brave enough," I repeated.

He let me go.

It wasn't until I was outside on the street that I realized I wasn't wearing any pants.

CHAPTER 35

Willa didn't answer when I knocked on her hotel room door.

She didn't answer any of my phone calls.

I paced back and forth in my perfectly clean hotel room. Holland's sweater lay over my chair, the only indication of who cleaned everything. I was grateful it was him and not the cleaning crew.

The longer I was alone, the harder it became to breathe.

I couldn't find my friend. The last thing I saw was blood. She looked dead.

Holland wanted to rip my throat out.

Holland was a vampire.

My chest constricted. I dug my nails into my palms to feel something other than terror. My whole body was in pain from running and falling down the stairs last night.

Willa was bleeding.

There was a bruise on my hip. I hadn't noticed it before.

How had Willa lost so much blood? How deep were her cuts?
Was Willa alive?

Twice, I picked up the phone to call Holland. The second
time, I made it as far as it ringing before I hung up and threw the
phone across the room.

Fuck, I couldn't breathe.

I tried Willa's door again, sobbing when it didn't open. There
wasn't even a noise from the inside to let me know she was alive.
The whole hotel seemed too quiet. I swore, clutching my chest on
the way back to my room. With the door shut and locked, I fell
onto the bed and rolled onto my back to catch my breath.

My phone rang.

I sobbed, scrambling to reach for it. I prayed it was Willa.

It was Indy.

I wiped my face quickly, trying to plaster on a fake smile
while I answered her call. "Hey," I croaked.

Indy didn't answer immediately, her smile fading into suspi-
cion as she stared at me. "What's going on?"

I shook my head. "Nothing."

"Addie," she breathed. A tear ran down my face. I wiped it
away, sniffling. "What's wrong?"

"Just a bad day," I told her. "Everything's fine."

"It doesn't look fine. What is it? Did you hear from Donna?"

I laughed once, shaking my head. "If only it were that
simple."

Fighting with Donna seemed easy compared to what I dealt
with in Paris. It was easy, familiar. She would scream. I would
shut her out. I could handle her.

I didn't know what to do about this.

I opened my mouth twice to tell Indy I was coming home, but
the words never came. They caught in my throat each time. I
rested my head on the pillow in defeat.

I wanted to go home.

Phoenix didn't feel like home anymore. It was the place I grew up, where my family lived. It didn't feel like I belonged there anymore. I wasn't sure I had a home to return to.

"Boy trouble," I said finally, unsure what else to say to my sister.

"A boy?" She squeaked. I slumped into the pillow, exhausted. "What happened?"

I shrugged. "I don't know how to trust him."

"Makes sense, he's probably a fuckboy if he's hanging out in Paris." I laughed once. My sister paused. "I'm sorry about the last time we were on the phone. A patient died at work; I was upset and I miss you. I let my frustration get the better of me."

I brushed away another tear. "Is everything okay there?"

She sat down on her couch, sinking into it. "Work fucking sucks. Mom and Dad are on my ass for whatever reason. I'm tired."

"Well, you could always do what I did and run away," I said.

"Don't tempt me," Indy snorted. "So, you're going to stay in Paris?"

"That's the plan."

"Forever?"

I winced at her choice of words, remembering how Willa whispered it while she bled out. Truthfully, I had no idea how to commit to forever.

"Well," I said. "My savings account is draining faster than I expected. So, I'll have to get a job. And I'm sure I'll also need some sort of work visa. And an apartment, because I can't live in a hotel forever."

"That's a lot," Indy said quietly.

I nodded, staring at the wall as I thought about actually living in Paris.

I was happy here. I felt lighter, more free. If I could figure out a job, and a place to live, it seemed like an easy enough decision to stay. I worried, though, that it might lose its charm once I committed. I also wondered if I would enjoy Paris as much without Willa.

My heart lurched. God, I hoped she was okay.

I talked casually with Indy until she left to make dinner. She didn't bring up me going home again. I let her go, blinking through my exhaustion. My eyes burned from all my tears and my throat ached from sobbing. When I rolled onto my back, I felt the burn from the bruises on the backs of my thighs. Still, I didn't feel like sleeping.

I felt restless. Scared.

I dressed in Holland's sweater and a pair of leggings. The sun would be up for a while longer. I thought I would go for a walk and grab a sandwich. I could try to find Willa again when I got back.

I left the hotel with a slight limp, deliberately avoiding eye contact with the receptionist who had seen me come inside wearing no pants earlier today. That was embarrassing. It was chilly and overcast. I hugged my sweater to my chest. My whole body resisted every step I took up the hill.

I walked up to the small roundabout at the top of the hill. The restaurants overflowed with people and there was a line out the door of the gelato shop.

That wasn't what stopped me, though.

Willa sat in the middle of the roundabout, on a bench, laughing as the fountain splashed water on her face.

CHAPTER 36

I stopped mid-step and almost got run over by a bicyclist. Willa shook water out of her hair, looking happier than I'd ever seen her. Thierry sat on the ground at her feet. He seemed bored, picking at his nail beds.

And Holland.

Holland leaned against a tree nearby, his arms crossed while he watched Willa carefully. He seemed to be waiting for something. Willa leaned down to kiss Thierry's forehead. When she looked up, her eyes settled on me standing in the middle of the street.

"Addie!"

All eyes were on me.

My stomach dropped to my feet and I took a single step backward before correcting myself and crossing the street. Willa barrelled into me half a second later, her arms winding around me so tightly I thought my ribs would break.

"I haven't been able to get a hold of you all day," I said

weakly.

"I know!" Willa pulled back to place both hands on my shoulders. "Thierry has been such a buzzkill."

I glanced between my overly excited friend and the two vampires standing behind her. They both shifted nervously. "Where've you been?" I asked.

Willa grinned. She opened her mouth to say something, then her eyes roamed over me in confusion. "Are you bleeding?"

I paused. "No?"

Willa's smile faded as she stared at me. "You smell good."

"Willa?" I croaked.

Thierry came up behind her, swinging his arm around her shoulders. "New perfume, Addie?" He asked, his eyes wide in concern.

I shook my head. I swore the whole square heard my heart racing. Holland walked up behind me; I jumped when his arm wound around my waist. I hated that I stepped back into him so effortlessly. My palms were sweaty. The lump in my throat grew so large I couldn't breathe.

Willa wasn't paying attention to me anymore. She stared at Holland, her eyes dark. A low growl rumbled in his chest. "Mine," he said.

Willa smiled. "She doesn't smell like yours."

"Willa," Thierry said sharply.

My mind reeled in a thousand directions. I watched Willa look between me and Holland again.

And her eyes turned red.

Willa was a vampire.

I tried to contain my shock and horror to avoid people taking notice, but my head spun and my vision blurred. Willa grinned, displaying a razor-sharp pair of fangs.

"Willa," Thierry said again. "Why don't we go find something to eat?"

Willa smiled at me. "Care to join us, Addie?"

"Adalyn stays with me," Holland spoke up. His grip on me tightened.

Willa's smile faded. I hated the unnatural growl that escaped her. Her eyes flicked to me. "I'll see you later. Breakfast tomorrow?"

"Sounds great." I forced a smile.

Thierry beckoned her away. My knees gave out the instant she turned to leave. I would have fallen if Holland wasn't holding me so tightly. Willa and Thierry disappeared around the corner. My breaths came faster, harder. Holland took a few steps back, drawing me with him.

I followed him as my world fell apart.

Willa was a vampire.

As soon as they were gone, I spun towards Holland. "What the hell happened?" I cried. "You said she was dead."

"She is dead," Holland said.

I shook my head, reaching up to tug at my hair with a sob. "No, that's not dead. That was-"

"You have to die to become a vampire, Adalyn," Holland reminded me.

I hiccuped. "She *died*?"

Holland's face softened. "Yes, my love. She had already lost so much blood. I'm sorry, I thought you understood."

I shook my head, gripping a bike rack to keep my balance. "I don't understand any of this. Why did she act like that?"

"Because all new vampires can think about is blood. The taste of it. The smell of it."

I clutched my stomach, worried I would be sick. "My blood?"

"Of course yours," Holland said. "She will return to the normal, vivacious, and carefree friend you care for. But right now, Willa is dangerous. She doesn't see you as a friend. She sees you as her next meal."

"And what about you?" I whispered, raising my eyes. "What do you see me as?"

Pain flashed on Holland's face. "I'm sorry, Adalyn."

"Answer the question," I snapped. Or, I tried. It came out more as a desperate cry of a trapped, feral animal.

"You want my honest answer?" Holland growled. I flinched when he walked forward to loom over me. "I see you as *mine*," he whispered. My eyes snapped up to meet his. "I look at you and I see a beautiful, confident woman, and I want you to fall into my bed so I can kiss you and fuck you senseless." I shivered. Holland's eyes turned red. "And I won't ever touch you unless you ask me to, but yes, Adalyn, there is a part of me that longs to know how sweet your blood tastes."

"And what about last night?"

"I won't let anything like last night ever happen again," Holland said. "There was a lot of blood and I was overwhelmed." My stomach flipped. "I'm sorry I scared you. I'm even more sorry I hurt you."

I sobbed suddenly, clutching my chest. "You promised you wouldn't, Holland."

"I know." His voice cracked.

I took a few steps back. "I love you," I blurted.

Holland's face went white.

I laughed once, shaking my head and tossing my hands in the air. "How fucking pathetic is that? You almost *killed me* last night and all I can think about is how desperately I want to fall into your arms. I wasn't even supposed to fall in love here. I was supposed to find myself, whatever the fuck that means. Instead, I'm bruised and I'm scared and in love with a fucking vampire."

I fell to my knees, hardly able to catch my breath.

"I love you," Holland murmured.

I fell prey again to his honey eyes and his satin lips. One look and he was everything I ever needed and more.

He was everything.

Holland dropped to his knees in front of me, in the middle of the street. The world pulsed around me as I stared at the vampire begging me to forgive him.

"Please don't leave Paris," he said quietly. "Please, Adalyn."

I wrapped my arms around my torso, whimpering.

I wanted to go home.

I wanted Holland.

I wanted... I wanted...

"I'm going back to the hotel," I murmured. "I can't do this today."

Agony flashed on Holland's face. His voice broke. "You're not leaving?"

"I don't know." I took a step back, shaking my head. "I can't, I don't."

I backed up further, nearly tripping over the bike rack. Black dots flooded my vision and my chest felt like I was being crushed by bricks. My back hit the wall of a building and I whined. Holland stood, grimacing as he watched me retreat.

"I'll walk you back," Holland said.

I paused, staring at him for a long moment. At least, if I let him walk me back, I would get there without falling. Holland approached, holding out his arm. I reached for him. He held onto me tightly, walking at my pace.

He said nothing else on the walk back to the hotel. I clung to him until we reached my room. With a shaking hand, I flashed my key over the lock. Holland pushed the door open.

I stepped inside. He paused in the doorway.

I turned towards him, my eyes wet and my chest heaving. "Do you have to go back?" I murmured.

Holland tilted his head. "Depends on whether you need me here."

My lips quivered. I stepped back into the room, wincing at the pain in my hip. I nodded. I hated how much I needed him. Every part of me wanted to fall into his arms. Holland's shoulders slumped with relief as he stepped into the room, shutting the door behind him.

"Don't leave me," I whispered.

Holland nodded.

I barely covered my next sob when I spoke. "I'm going to shower."

Holland kept his distance as I limped towards the bathroom to start the shower. I left the door open as I shrugged out of my sweater, laying it over the counter. My hands shook as I pulled my shirt over my head, exposing the bruises on my arms and the big one on my shoulder. I heard Holland move behind me and raised my eyes to watch him through the mirror reflection. His brow furrowed in concern as he took in the bruises covering my skin. Determined to seem stronger than I felt, I watched him as I pushed my jeans over my hips to reveal the worst bruise of them all on my hip - as dark as the night and swollen. A few others littered my thighs.

"Fuck," Holland whispered.

I turned to face him. Fear pricked my skin as I watched his eyes darken and turn red. I took a step back. He only lifted his hand and dug his fangs into the skin of his wrist. He held out his hand. I watched blood bead on his wrist, dripping down the side and onto the ground.

Without hesitating, I walked forward and closed my mouth over the wound he created. Vampire blood healed all wounds, and I couldn't stand another moment in pain. Holland's blood filled my mouth, and I nearly collapsed in relief as the pain faded. Holland wrapped his free arm around me, holding me close as I drank.

"Everything's going to be okay," Holland whispered. "I promise, I'll make it okay."

CHAPTER
37

I raked my fingers through my hair and let my phone fall onto the bed in front of me. For hours, I'd researched how to stay in Paris. The more I searched, the faster my heart beat.

I didn't have any more time to figure this out. My savings account was draining faster than I expected and I couldn't afford another week in this hotel with no other sort of income. Besides, I wasn't sure how many more times I could walk through the lobby in tears without the hotel asking questions.

I was in love with a vampire.

My friend was dead.

I shook my head, trying not to think too hard about Willa. If I did, I would dissolve into hysterics again.

Across the room, Holland's eyes drooped when he looked up from his book. He stayed with me last night, but never came into the bed. He didn't touch me again after healing my bruises. My stomach twinged wondering if he sat in the chair near the wardrobe all night long - waiting, watching. Instead of saying anything, I picked up my phone again, and the notebook next to me on the bed - scribbling down more notes.

First, I would have to find a job with a company that didn't mind me working from France. I didn't particularly care what the job was, as long as it paid well enough for me to stay here.

I would need to get a long-term visa, which would require going home for the application process. A little voice in the back of my mind warned me that if I went home, I might not come back. I might lose my nerve... I might let my mother convince me I belonged there... something, anything. I was a fucking coward.

I needed to get an apartment.

My stomach growled, and I sighed. It was late morning; I needed to find food, especially since I hadn't eaten dinner. I buried my face in my pillow, resisting the urge to scream into it.

"I could offer a simpler solution, though I imagine your answer is no," Holland spoke, his voice raspy from his silence.

"I don't want to go home," I said, harsher than I intended.

He raised an eyebrow. "No, my love. You could die."

A laugh bubbled up in my chest. Holland sat back in his chair, watching me laugh. The idea sounded so absurd for a moment that I couldn't contain my amusement. Except, the moment ended and he still watched me seriously. My hands fell to my sides. I gaped at him.

"What?" I asked.

Holland shrugged. "The dead live entirely under the radar. We don't need visas, or citizenship, because we don't exist."

I shook my head, clenching my hands into fists and pushing myself out of bed. "That's ridiculous. That's not an option."

"I figured, just throwing it out there," he said.

I placed my hand on my forehead. "No, I'll figure this out. Plenty of people do it, right? Even if I have to go home for a little while, I'll figure out the visa and I'll be on the next flight out."

Holland stood, walking to stand in front of me. I gulped when he tilted my chin up. I couldn't escape the desperation on his face. "Don't leave me," he whispered.

I jolted in surprise. Holland's eyes were wide; a thin red line on his waterline betrayed his fear. I reached up to brush his hair off his forehead and rest my hand on his cheek. "Nothing has to be decided today," I told him, even though my stomach clenched with nerves.

Holland drew in a shaky breath. "Go somewhere with me tomorrow," he said.

I tilted my head. "Where?"

"I'll pick you up in the morning?" He asked, taking a step back. Then another towards the door.

"You're leaving?"

"I have plans to make." He smiled, and it reached his eyes, glittering gold. I wasn't prepared to be breathless at the sight.

I nodded. "Can I call Willa?"

"Yes. You can see her if you'd like, but only if Thierry is there too." Holland approached me again, leaning down to kiss my cheek.

I turned my head at the last moment, catching his mouth with mine. I couldn't resist. Holland *whimpered* into the kiss, the noise sending shivers down my spine. I pushed myself up on my toes to kiss him harder, tracing my tongue over his lip. He opened his mouth to me, one arm winding around my waist and the other tangling in my hair.

Then, he pulled away.

I gasped at the disconnect, nearly stumbling backward. Holland cleared his throat. Black veins rippled across his face. He retreated, shaking his head and taking a few deep breaths. I sobered, sitting on the edge of the bed.

"I'm sorry," I breathed.

"Believe me," he murmured. "I would love to throw you into that bed if you asked me to, but I'm starving - and I don't-"

"Okay," I interrupted. "I'll see you in the morning."

Holland's fangs retracted when he smiled. He retreated, pausing at the door before turning again. "I love you, Adalyn."

My cheeks burned red and my heart skipped a beat. It had been so long since I believed someone when they said that to me. Holland's eyes glistened when he spoke. He meant it.

He was gone before I could respond.

I knocked quietly on Willa's hotel room, hoping she would be there.

When I heard the noise from inside, my stomach flipped. There wasn't enough time to back out of my decision to check on her. The door opened a moment later.

Willa beamed when she saw me. I barely heard her babbling about going shopping. My heart beat in my throat when I stepped into her room. Thierry lounged back on her bed and offered me a cool smile.

Willa paused mid-sentence, raising an eyebrow. I tensed when she looked me over from head to toe. "You smell like Holland. How strange," she said. She wrinkled her nose, like the smell was distasteful.

"Sorry," I said nervously. "How are you doing?"

Willa beamed, sitting on the edge of the bed. "I've never been better. I feel invincible."

I glanced at Thierry again. He paid no attention to either of us. He scrolled through his phone idly.

"Willa, what happened?" I asked.

Her smile faltered. She crossed her hands in her lap and inclined her chin. "My father drowned my older brother because he didn't want to inherit the ranch one day," she said quietly. "If I went home with my mother, there would have been an *accident* in six months or so, and I would be dead. I didn't want to go back just to die. I didn't know what else to do."

"Where's your mom?" I asked.

"Oh, I gave her the fright of her life and she boarded the next plane home." Willa grinned again. The red rim appeared around her eyes and her fangs extended. "My family is excruciatingly Catholic. I'm sure the sight of her daughter with fangs was enough to get her to pray for weeks."

I swallowed thickly. "So, what are you going to do?"

Willa shrugged; her features returned to normal. "I'll stay with Thierry for a while until I figure it out. What are you going to do?"

I opened and closed my mouth a few times before sighing. "I don't know yet."

Willa stared at me for a moment too long. "Have you always smelled sweet?"

I tensed.

"Willa," Thierry warned behind her.

She ran her hands through her hair. "I'm sorry, I don't mean it. It feels like there's a lot going on." She took a deep breath and smiled again. "Thierry and I were going to the Champs-Élysées, want to come?"

"I would love to," I said.

I walked arm-in-arm with Willa, thinking that there was no way this girl was dangerous. She chattered about the fall leaves, and the pleasant breeze, and bought us both macarons to snack on. Thierry walked a couple of steps behind us, hardly interested. We ducked into a few stores, only to walk back out quickly when we realized we couldn't afford a single one of these.

"We want to do the Arc de Triomphe," Willa told Thierry. He waved us off.

Willa's face fell at his dismissal. I took her arm again, dragging her towards the monument. She skipped next to me as we walked below the street, resurfacing in the heart of Paris.

Two hundred and eighty-four stairs later, we reached the top.

My breath caught as I looked around. I could see every part of the city.

Willa was crying.

"Hey, what's wrong?" I touched her arm, immediately pulling a tissue from my bag to help her wipe away the bloody tears.

She turned towards me. "I didn't want to die," she whispered. I blinked in shock. "I didn't see another option. And, I thought Thierry would be excited. He's less interested in me than he ever has been, and is treating me like I'm an inconvenience. All he cares about is getting his sister to answer the phone."

My heart ached for her. She'd lost everything.

Including her life.

Willa gulped. "Can I tell you something, and you promise not to tell Holland?"

I sucked in a breath. "Willa," I started.

"Thierry didn't save me," she blurted, interrupting me. All the blood drained from my face. I felt dizzy. "He sat there and watched me bleed out until my heart stopped."

I trembled.

Willa shook her head. "The only thing I can think of is that Holland gave me his blood to heal my bite marks a few days ago.

I didn't think it was still in my system, but Thierry did nothing. I died and still woke up hours later. I love him, and he let me die."

"Can I hug you?" I asked.

She nodded, sniffling.

I wrapped my arms around my friend and promised I'd never leave her behind.

CHAPTER 38

"So, he didn't tell you where he's taking you?" Willa asked.

"Nope," I replied, shifting uncomfortably in front of the fitting room mirror.

"Come out, please," she chirped, as if she anticipated my discomfort in the golden slip.

I let out a long breath, poking my head out to make sure no one else was around before stepping fully out of the fitting room. The satin slip left little to the imagination, hugging every curve of my body. Willa beamed as she took in the sight of me.

"Now, that'll have him on his knees," she whistled.

I gulped.

"Are things okay with you two?" She asked.

I shrugged. "There's just a lot going on, I think."

"Dead best friends?" Willa teased.

My shoulders slumped. "How are you okay with this?"

She stiffened. "Because if I'm not, I'll break. If I think too hard about the pulse in your throat, I'll lose my mind. Or if I think about how the man I love let me die, I'll shatter. So, I'm focusing on helping you pick out lingerie to seduce the vampire who worships the ground you walk on."

Forcing away the quiver in my lips, I straightened and spun in a circle. "Okay, gold or black?"

"Definitely gold." She grinned.

I went back into the changing room to take off the slip.

"So, I'm thinking I'm gonna stay," Willa said through the door.

"In Paris?"

"Yeah. Why not, right? I was thinking I could restart my candle business here."

I paused at her words. "That's a great idea."

"I thought so."

"I'm sure there's a market for it," I told Willa, leaning over her laptop. "It might take time, but you have a huge following. Would they pay for international shipping?"

Willa pursed her lips and took a sip of champagne. "They might," she shrugged.

It was well after dark. We sat in Willa's hotel room, flipping through her business plans and what it would take for her to start over in Paris. It seemed easier to help her than it was to figure it out for myself. I wanted to ask how being a vampire played into this, but I wasn't sure she knew the answer - so I didn't bring it up.

"What if you helped?" Willa asked suddenly. I tilted my head in confusion. "You need a reason to stay, right? We could get an apartment and run this business together. And I promise I won't terrorize Holland too much."

I stared at my friend for a moment, piecing together what she said. "You're serious?"

Willa grinned. "Of course, I am."

If I had questions before about how being a vampire would change Willa, they were gone. She was still Willa. Her smile was the same. Her laugh was the same. Sure, she watched people a little more intently - sometimes longingly like all she wanted was them. And I caught her watching me like that twice today. Each time, she cleared her throat and pushed away whatever she was thinking.

"Say yes, Addie," she begged. "Stay in Paris with me."

Don't leave me, Holland said.

I sighed. "I still don't know about a visa."

Willa rolled her eyes. "My parents are millionaires, I'm sure I could pull some strings for you. Say yes."

My shoulders slumped and I took her outstretched hand. "Okay," I agreed.

Willa leaped out of bed with an overjoyed cheer. I barely caught the bottle of champagne before she knocked it over.

My phone dinged; I reached for it to read the text from Holland.

Picking you up at 6. Pack an overnight bag.

"Is that lover boy?" Willa fell back on the bed, snatching the bottle from me and taking a big drink. She peered over my shoulder at the text. "He won't spill?"

I shrugged. "Nope."

Willa patted my leg excitedly. "Take the lingerie!"

I blushed, laughing as I responded. **See you soon.**

I set down my phone and turned to Willa. She crossed her hands in her lap and wiggled her eyebrows at me. "He said he loves me," I blurted.

Willa threw her arms in the air and howled. A warm, fuzzy

feeling spread through me as I watched my friend cheer and thought about the vampire who loved me.

I came to Paris to find myself.

While I wasn't sure I had yet, it was starting to feel miraculously like I'd found people to call my family. And... I liked how that felt.

CHAPTER 39

I sucked in a deep breath as the phone rang in my hand. One ring. Two. Three.

Please, answer.

"Hello?" Donna's voice echoed through the room, piercing my heart.

"Hey," I whispered.

"Addie? Why are you calling me?" Immediately, she sounded guarded.

I rubbed my hands on my thighs. A single tear dripped down my cheek. "To apologize."

Silence.

I gulped down my nausea and started talking. "I started running from you the day I spilled wine on your grandmother's quilt. You were heartbroken, angry, and we didn't know if it was fixable yet. That was the first time you told me you hoped I drowned."

"We'd only been together six months," Donna breathed.

I nodded, knowing she couldn't see me. "I spent the next five years running, hiding, and pushing you just far enough away that you'd come back to me again. It was the only way I knew how to love you."

"Why are you telling me this?"

"Because I'm going to stay in Paris," I said. "Live here, work here, maybe even die here. I'm moving on, and I didn't want to move on without telling you I'm sorry for my part in how we ended."

"I never wanted you to drown, Addie," Donna whispered. "I always wanted you to breathe."

I struggled to take another deep breath. "Goodbye, Donna."

"Goodbye, Adalyn. I hope you find happiness."

The line went dead.

Pulling my knees to my chest, I sobbed quietly. I shook my head, not wanting to wallow. I leaped out of bed, shoving things into a backpack - a couple of changes of clothes, my toothbrush, and the lingerie I'd bought earlier in the day. Blinded, I ran out of the hotel room and out onto the cold Paris streets.

I took the metro since it was faster than walking.

Holland was waiting when I made it up the stairs to his apartment door. He leaned against the doorway, concern filling his face. He wore a pair of pajama pants, but no shirt. His hair was messy from sleep. My heart skipped a beat, feeling lighter somehow. I dropped my backpack on the ground at our feet and threw my arms around his neck.

Holland kissed me hesitantly, stiff with shock. He tasted like chocolate.

"What are you doing here?" He breathed, resting his forehead on mine. "Are you okay?"

I nodded, a stray tear running down my face. "I feel like I can finally breathe."

Holland smiled when he leaned down to kiss me again,

drawing me into his apartment. He kicked my backpack into the room without releasing me. His kiss deepened once the door shut behind us. I opened my mouth to his tongue, shivers running through me at the feel of him against me. I yelped when Holland hoisted me into his arms, carrying me across the room. He rested me back on his bed, the blankets already ruffled from his sleep. He sat up a moment, popping the buttons of my pants and pulling them off in one fluid movement. I let him undress me, high off the feeling of his mouth over every inch of me.

Holland's tongue left trails over my skin as he kissed and licked his way down my body. He groaned as he settled himself between my thighs. I gasped when he took me in his mouth, his tongue dipping inside me before swiping up to my clit. He sucked deeply, sending shocks through me like lightning.

Holland sat up, running his fingers over my lips, asking for entrance. I stuck my tongue out and took him in my mouth, sucking gently and swirling my tongue around. He groaned, his eyes wide. I watched as he moved his hand to my core. A deep, desperate moan escaped me as he pushed into me. His fingers curled inside me, pulling another gasp of delight.

"Would you like me to make you cum with my hand or my tongue?" He asked.

"Yes," I whispered, clutching the sheets. Holland chuckled, laying back down. His tongue joined the movements of his fingers, lapping against me hungrily. Holland licked and sucked while the heat built in my stomach. His fingers pumped into me quickly, his tongue flicking against my clit in perfect unison.

As soon as my orgasm built, it ripped through me. Holland raised his head with a gasp for air, fucking me with his fingers as I rode out my high.

"That's it, come for me," he growled. "Again, Adalyn."

He lowered his mouth, finding the perfect spot that made me

come again before my first one was through. My back arched from the bed; I pushed myself against his face. I think I screamed. Holland sat up when I stopped quivering. He kissed his way up my body again, groaning into our kiss.

He rolled off me and stripped naked. I rolled onto my back on the edge of the bed near where he stood, eagerly opening my mouth. Holland pushed his length into my mouth, thrusting slowly. I slid my tongue along him, moaning when he leaned forward to slip his fingers between my thighs. He rubbed circles on me in rhythm with his thrusts into my mouth.

"You're a fucking godsend," he growled. "I wish you could see how well you take my cock."

Oh, my god.

I'd never been with someone who talked like Holland. Every one of his words went straight to my core, pulsing through me and making me more desperate for him. I never would have expected it from him, always so polite and poetic. He growled as he thrust into my mouth. Saliva dripped down my face as I struggled to keep myself from gagging.

Holland pulled back, taking himself in his hand. "On your knees." He growled.

I rolled over, bending low and shaking my hips. Holland laughed, gripping my thighs. I felt him behind me, jumping when he swiped his length up and down my entrance. I sat back suddenly, pushing myself onto him. Holland snarled as he sank into me all at once.

"Fucking desperate, aren't you?"

"For you? Yes," I gasped.

Holland gripped my hips, thrusting into me. He pulled all the way out before sliding back into me again. Frantic whines escaped me with each torturous movement.

"Please," I whined.

"Tell me what you want," Holland growled. His hand came down on my ass with a loud *smack*. I yelped, pushing back into him. He hummed, raising his hand again. I sobbed with the next smack, my eyes rolling back in delight.

"Fuck me harder," I begged.

Holland obliged.

Instantly, his hands gripped my hips as he pounded into me hard and fast. I dropped one hand between my thighs, rubbing circles on my clit as Holland's hips slapped against mine. He reached down suddenly, wrapping one arm around my waist and pulling me up so my back pressed against his front. I let my head fall back on his shoulder, my cries echoing through the room. Holland dropped his head, kissing over my throat hungrily. With his free hand, he replaced mine between my thighs, humming when I gasped at the sensation.

Every nerve was on fire after two orgasms; I writhed in Holland's arms, unsure whether I pushed into his touch or pulled away from it. His arm around my waist slid up to my throat, holding me tightly against him.

"I want you to come. Now," he whispered in my ear.

Holland sped up the movements of his fingers, tilting me over the edge for the third time. He followed me over it, clinging to me like I was everything.

I fell forward onto the pillows as soon as his grip on my throat loosened. Holland swore, falling after me and apologizing. I laughed, my throat raw. I accepted the gentle kisses he peppered over my face, curling into him.

"What time is it?" I asked.

"Almost three," he hummed.

I sighed. "I want to sleep so badly, but I'm sticky and want to shower."

Holland smiled. "Want help?"

"Can you keep your hands to yourself for ten minutes?" I teased.

His eyes flashed with delight. "Probably not."

I grinned, sliding out of bed and holding out my hand for him to join me. He took it.

CHAPTER 40

My eyes were heavy when Holland kissed me awake the next morning. I whined deeply, shaking my head and trying to pull the blanket over my head. Holland chuckled and tugged it away, flicking his tongue against my jaw with several warm kisses.

"Good morning," he hummed. "You look ravishing." I snorted, blinking up at him. "Come on. Coffee will be ready in a moment."

I rolled with a groan, checking the time. It was five-thirty. We'd only slept for two hours. Resisting the desire to cry, I pushed myself out of bed. Thankfully, Holland left me alone while I did my makeup and pulled my hair into a high ponytail. I dressed quickly, walked out of the bathroom, and accepted the travel mug of coffee he offered me. I gripped it like my life depended on it.

"It's a bit chilly out this morning, do you have a sweater?" Holland asked.

"Yeah," I said. Holland raised an eyebrow. I realized, after a delayed moment, that he was waiting for me to get it. "Sorry," I mumbled, walking to my backpack. "It's early."

"Promise me something," he whispered, wrapping his arms around my waist from behind me when I stood again. I sighed, leaning back into him. "For the next thirty-six hours, don't worry about anything else."

I opened my mouth to protest.

Holland didn't let me speak. "I'm serious, Adalyn. I'm only asking for thirty-six hours. Give us a chance for that long, and we can worry about everything else when we get back."

I turned to face him, reaching up to brush a lock of hair out of his face. "I promise," I said.

A smile spread across his face. He kissed the tip of my nose. "Great, let's go."

"When will you tell me where we're going?" I asked, grabbing my backpack and slinging it over my shoulder.

"When we get there." Holland grinned.

He took me to Versailles.

We barely spent a moment in a hotel room covered in floral and butterfly wallpaper. Holland opened a box on the bed and offered me a pink satin dress to wear for the rest of the day. I changed in the bathroom. When I came back out, Holland wore slacks and a black button-up. He looked dashing. I blushed bright red at the sight of him, accepting the gentle kisses he offered me.

I trembled in excitement one step behind Holland on the way to breakfast, eager to explore the grounds and the palace. It was chilly out today, but the sun felt warm. I held Holland's hand and my jaw nearly hit the ground at the breakfast spread. There was even a pitcher of red liquid in the middle of the table - blood. Holland held my chair for me before sitting across the table.

"What is this?" I asked with wide eyes.

"Breakfast," Holland said, pouring both of us a glass of champagne.

"No, this. What are we doing here?" I gestured to the grounds around us.

Holland paused, licking his lips. "I'm showing you what life would be like if you stayed." My breath caught. I opened my mouth to respond, but he continued. "I want you to stay, Adalyn. I want you to know that, if you stay, I'll make every day feel like this one."

"Holland," I laughed once.

"Let me finish," Holland said. "The first day I saw you, I thought that I'd never seen someone look so alone in a place so beautiful." I winced. "And now - there's a sparkle in your eye that I could drown in. This isn't about me, my love. Well, that's a lie, it's about me a little because I love you, but it's more about me being afraid that, if you leave, the sparkle in your eyes will die and you'll forget how you felt with me, with Willa, in Paris."

I brushed a tear before it escaped.

"You don't have to have an answer today, or even this week, but give me today to prove to you how happy you could be here," he begged.

I pushed out of my chair, walking around the table. Holland seemed confused until I leaned down and crushed my lips against his. My whole body vibrated with excitement.

I decided not to tell him about my discussion with Willa. If I could get a visa and an apartment with her, and invest in being a co-owner of her candle business... this could work.

Don't leave me, Holland had said.

I would let him have today.

I returned to my chair across from him, my cheeks bright red. Holland lifted his glass of champagne for a toast. I clinked mine against his with a smile.

After breakfast, I walked hand-in-hand with Holland for a tour of the Grand Trianon. Every chance he got, when our tour guide's back was turned, his hands were on me. On my back, my neck, my wrist - brief, delicate touches that set my soul on fire. I tried to pay attention to the history and architecture; all I could think about was Holland.

Especially after he placed a gentle kiss to my throat and his lips grazed my ear.

"You're a fucking tease," I whispered, lacing my arm through his.

"I have no idea what you mean," he said, unable to hide his smirk.

I whined quietly, squeezing his arm. Holland chuckled, keeping his eyes straightforward. A couple of the other people in our group asked questions. I moved to follow them and the guide; Holland squeezed my hand and stopped me. I opened my mouth to argue. He placed one finger over his lips, watching the tour group walk further and further without us.

I tilted my head in confusion.

Holland gripped my hand, taking a few slow steps back before dragging me with him. We turned a few corners into a large room with an extravagant golden chandelier, accented by turquoise blue chairs and curtains.

Before I could ask what was happening, Holland stepped over the ropes and nudged me up against the wall. His mouth covered mine in a hungry, frantic kiss. I melted into him with every ounce of myself, already tingling after his relentless teasing the last few hours. He tasted like champagne and chocolate.

He felt like home.

I kissed him harder, tangling my fingers in his hair and holding him against me. His hands explored every inch of me, like he could never get enough. Holland ground his hips against mine, sending waves of desire through me. Right then, I would have done whatever he wanted. I wanted whatever he offered. I wanted it then... I wanted it forever.

Holland trailed wet kisses down my neck and over my chest. I covered my mouth, afraid I would whimper and it would echo through every room of the Trianon. Holland knelt, his hands tracing up the outsides of my thighs. My eyes widened.

"What are you doing?" I gasped.

Holland's hands traveled higher. "I was hoping to taste you."

I glanced around. "Here? We could get caught."

He smirked. His fingers looped around my underwear. I didn't stop him from pulling them down. I placed my hand on my chest to calm my racing heart.

Holland licked his lips. "The tour group is six rooms ahead of us, and the next closest group of people is outside. I'll be quick - yes or no?"

"Yes," I said without thinking.

Holland grinned, lifting my dress around my hips. I barely had another moment to worry about getting caught before Holland buried his face between my thighs, his tongue swiping over the warmest part of me. He groaned deeply, boosting one of my legs to rest over his shoulder. I tangled one hand in his hair, gasping at the feeling of his tongue tracing circles on my clit.

I caught sight of myself in a mirror across the room, my eyes widening. I blushed bright pink, my hair a mess, a man between my thighs - and I looked... beautiful. Happy.

My eyes fluttered shut and I let my head fall back against the wall. Holland held onto me tightly with one hand. His other one joined his tongue between my legs. He pushed one finger, then two, inside of me. My cry echoed through the halls. I covered my mouth again. The vampire on his knees chuckled deeply, pumping his fingers in and out of me with the rhythm of his tongue - slow and steady. I felt him curl his fingers inside me and I moaned at the sensation.

Sunlight burst into the room from behind a cloud, warming my skin. Holland consumed me like the sweetest dessert, his moans echoing through the room as he coaxed the dawn from within me.

I forgot we were in a public, historical palace. The brighter the sun grew within me, the closer I came to letting go of everything. I forgot the blush on my cheeks when Holland pushed my dress further up around my waist, both exposing me and giving himself better access. The sunrise ignited.

Yes, yes, yes.

Another pump of his fingers and curl of his tongue and I saw daylight. My cries echoed as I clung to Holland, my mind fracturing. He held me up, still rubbing his tongue against me as I came down from my orgasm.

"Fuck," I whispered.

Holland glanced up, his lips pink and swollen. A smile pulled at his mouth as he stood, letting my leg fall. I moved to step away from the wall; Holland held me there, undoing his belt.

"Holland," I warned.

"No one's coming," he murmured, his mouth brushing mine.

I smiled, reaching up to trace his jaw. "Well, fuck me then."

Holland growled, kissing me deeply. I felt him undo his pants, pushing them slightly over his hips. I wrapped two arms around his neck, giggling when he lifted me like I weighed nothing. My legs wound around his waist. He pushed into me, both of our moans blending with our kiss. Holland broke our kiss, reaching up to wrap one hand around my neck and hold me against the wall as he thrust into me. My eyes rolled back in delight.

"I love how your blood rushes when I fuck you," Holland growled. I shivered at the sight of his red-rimmed eyes. "My pretty, pretty girl."

"Your girl," I echoed, dazed.

Holland's grip tightened and his thrusts came harder. "Yes, my love. Mine."

I watched Holland's mouth as he let his head fall back with a groan. His lips parted, revealing two perfectly sharp fangs. A shiver ran through me as I thought of what they could do... what I wanted them to do.

I wanted to belong to Holland, in every way he would have me.

He came back to me, his mouth covering mine in a long kiss. "As much as I'd love for you to come again, we're running a bit low on time," he murmured.

"Bend me over a table and use me for yourself," I said.

Holland snarled, pulling away from me so quickly I wanted to cry. He kept his hand around my throat, dragging me to the closest table. I tried not to think about how old the furniture might have been, or how many laws we were breaking. Instead, I let my hand fall between my legs as I bent over the table. Holland peppered kisses down my cheek to my shoulder. His hands gripped my hips when he rubbed himself against my entrance and pushed in, filling me.

This time, I let my cry echo.

"You're dripping wet for me," Holland whispered. "It feels fucking amazing."

I rubbed my fingers over my clit as Holland fucked me. The table creaked beneath my weight. Holland's growls echoed with my cries and the slap of skin-on-skin contact. The room became a cacophony of our love. I touched myself harder and faster, feeling another sunrise within me... another orgasm within reach.

Thrust after thrust, I lost myself to Holland.

When my second orgasm crashed through me, I forgot my own name.

Holland finished with a roar seconds after I did. I swore our cries made the windows rattle.

I was still shaking when Holland stepped away. He pulled a handkerchief from his pocket, kissing my shoulder while he cleaned me up. I fixed my underwear and brushed my fingers through my hair, blushing brightly.

He paused, tilting his head. "We gotta go."

Then, it was our laughter that echoed as he took me by the hand and dragged me outside.

CHAPTER 41

H ours later, I lay on a blanket in the grass with Holland. After our tour of the Grand Trianon, and our rendezvous, Holland drove a golf cart around the grounds of Versailles for most of the day. Our exploring was constantly interrupted with kisses in the shadows - deep in the gardens, behind the trees at the Queen's Hamlet, in the quiet hallway of the Petit Trianon. I felt like I was on fire, glowing from Holland's attention.

We had a private tour of the main castle and the Hall of Mirrors in a couple of hours. While we waited, we lay in the sunshine and watched the swans on the lake. Holland lay next to me. I used his chest as a pillow, my eyes heavy. I'd been here for a while, listening to his impossibly slow heartbeat. The rhythm was hypnotizing.

"Don't fall asleep," Holland's voice startled me.

"Sorry," I laughed once, rolling onto my back and stretching on our blanket.

Holland rolled to face me, his eyes soft. I accepted the kiss he offered with a delighted hum.

"Tell me something I don't know about you," Holland said quietly.

I pursed my lips, watching a swan skid across the water as I thought of something good enough. My breath quivered when I turned back to him, watching the sun dance in the gold of his eyes.

"My favorite book is about a girl who sells her soul to live forever," I told him. "It explores what makes life worth living."

"What do you think makes life worth it?"

I shrugged. "I think anyone can cling to anything to find a reason to live. Love. Pain. Alcohol. Painting."

"And you?"

My heart skipped a beat. "You first, you've lived much longer than me."

Holland lay back on the blanket, blinking up at the sun. "It changes every day. What keeps me alive now certainly wouldn't have done it a decade or a hundred years ago," he said. "The breeze through the park, the couple in new love at the Trocadéro, fine wine, a girl made of midnight rain." Holland looked at me with soft eyes. "The way the sun makes her hair burn like fire. The shadow of the tattoos on her leg. The curves of her hips. The way she tastes. The pink of her cheeks when she realizes I'm talking about her."

I laughed.

"I love you," Holland murmured. Something sad flashed on his face.

My heart swelled. "Say it again."

He sat up, pulling me up to straddle his lap. He brushed my hair out of my face. "I love you," he said, and kissed me.

He said it between every kiss. Each one grew deeper. His tongue danced against mine. His hands tangled in my hair. I clung to the collar of his shirt. His mouth fell from mine to my jaw, to my neck, to my chest, and back to my throat. He groaned deeply, dragging his tongue across my skin. I shivered nervously, well aware of what went through his mind. I realized, with a shaking breath, that I wanted him to bite down and take what he needed from me.

He pulled away with a soft hiss. I reached up to tilt his chin up. Holland blinked up at me with red-rimmed eyes.

"I'm sorry," he whispered.

I traced my fingers over the blackened veins of his face before leaning forward to kiss him again. "Later," I murmured against his mouth.

Holland stiffened beneath me, pulling back to search my face. His brow furrowed. "Adalyn, you don't have to-"

My eyes dropped to his mouth. A new desire coursed through me. "I want you to."

"Fuck," he swore, leaning up to kiss me again.

I fell off Holland's lap when someone whistled nearby. My cheeks burned bright, but I laughed with Holland. I leaned over to pepper his face with kisses; his laugh gave me butterflies.

"I love you," I said.

Holland smiled.

And I was home.

Our tour of the Hall of Mirrors was private. Holland nodded to the man at the entrance to the hall, reaching over to shake his hand. I barely saw the flash of the bills and tried to cover my smile.

The room glittered in the sunset. Immediately, I felt warmer and lighter, turning in a circle and watching the sun dance off the gold and the mirrors. Holland walked a step behind me, quiet as I resisted the urge to cry. When I turned to him, my eyes watered when he held out his hand for a dance. I smoothed out the front of my dress, approaching and stepping into frame with him.

"Where'd you learn to waltz?" he asked as he stepped forward to a silent count.

"My ex-fiancé and I took lessons years ago. I can foxtrot too, if you're interested."

Holland smiled. "I can't foxtrot, but I would learn for you."

I laughed, stepping into the turn he set up for me. To my shock, instead of finishing the box, he dipped me backward. His mouth covered mine in a deep kiss. I beamed when he pulled me up, moving into perfect step again. I alternated between getting lost in his eyes and watching us in the mirrors. The room grew brighter and more golden the longer we danced, lost in our own world.

"I'm going to stay," I said suddenly, mid-step.

Holland's lips parted in shock, and he stopped the dance. He didn't let go of me. I sucked in a deep breath, my heart racing as I stared up at him.

"Don't say things you don't mean," he whispered.

I shook my head. I brushed a strand of hair out of his face. "I'm going to stay, Holland. Whatever it takes."

A red tear escaped, trailing down his face. He leaned down, kissing me deeply. When he pulled back, he smiled from ear to ear and spun me in a circle again. Our laughter echoed through the hall. I fell into his arms, burying my face in his chest.

"I will love you till the sun dies," Holland murmured, holding me tight.

In his eyes, I somehow found everything I'd ever wanted. "And then I'll love you in the dark."

CHAPTER 42

Holland held the door open for me, his eyes never leaving my face as I stepped inside the room before him. My heart pounded in my chest as I remembered what I promised him tonight. My blood.

Except, I'd given him so much more today. I gave him me, for as long as he'd have me.

He walked into the bathroom, and I heard the water start. I glanced from the bathroom to the bed, to the last of the dying sun outside our window. After a moment's hesitation, I followed Holland into the bathroom. I lingered in the doorway, watching him sprinkle bath salts and bubbles into the tub.

"Dinner will be delivered in about an hour," Holland said.

"Okay," I breathed.

Holland pursed his lips, crossing the bathroom to pull a robe off the hook and rest it on the chair next to the bath. He held out his hand to me. I took it, humming into the kiss he immediately pressed to my cheek. He stepped behind me, undoing the zipper of my dress and nudging the straps over my shoulders. His fingers were gentle on my skin, but left trails of fire behind them. The dress fell in a heap around my feet and Holland snapped the clasp on my bra too.

A moment later, I stood naked in front of him. His eyes stayed on my face as he held out his hand to help me into the bath. I sank into the warm, lavender-scented water with a sigh.

I rested my head on the back of the tub, breathing evenly. My eyes slipped closed. Holland sat in the chair next to the tub, his hand on my shoulder. I smiled when he leaned down to kiss my jaw and my cheek.

"Whatever happens tonight," he whispered. "You're in control, okay? I will do whatever you ask of me."

I blinked up at him. "Thank you."

He smiled slightly. I could have sworn he was nervous. I reached up to take his hand, letting my eyes slip closed again. Holland sat with me for a while, rubbing my shoulders and brushing my hair while I rested in the bath. He brought me a rag to wash the makeup off my face, and a glass of champagne after a while.

"I'm going to shower," he said, kissing my shoulder.

I watched him cross the bathroom and start the shower. Sipping my champagne, I shifted beneath the water as I watched my vampire undress. His clothes fell to the floor piece by piece until he stood completely naked. He brushed his hair in the mirror. If he knew I watched him, he didn't acknowledge it. Instead, he stepped into the shower and let the water rush over his skin. I licked my lips, my heart beating faster. Holland washed his hair, soap leaving trails in every crevice of his skin. He faced away from me, mostly, the muscles in his back rippling as he moved.

"Fucking hell," I whispered to myself, letting my head fall back.

In the shower, Holland chuckled. I turned pink.

I looked over at him again when the water stopped and he stepped out, wrapping a towel around his waist before my eyes could explore lower than his waistline. He dried his hair with a towel in the mirror, crossing the bathroom again to sit behind me.

"Miss me?" he murmured, kissing my cheek. I nodded. "How much?" His voice darkened.

I shivered. "Desperately."

Holland leaned down, his lips brushing my ear when he spoke. "Show me."

I wanted to turn towards him, desperate for him to kiss me, touch me, anything. Holland stopped me; catching my hand and guiding it beneath the water, between my thighs. My heart beat in my throat, but I did as he asked. My breath caught as I touched myself. Holland released me and sank into the chair behind me. I could hear his breathing, but I couldn't see him. I jumped when his hands traced my shoulders.

"Go on," he coaxed quietly.

I focused on tracing my fingers in circles where I ached for him. Small gasps escaped me in unison with the splashes of pleasure I gave myself. I took my time, feeling every inch of myself with my fingers, knowing Holland watched. Carefully, I pushed one finger inside, then two, and didn't bother to stop my deep moan. Behind me, Holland's breath shook.

I was hyper-aware of the man behind me as I coaxed the knot to build in my stomach - alternating between rubbing circles on my clit and pumping my fingers inside me. I let my gasps and moans echo through the hotel room with each new sensation.

"That's my girl," Holland whispered, his voice breaking. "Make yourself come."

I nodded, whining frantically. I moved my fingers faster, shifting my hips beneath the water like it would help me get there sooner. Holland leaned down, his lips brushing my jaw. I tilted my head back into his delicate kisses, my back arching as the knot in my stomach grew tighter and tighter.

"Fuck, Holland, I-" I broke off mid-sentence as the world shattered around me.

I trembled as I came down from my high. Holland kisses my cheek, his hands on my shoulders the only sense of reality I had for an extended moment. My eyes finally opened when my body stopped shaking. Holland leaned down, kissing me deeply.

"My turn to make you come," he whispered against my mouth.

Oh.

He helped me out of the tub, his eyes dark while I dried off and wrapped the robe around myself. Holland took my hand, leading me towards the bedroom. I held his gaze, my heart pounding with anticipation. Holland backed me up until my calves hit the back of the bed. I fell back against the mattress, giggling when Holland caught my hips and pushed the robe aside.

He trailed kisses down the insides of my thighs, wasting no time in swiping his tongue up my core. I gasped, clutching the blankets on either side of me as Holland buried his face between my thighs. His tongue worked quickly against my already-sensitive clit, sucking and licking. His hands dug into my hips as he held me still for his work.

His moans were music to my ears as he pleasured me. I felt every move he made. Each time his fingers pushed against my skin, every flick of his tongue, every breath he made. He glanced up at me, taking a deep breath.

"You're a beautiful mess," he murmured. "Say my name when you come again."

His mouth found me again, and the world imploded.

I didn't say his name when I came.

I screamed it.

"How do you even ask for that?" I asked Holland over dinner, motioning to the carafe of blood sitting next to him on the table.

He hummed. "Money keeps secrets, my love."

"You don't even work," I said.

"I'm almost two centuries old, my love. I have investments that keep me comfortable."

Laughing once, I reached for my glass of champagne. "Investments in what?"

"Right now?" Holland said. "Major tech companies, mostly. I've invested in oil, cars, and a few other things that have gone dormant and left money sitting in accounts."

"So, now you spend your time in Paris parks, painting pretty girls?" I teased.

Holland brought his glass to his lips, a devious glint in his eye. "Fucking them too."

My laughter rang through the room. Holland grinned. I finished the rest of my glass, setting it on the table and pulling my robe tighter around myself. I wore the golden slip beneath the robe, and each time I felt it brush my skin, I thought about how it would feel beneath Holland's hands.

"Did you get enough to eat?" Holland asked.

"I think so," I said. Holland poured himself another glass of blood - his third, I thought. His hand shook ever so slightly when he lifted the pitcher. "Are you alright?"

He cleared his throat. "I'm fine, why?"

"You seem anxious," I said.

"I am," he sat back.

I paused, setting down my glass. "Why?"

Holland took a long drink, his eyes trailing over me. It was unmistakable where they landed - on my throat.

"I trust you," I said.

Holland's eyes met mine. "That makes one of us."

I stood and walked around the table. I placed my hands on his shoulders and leaned down to kiss his cheek. "You don't have to if you don't want to, but I would like to know what it's like when you're ready," I said.

Holland nodded. I kissed his cheek again, harder this time. He leaned into the touch, his eyes closing. I returned to my spot across from him, downing the rest of my glass of champagne. My mind buzzed from the champagne, making the world seem rose-colored. Holland looked between me and his glass again, nodding to himself. He tilted the rest of it back before standing from the table and disappearing into the bathroom.

I left the table, hesitating only a moment before shrugging out of the robe I wore to reveal the golden slip beneath it. Taking a deep breath, I smoothed the fabric over my stomach. I crawled onto the bed, laying back against the pillows.

When Holland returned, he reached for a piece of chocolate from the table - popping it in his mouth. His eyes found me a moment later and he cleared his throat, his eyes widening considerably. He sat on the bed next to me as he rolled chocolate on his tongue, watching me with a curious glint in his eyes.

"That's pretty," he said, his eyes darkening. I blushed, watching them rim with red before returning to normal.

"I thought you'd like it," I breathed.

"Was it expensive?" he tilted his head.

I shrugged. "You just told me you're rich. If you destroy it, you can buy me a new one."

Holland's laugh was the sweetest symphony. I hummed in delight when he finally moved to lie with me. I rolled to rest my head on his chest. Holland seemed to relax, wrapping his arm around me and kissing the top of my head.

"Thank you for today," I murmured. "And for every day."

"Are you happy?" he asked.

I tilted my head back to look at him, smiling softly. "Yeah, I think I am."

Holland caught my lips with his, kissing me delicately. I ran my hands up his bare chest. Holland's tongue traced mine, the taste of chocolate invading my senses.

With each moment that passed, our kiss grew deeper. Holland rolled to lean over me, his hand gripping my hip and holding me against him. I kissed him harder, faster. His heart beat hard under my hands. Mine echoed in my ears. Holland only wore a robe. When he moved again to rest between my thighs, I felt his hard length pressed against my center. The sensation sent shivers through me. I bent my knees, wrapping one leg around him and shifting to pull him impossibly closer.

Holland chuckled deeply, pulling back from our kiss to lick his fingers. I gasped when he touched between my thighs, wetting me for him. He did not kiss me when he pressed forward, inching into me impossibly slow. Instead, he watched my eyes roll back and my mouth fall open as he filled me.

"Fuck, Adalyn," he growled. "You drive me mad."

I couldn't respond.

"Open your eyes," he warned.

I did as he asked, whining as he thrust into me, pulling completely out before pushing in again. The veins beneath Holland's eyes rippled and turned black as he watched me writhe beneath him. I held eye contact, gripping his biceps as he picked up the pace - fucking me harder and faster. With each thrust, I melted further into him, beginning to forget where I ended and he began.

I dropped my hand between my thighs where we met, my

back arching at the added sensation. Holland growled above me. I watched him clench his jaw. He bit his lip in desperation, his fangs drawing blood.

"Holland," I whispered, bringing his attention back to me. I tilted my chin up, further exposing my throat. "Please. Taste me."

My vampire whimpered as he kissed me deeply. I tasted his blood on his mouth, smooth and warm. Holland trailed his mouth over my jaw, placing gentle kisses on my throat.

"Fuck," he breathed. "Adalyn, tell me to stop if you don't want this. Tell me now."

"Please," I said instead, ignited by every other delicious sensation he offered me. I felt his tongue on my throat - kissing, licking. Holland's thrusts slowed, but never stopped. I opened my mouth to tell him again it was okay. I didn't need to.

There was a sharp pain when Holland bit down. Instinctively, I reached up to grip his arm, my cry echoing through the room. For a moment, I remembered the horrible ripping and tearing sensation from the last vampire, and a scream built in my throat. In the same instant, the pain faded entirely. I relaxed beneath him and my eyes fluttered. I felt small shocks as Holland's tongue traced over the wound he'd made repeatedly. Instead, I listened to him moan and set the world on fire. Holland held me like I was everything. I'd never felt so desired.

Holland thrust into me at a torturously slow pace. I touched myself in unison with his movements, gasping each time. He cradled me against him, like he worried I would break.

With a groan, Holland lifted his head again. My eyes widened at the sight of my blood dripping down his lips and chin. He paused his movements entirely, searching my face for any signs of pain or fear. He found only pleasure.

"How prettily you bleed for me," he whispered.

Holland sat up slightly, hooking my legs over his arms. Mischief flashed on his face before he sped up his thrusts -

pounding into me relentlessly. With each thrust and touch of my own fingers, I came closer to another orgasm. My eyes never left Holland's face, somehow so monstrous and full of love and adoration for me.

His thrusts faltered again as he came closer to his own release.

More.

Please, please, please.

As soon as my orgasm crashed through me, his followed.

CHAPTER
43

Holland lay next to me in bed, tracing circles on my bare chest.

"Are you sure you're alright?" He asked.

I smiled drowsily. "I'm fine, I promise."

Holland's gaze dropped to the small mark he'd left on my neck. His eyes darkened for a moment and he reached up to prick his thumb on his fangs. I paused, sighing when he reached over to brush his thumb over my lips. I licked off the blood, immediately feeling the tingling sensation as my wound healed.

"Thank you," I murmured, feeling sleep tug at me. I blinked. "Is there water?"

"I'll get you some," Holland said, kissing my cheek.

I watched him as he crossed the room, pouring me a glass of water. I sat up to drink it, relieved it was cool enough to quench the heat beneath my skin. When I was finished, Holland poured another glass and set it on the stand next to the bed. He turned out all the lights, crawling back into bed next to me.

I rolled to rest my head on his chest, sighing. "What happens now?" I asked.

"Thirty-six hours isn't up yet," he breathed through the dark. "We'll deal with it all tomorrow night."

I closed my eyes, comforted by his promise.

I never wanted to leave Versailles.

Holland held my hand on the walk back to the train, both of us quiet. Thirty-six hours weren't up yet, but it felt like leaving the golden palace meant returning to a real life that was infinitely more complicated. A hundred questions fought on the tip of my tongue, desperate for release.

What would happen with Willa?

I hadn't talked to my family in days. I needed to call them and tell them I'd decided to stay in Paris. What would they think?

What would Holland think of my apartment and working with Willa?

What did it mean if I stayed here with him? Holland was immortal, and I... was not. So what - I grew old in his arms and he watched me die? The thought made my stomach churn.

I sat with my head on his shoulder on the train. He pulled a sketch pad out of his backpack and I watched him draw me. I recognized the tattoos on my thighs instantly, blushing when I realized I was naked in the drawing. He'd started it some time ago, but worked on shading around the curves of my breasts. The drawing was hauntingly lifelike. My eyes were closed, my head tilted back and my mouth open in silent delight.

Holland sketched for the entire ride back to the Notre Dame train stop. A few times, my eyes slipped shut, only to be jerked awake again by the rickety train. Each time, Holland kissed the top of my head.

The walk to my hotel was silent. Holland held the front door open for me, placing his hand on my lower back while we walked to the elevator.

I paused outside my door. "We're not out of time yet," I said.

A smile tugged at his lips.

I opened the door and stepped in. "Run away with me, Holland."

He tossed his bag on the ground inside the room, his mouth covering mine. I laughed, stumbling slightly, only to be caught by him again. The door slammed shut behind us and Holland lifted me into his arms. I wrapped my legs around his thighs, beaming as he carried me to bed and tossed me backward.

I laughed, kicking my feet. Holland descended, beaming and kissing every inch of my face. I clung to him and our joy, returning his kisses and holding his body against mine. I kicked off my shoes and Holland shrugged out of his sweater. The bed sheets were cool beneath us, a welcome comfort after the unpleasant train ride.

Holland's kisses slowed and trailed over my jaw. I hummed into the sensation, my eyes fluttering. Delight coursed through me when Holland's tongue flicked against my throat, silently asking for permission.

"Yes," I whispered.

He bit down.

My cry echoed through the room; I arched into Holland. He wrapped one arm around me, cradling me against him. I felt like his queen and his goddess, his moans of pleasure echoing in my ears.

Holland lifted his head a moment later, licking my blood from his mouth. I blinked up at him, dazed. He pressed the pad of his thumb to one of his fangs and offered the bead of blood to me. I took it, wide-eyed. Immediately, the wound on my throat healed.

"Am I yours now?" I whispered, sinking into the pillows.

Holland chuckled and pulled me into a sitting position to take off my coat. "You've always been mine." I blushed. "But, yes. Now any other vampire that comes near you can sense that you're mine."

I hummed, pursing my lips. "That's kinda sexy." My vampire rolled his eyes and adjusted the blankets so we both lay beneath them. I rolled towards him. "What happens now?"

"We could travel," Holland said, resting next to me.

"Where?" I asked.

"Anywhere you'd like. Have you done much traveling?"

I shook my head. "Just this."

He kissed me deeply. "Let me show you the world, Adalyn."

I brushed his hair back, pulling him in for another kiss. "Tell me about your favorite places."

Holland smiled.

I lay on my back for a long time, listening to him talk. He told me about castles in Scotland and pizza in Italy. He talked about the blue roofs in Santorini, and how much he'd love to kiss me senseless on the beach. While I lay there, listening, I realized this was the life I was choosing if I stayed with Holland.

I was choosing the world. And perhaps it was everything I'd ever wanted.

Holland fell quiet after a while, kissing my shoulder.

"Stay with me," he whispered.

I looked at him. "I am."

He sucked in a breath, his eyes wide. "Even after this time is up?"

"Of course," I rolled closer, so we were face-to-face. "Why don't you believe me?"

"Because, you have a life, Adalyn. You have a family, and a home," he breathed.

I shook my head. "I left Phoenix because I was drowning. I left because it had been so long since I felt *human* that I forgot."

"Why'd you come to Paris?"

"It's the city I dreamed about as a little girl. The ultimate fairytale," I admitted. "I thought if I could find myself anywhere, it would be here."

"And have you?"

"I don't know," I said. "I found fresh air, though, and sunlight." Holland kissed me again. I curled up against his chest, listening to his slow heartbeat. "I'm choosing to stay. Not just because of you, but because I think it's the right thing to do."

"Okay," Holland whispered.

"I only have one question," I started.

I didn't finish. Holland sat up suddenly, his features hardening. His whole body went tense and he shoved himself out of the bed.

"What's wrong?" I asked.

"Willa," he said.

Without pausing another moment, Holland darted towards the door and threw it open. I scrambled after him, dashing into the hallway as Willa's hotel room slammed open and Willa fell out of the room.

"I don't know what you mean, Thierry!" Willa sobbed.

"You're the only one who knew she was here!" Thierry roared. "What did you do, Willa?"

"Nothing!" My friend cried.

"What's going on?" Holland demanded. He grabbed my arm when I approached, holding me one step behind him.

Thierry spun on Holland in fury. "My sister is missing."

My heart stuttered.

Thierry's sister. The vampire who attacked me. The one Holland killed.

"How does that involve Willa?" Holland asked.

"We had dinner with her. Willa was the only other person who knew she was in Paris," Thierry snarled. That wasn't true. Holland and I saw her when they got ice cream. Thierry didn't seem to remember that.

Holland scoffed. "Your sister doesn't have friends?"

Thierry rolled his eyes. "What do you know?"

"Enough," Holland said.

It was the wrong thing to say. My blood ran cold. Thierry turned his attention from Willa to Holland.

"Where's my sister, Holland?"

Holland shrugged, like he couldn't be bothered with the answer. "Her body's at the bottom of the Seine somewhere."

CHAPTER 44

Holland stepped in front of me when Thierry descended like a rabid dog.

"Willa," Holland snapped, grunting when Thierry landed a punch to his chest. I yelped at the sight. "Get Adalyn out of here, now."

I was frozen in shock when Willa skidded across the hall, grabbing my arm and pulling me from behind Holland - away from where I felt safe. Still, when I looked at the other vampires in the middle of the hall, fangs bared and eyes bright red, I wanted to run.

"Get it together, Thierry," Holland snarled. Willa propelled me toward the stairs.

"Did you kill her?" Thierry screamed. He lashed out at Holland. A cry caught in my chest when I watched blood well on Holland's cheek. Thierry had scratched his nails through Holland's skin.

"She tried to kill Adalyn," Holland said with a shrug "Of course, I killed her."

"I'll tear the throat from your human toy," Thierry roared.

"Run, Adalyn," Holland yelled.

Willa dragged me down the rest of the stairs. My heart galloped in my throat as I stumbled behind my stronger and faster best friend. The roars of the vampires behind us felt distant as we skidded through the empty lobby, and out to the midday streets. Willa never let go of me.

We made it to the square up the hill before Thierry found us. He was splattered with blood, and I tried not to be afraid that it was probably Holland's. He stood in the middle of the town square, in front of the fountain.

"Give her to me, Willa," he growled.

Willa stepped in front of me with an inhuman snarl. "No."

God, where was Holland?

Willa pushed me into the nearest alleyway. "Run, find Holland."

I didn't hesitate before I took off as fast as I could. Thierry snarled behind me, and Willa cried out in reply. I didn't look back.

They were immortal. I was not.

I thought I turned towards the hotel, but in my terror, I couldn't entirely tell where I was. I ended up at the Luxembourg Gardens. I swore at the entrance, clutching my stomach as I struggled to breathe.

Someone grabbed my shoulder.

I nearly screamed, spinning toward them in terror.

I came face to face with my best friend. Willa's hand closed over my mouth. Blood splattered on her face. Her eyes were as red as the blood, haunting black veins stained beneath her skin.

"It's okay," she whispered. "I've got you."

I nodded quickly. She released me. "Where's Holland?"

"Here."

I turned to watch Holland step through the gates of the gardens. He nodded to Willa, his eyes searching me for any injuries. "Go with Willa," he said. "I'll take care of Thierry."

"Are you going to kill him?" Willa squeaked.

"Unless he kills me first," Holland answered.

"Wait, what?" I gasped.

Holland placed his hands on my shoulders, turning me to face him. "My love, run with Willa. She'll keep you safe."

Willa screamed.

I turned to watch Willa drop to her knees. Something jutted out from her stomach, covered in blood and flesh. A wooden stake.

Thierry stepped out from behind her.

Chaos erupted.

Holland released me to meet Thierry's attack. I skidded along the sidewalk to Willa, who vomited blood.

"Get it out, please," she rasped.

My stomach rolled. I had no other choice. My hands closed around the stake jutting out from her back, and I pulled. The squelching sound would haunt my nightmares, but at least it was out. Willa slumped into my arms. I held her like a child, sobbing.

"Run," Willa whispered. "If Holland falls, I can't stop Thierry. Please run."

I watched the battling vampires for a moment. Each time Thierry landed a hit on Holland, my whole soul cringed. Holland jerked his knee up between Thierry's legs, holding onto his head and head-butting him hard. The younger vampire stumbled back, blood dripping from his nose. Holland looked deadly. I should have been afraid of him.

He fought to keep me alive.

Holland glanced over, nodding once to acknowledge he agreed with Willa. I stood slowly, making sure Willa could sit on her own. Already, her wound was half-healed. I closed my hand around the stake, backing up a few feet. Holland leaped towards Thierry, who braced himself against the older vampire's attack. I didn't see the second weapon, a knife, until it jutted out from the center of Holland's chest. Holland dropped to his knees, blood leaking from his mouth. A scream threatened to drown me.

Thierry's eyes flicked to me.

I ran.

I only made it a dozen feet before he appeared in front of me, his fangs bared. His hands caught my arms, knocking me off my feet and pushing me down - hard. I think my head hit the ground. The world spun. I yelped, hearing the clatter of the stake but unsure where it had fallen.

"A life for a life, Holland. Now, I'll kill your girl," Thierry snarled.

I tried to gain my bearings enough to run. Everything spun. I reached for the stake with one hand, whimpering. I was going to be sick. Where was Holland?

I blinked and focused enough to watch him push himself off the ground, shaking. His hands closed over the weapon in his chest.

Thierry descended.

There wasn't time for me to run. Instead, I rolled and held the weapon up at the last possible second and squeezed my eyes shut. I felt it when it pierced his skin; I would never forget the cracking noises his bones made and the squelch of his flesh.

Willa's gut-wrenching scream echoed through the streets.

I watched Thierry's skin turn gray. He blinked slowly, looking down at the weapon in my hands. I stared at what I'd done - it had pierced his chest.

I staked a vampire.

Thierry gurgled, his weight collapsing on top of me. I whimpered, trying to push him off. His weight disappeared suddenly, and I came face-to-face with Holland. He shoved the dying vampire off me, pulling me into his arms. He was covered in his own blood and there was a large gash in the front of his shirt. I pushed him away quickly when my stomach flipped. I was sick on the sidewalk.

When I sat up again, Holland lifted me in his arms. I clutched my stomach and chest, unable to breathe evenly. Holland bit down on his wrist and offered it to me.

"You have a concussion," he murmured.

I closed my mouth over his wrist for only a moment before everything went dark.

CHAPTER
45

I set my bag down in Holland's apartment, taking a few mechanic steps inside and standing in the middle of the room. Holland was one step behind me, setting down my other bag and locking the door behind me. Returning to the hotel covered in blood was a blur. I think there was screaming. I vaguely remembered the police asking questions. Mostly, I remembered standing next to Holland, gripping his hand because it was the only thing holding me upright. My whole body ached, despite the vampire blood I drank to heal my wounds.

Holland poured a glass of water in the kitchen, walking over to offer it to me. I didn't acknowledge him. He set it down on the table.

I killed someone tonight.

I felt the weapon pierce his skin and break his bones. I felt him die.

My stomach churned again.

I barely made it to the bathroom before I was sick, falling to my knees in front of the toilet. I vomited up whatever was left in my stomach before sinking back and resting my head against the wall with a sob.

Holland was there a moment later to flush the toilet and kneel next to me with a warm rag. I cried as he wiped my face clean. My bloody clothes were sticky with blood. The hotel hadn't been willing to let us stay long enough to change them. Holland pulled my dirty shirt over my head, tossing it on the ground. I tried not to focus on the wet slap it made against the floor. Holland helped me to my feet again, unbuttoning my pants and pulling them off. They stuck to my legs, peeling off like a second skin.

A moment later, I was bare and stained red.

Holland started the shower. I watched him undress, his bloody clothes joining mine on the floor. Every move Holland made was slow and deliberate. He took both my hands in his, coaxing me towards the shower.

I hissed when the warm water touched my skin. The water ran red.

"Can I wash your hair?" Holland rasped.

I nodded.

I killed Thierry.

It was all I thought about as Holland's hands ran through my hair, washing away all the blood.

I killed him.

I killed him.

I killed him.

I didn't mean to.

Or, maybe I did? He would have killed me first if I didn't hold the stake up. It was instinct, and the stake broke through his skin like he was made of nothing. I felt it when it broke his ribs and pierced his heart.

And the way Willa screamed...

I gripped Holland's arms. Holland wrapped himself around me, holding me tight.

"I'm sorry I wasn't fast enough," he whispered. "I'm so fucking sorry."

I shook my head, burying my face in his chest. I didn't have the strength to answer.

When the water finally ran clear, Holland helped me dress in a pair of soft pajamas. I stood blankly while he toweled me dry and helped me into clothes. Finally, I raised my eyes to look at myself in the mirror. Holland brushed my hair and braided it back.

I followed him to the couch. Holland wrapped me in a blanket and offered me a pillow. I rested my head on it, watching him tiredly as he brought a water glass over to sit on the coffee table. I expected him to leave, but he sat on the floor next to me and buried his face in his hands.

"I'm sorry, Adalyn," he whispered.

I reached over to place my hand on his shoulder.

I didn't have it in me to say anything, but I wanted him to know - at the very least - that this wasn't his fault. I didn't blame him. Holland reached up with a shaking hand and covered mine.

It was midnight before either of us said anything else. My stomach rumbled, despite my misery. Holland raised his head from where he dozed on the ground at my feet.

"Are you hungry?" He mumbled, his voice catching.

I shrugged. "I can't remember the last time I ate anything."

"How about a sandwich?"

"I can try."

Holland pushed himself off the ground, his eyes lingering on me for a prolonged moment before he padded into the kitchen. Finally, I reached for my water on the coffee table, taking a long drink. Holland turned the kitchen light on, pulling a few things out of the fridge.

"Do you want help?" I asked quietly.

"No, I'm fine," Holland replied.

I said nothing else, closing my eyes again while he moved around in the kitchen. Holland returned, his fingers brushing my arm to pull me from the half-sleep I'd fallen into. I sat up slightly. He placed a plate on my lap, sitting next to me on the couch. My eyes dropped to the glass of red liquid in his hands and I sighed in relief. He needed to eat too. We were both drained.

I picked up the sandwich twice before gathering the strength to take a bite. I chewed slowly to avoid the nausea. The more I ate, the more it faded along with my headache.

I finished, and Holland took our dishes to the kitchen.

"You don't have to stay if you've changed your mind," Holland said when he returned.

"I haven't," I croaked.

A couple of red tears dripped down his face. "How the fuck not? You could have died tonight, Adalyn!"

I winced at his change in tone. "Because I love you," I whispered.

"You almost died," he repeated himself. "Again. Because of me."

I shook my head. "Don't put this on you. I'm alive because of you - and I don't just mean tonight."

Holland shook his head. "You don't have to live like this. You don't have to live in this world."

I stood. "I want this. I want you."

He scoffed. "You're young, you don't know what you want."

I looked around the room in anger, my eyes settling on the letter opener on the coffee table. I picked it up, storming over to

Holland and slashing it over the palm of my hand before he could stop me. With all the pain in my heart, I didn't notice the burn in my palm. My blood spilled over my palm and Holland's eyes widened and turned red.

"Why the fuck-" he started.

"I am *not* afraid of you," I said, holding my hand out to him. "I am not afraid of this world, not anymore."

He shook his head, his eyes fixed on the blood leaking from my wound. I raised it closer to his face, daring him to let me into this world... to let me stay despite everything that happened tonight.

"I want *you*, Holland," I cried.

He stood, ignoring my bleeding hand and kissing me. I stumbled back at the force of his kiss. He held me tight, winding his arm around my waist. Holland cried as he kissed me, smearing his blood across my face. I didn't care. I frantically returned his advances, holding onto the collar of his shirt with my free hand.

"I'm staying in Paris whether you'll have me or not," I mumbled against his mouth, gasping as he trailed kisses over my jaw and neck. "But, I hope you'll have me."

Holland dropped to his knees, clinging to me like I was everything he had left. I lowered myself after him. His eyes found mine. I smiled softly.

"I'm already home," I whispered.

"I love you," he rasped.

"Until the sun dies," I replied.

Holland kissed me again.

And that was it.

CHAPTER
46

Willa sank into the chair across from me. She looked exhausted, her hair hanging in loose messy waves. She wore a matching set of sweats, her face bare without makeup. Immediately, I opened my mouth a few times to apologize, to ask if she was okay - something, anything. Nothing came.

The server came over. Willa ordered a cup of coffee. I stared down at mine, placing my shaking hands on the table.

"I'm not angry with you," Willa said quietly.

I stiffened.

Willa swallowed like she tried to resist tears. "I'm hurting, and I'm lost, but I don't blame you even a little."

"But I-" I couldn't even say it.

I killed Thierry.

The server returned and set some coffee in front of Willa. She sipped it once. "I love him," she muttered. "Loved, I guess. And still, if he would have hurt you-" Willa paused and took a steadying breath. "I'd lose Thierry a thousand times over if it meant I kept you. You're my best friend." She reached for the messenger bag she'd brought with her, pulling out a large binder and setting it on the table in front of us. "I have a plan."

"A plan?" I tilted my head in confusion.

Willa pushed it forward.

I took it and opened it in my lap, my eyes widening. I flipped through charts, projections, graphs, budgets, and half a dozen other things I didn't understand. All of them were tied to Willa's candle business.

"It's all put together. All I need is an apartment to work in, and you," Willa said softly.

I looked up at her in shock. "Me?"

"It's ambitious. I could probably do it to myself, but I don't want to. It would be easier with a business partner. You could do whatever you wanted - social media, accounting?" Willa stared at me hopefully.

"Are you offering me a job?" I gasped out.

"A job, my friendship, forgiveness, whatever you want it to be," Willa said softly. "Please stay in Paris."

Laughter bubbled in my chest. Instantly, I covered my mouth to hide the noise. Willa gaped at me, glancing around to see if there was anything else I could laugh at. I didn't blame her. She said nothing funny.

But, I was drained and overwhelmed. And I was staying in Paris.

With a job. A friend. A man I loved. And vampires.

I sat back in my chair, my laughs rattling my chest as I shook my head. Three weeks. That was all the time it took for my life to turn into something unrecognizable. Three weeks. I wouldn't have it any other way.

My laughter faded and I reached across the table to take

Willa's hand. She stared at me, slightly shocked and mostly worried.

"Of course, I'm staying," I said. "And, I would love to work with you."

Willa leaped out of her chair. I stood to catch her embrace. The whole cafe stared in disgust and shock. I didn't care about any of them. I buried my face in Willa's shoulder - laughing, crying, flying.

The further I stepped into this decision, the more it felt right.

When Willa and I could both breathe again, we settled into our chairs. Willa opened the binder again, moving to sit next to me. She pulled a pen from her bag. I smiled when she began to talk through the details.

We were at the cafe for hours.

Coffee after coffee, we talked through ideas, budgets, and realities. Willa turned out to be excellent with numbers, and I wanted to talk through marketing and design ideas.

We were going to be great together.

I watched the sunset as I waited for my mom to answer the call. My phone sat on the couch in front of me. I'd returned to Holland's apartment a couple of hours ago, vibrating with the excitement of working with Willa. She made an appointment to go apartment hunting tomorrow. We could get started with this business as soon as she was out of the hotel.

Across the apartment, Holland sat at his desk, hunched over a sketchbook - like me being here was the most natural thing in the world. I wanted to ask him about what happened now. Did I stay here with him? Should I ask to live with Willa? I couldn't afford my own place yet, but I wasn't sure where we stood.

My mom's voice came through the phone, interrupting my thoughts. "Addie? Are you alright?"

Immediately, a lump formed in my throat. I took a deep breath. "Hi, Mom. Can you talk?"

"Of course." Her voice was softer than I expected, full of worry.

"I've decided I'm going to stay in Paris."

There was a long moment of silence. I glanced across the room when Holland sat up in concern. His eyes found mine. I shook my head, gulping.

"You're sure?" Mom finally said.

I licked my shaking lips. "Yes."

"And you have a plan?"

"Yes, my friend Willa and I are going to restart her business here. In the meantime, I'll do some freelance, remote work. I'm staying with her," I said.

Holland tilted his head, watching me. I focused on my phone call.

"You'll come home for the holidays, right?" My mom's voice cracked.

I smiled softly, pulling my knees to my chest. "Of course, Mom. And you can come here too once I'm a bit more settled. And, I'll be home in a few weeks to get things figured out with my visa."

"You really want this? You're sure?" Indy's voice came through the phone, quiet and worried. I didn't realize she was there. I checked the date. It was Sunday. Indy and I always spent Sundays at Mom's house - lounging on her couch, playing board games, and watching TV. Like we'd never grown up at all. The memory created another lump in my throat and I placed my hand on my chest. "I have an extra room."

"I want this," I said firmly.

More than anything.

Across the room, Holland smiled.

"Well, if you're sure, then we're entirely on board," Mom said.

I talked with my family for a while longer about the details of my decision to stay in Paris. Their acceptance shocked me. I still felt some of their skepticism and confusion, but they didn't fight me on my decision. The longer I talked, the more I understood it was because I was sure I wanted this. They'd fought me before because I didn't know what I wanted and they didn't know any different.

I was sure.

So they were too.

My mom was still crying when we hung up the phone.

I tossed my phone on the couch, crossing the room to rest my hands on Holland's shoulders.

"Staying with Willa?" He hummed, not looking up from his sketchbook. I peered over his shoulder to watch him drag his pencil along the trunk of a tree.

I gulped. "I don't know."

Holland turned to face me, positioning me so I stood between his thighs. "Stay with me instead."

I blushed brightly and laughed once. "I hardly know you, Holland."

He shrugged. "So? I love you, Adalyn. I want to fall asleep next to you, and use my tongue to wake you up every morning. I want to make you dinner. I want to see your smile every day."

I looked around his apartment. I spent so much time within these walls - both afraid and in love. I loved the view of the sunset from his couch and the flower decals on the kitchen walls. Every inch felt like home, from Holland's guitar in the corner to the fleece blanket on his bed. The thought of coming back here every day and falling into his arms seemed like a fairytale I didn't deserve. I brushed away another tear. "You're sure?"

"I've never been more sure," he breathed, taking my hands in his. He kissed my palms, then each of my fingers. "Say yes, Adalyn."

"Yes."

I smiled.

Holland leaped from the chair, throwing his arms around me with a whoop of joy. I laughed and let him spin me in a circle. Holland peppered kisses over my face. I kissed him wildly, recklessly, basking in the joy of my dashing vampire. Holland's kisses deepened. He took a single step back toward the bed.

"I have a question," I said seriously, placing my hand on his chest.

His smile faded. "Anything."

I clenched my fists a few times, gulping. Holland waited patiently for me to build up my courage. My stomach flipped.

"You're going to live forever," I said, my voice barely a whisper.

Recognition flashed in Holland's eyes. "Yes, I am."

I shifted nervously, unsure how to ask how this would work. I didn't want to grow old and die in his arms while he remained as young and strong as ever. But I wasn't ready to decide. It had only been three weeks.

Holland smiled gently, leaning forward to kiss my cheek, then my mouth. "We don't have to decide anything right now."

"But, what-" I tried.

Holland led me over to sit on the bed with him. "How about this?" He started, holding my hand tight. "Every year, on this day, we will talk about this. If you decide, one day, that you'd like to spend eternity with me, I will make it happen. If you decide you want to leave-"

I interrupted him. "I won't."

He shook his head. "Neither of us know that, my love. That's why we're going to talk about it. As long as you'd like to remain human, I will stay with you. If you decide you'd like to join me in immortality, I'll give you eternal life. And, before or after, if you decide you don't want me - that's okay too."

I placed my hand on his cheek. "Once a year, then."

"Once a year," he echoed.

I kissed him. "I'll love you till the sun dies."

"And then in the dark." Holland drew me into his arms again.

Outside, the last of the sun faded to night.

ACKNOWLEDGMENTS

I love every book I've ever written, but this one is more personal than most. I poured pieces of myself into Adalyn, every unloveable and prickly part, and then I gave her a handsome, charming vampire that loved her even in her darkest hour. I hope others find familiarity in the way Adalyn experiences the world and solace in her emotional journey - I certainly did.

As with every book, I never would have ended up here without the help of some very special people.

To Matthew - whose smile is like sunshine and love is golden. Thank you for loving me even when I don't love myself, and for always encouraging me to reach for the stars. You truly are the light of my life. I love you till the sun dies.

For my mom. I came up with the idea for Till the Sun Dies when we visited the Palais Garnier. While we explored the opera house for the first time, I came up with the scene where Addie and Holland met for the first time. Pretty cool how it all works out, right? Anyway, thank you for traveling the world with me, for believing in me, and for always feeding me so I don't die. I owe it all to you.

Thank you to my beta readers - McKenna, Adele, Lauren, and Jess. You all are the best A-Team an author could ask for. Thank you for every minute you spent helping me turn Till the Sun Dies into a story worth telling. I appreciate your support, and your excitement so much.

For Crystal and Nicole - who helped make this book look its best inside and out.

And thank you to every person who has shown support, whether it be words of encouragement, listening to me ramble, buying a copy, leaving a review, or sharing on social media. I would not be here without all of you.

Most of all, thank you, dear reader, for giving this book a chance.

ABOUT THE AUTHOR

 H.M. Darling is a new adult indie author that lives and burns in Arizona with her scrooge of a cat named Tobey. She has a bachelor's degree in English Literature and Creative Writing. She writes books full of morally gray characters, villainous love interests, and tops it all off with lots of spice!

When she is not writing, you can usually find her collecting houseplants, listening to Taylor Swift, or reading a book from her never-ending TBR list.

Stay Connected:

Click the link below and you can sign up to stay updated with all things H.M. Darling. There is no charge and no obligation.
https://www.subscribepage.com/hmdarlingnewsletter

Follow H.M. Darling's writing adventures on:

facebook.com/hmdarlingauthor

instagram.com/writerhdxrling

tiktok.com/@writerhdxrling

CPSIA information can be obtained
at www.ICGtesting.com
Printed in the USA
BVHW081857090223
658229BV00003B/55

9 798985 452129